THE SILVER SKULL

ALSO BY LES DANIELS

The Black Castle

Living in Fear: A History of Horror in the Mass Media

Dying of Fright: Masterpieces of the Macabre

THE SILVER SKULL

A Novel of Sorcery

———————————⊂⊃———————————

LES DANIELS

CHARLES SCRIBNER'S SONS / NEW YORK

Copyright © 1979 Les Daniels

Library of Congress Cataloging in Publication Data
Daniels, Les.
  The silver skull.

  I. Title.
PZ4.D1878Si   [PS3554.A5637]   813'.5'4   79–10057
ISBN 0–684–16141–9

1 3 5 7 9 11 13 15 17 19 O/C 20 18 16 14 12 10 8 6 4 2

Printed in the United States of America

THE SILVER SKULL

1. City of Gold

T HE man with the skull in his sack looked down from the mountains toward the city in the lake.

Tenochtitlan was the most astonishing sight that Alfonso Martinez had ever seen. The lake, of salt water, was vast, stretching for miles in all directions; its borders were rich with fields and forests, and with gigantic gardens where flowers bloomed in dazzling profusion. A gleaming city rose from the waters, its pyramids mirrored in the shining surface of the lake. The brilliant sunlight and the thin air gave the panorama the quality of a vision, but however Martinez shook his head and blinked his eyes, Tenochtitlan would not disappear. The city was real, and Alfonso Martinez was about to enter it. It was a city of water, but to him it was a city of gold.

The men around Martinez stood awestruck, yet there was a disturbance among the soldiers far ahead of him, that handful of veterans who had first followed Cortez into Tenochtitlan months ago. What was wrong? The city seemed placid enough. No hordes of feathered Aztec warriors stood ready to attack the Spanish troops, and no war canoes skimmed the surface of the lake. And yet, as word drifted back to Martinez and the other new recruits, it became apparent that this very lack of activity was an ominous sign.

Last November, when Cortez and his men had approached Tenochtitlan for the first time, the inhabitants of the Mexican capital had greeted them with curiosity and even enthusiasm. The towers along the causeway had been thronged with onlookers, and the lake had been covered with boats. It had been almost a festival, but now there was no welcome at all. The quiet, shimmering city was suddenly frightening.

Like all the others, Martinez had heard talk of trouble in Tenochtitlan, and he knew that he and his companions in the second expedition were partly to blame for it. They had come to Mexico months after Cortez, their army led by other Spaniards who intended to take control of the newly discovered territory and its riches. Determined not to let these interlopers subvert his authority, Cortez had marched away from Tenochtitlan to stop them before they could reach the city, and such was his skill as a tactician that he had defeated their larger force in a few hours. Moreover, he had spoken to them so persuasively that he soon rallied his former rivals to his cause, thus doubling his forces. But the absence of Cortez had left Tenochtitlan in the hands of underlings who had not been equal to the task. Fighting broke out between the Aztecs and the tiny Spanish garrison; the messengers who reported it sent Cortez hurrying back from the coast to secure the city. Yet he still had only about a thousand Spaniards against a city so huge that Alfonso Martinez could hardly guess at the number of its inhabitants.

Nervously he fingered his pack, and felt the reassuring roundness of the skull hidden within it.

"What do you think, physician? Ever see anything like it?"

"Never," answered Martinez, turning to look at his companion. The man beside him was rangy and sunburned. His face, where it was not concealed by shaggy black beard, was scarred, and his armor was equally battered. Thick eyebrows met above his flat and broken nose.

Martinez squinted at the soldier suspiciously. "Should I know you?"

"I am Luis Garcia. Captain Cortez sent me to keep an eye on you."

Garcia grinned, exposing broken teeth, and Martinez wondered if he were already under suspicion.

"Cortez says you may be the most valuable man in this second expedition," continued Garcia. "The rest of these fellows are fortune hunters, not fighters—we proved that fast enough. You're a bit of a runt yourself, of course, but that's why I'm here to look after you. We can always use a doctor, and there will be work enough for you soon, if I'm any judge. Looks like there's trouble brewing here."

Martinez breathed a sigh of relief. It would be intolerable to come this far from Spain only to be exposed as an impostor. He was no physician, although he had signed on as one. It might prove troublesome to live up to his lie, but every alchemist had some knowledge of medicine, and it would be easier to mix a potion or even amputate a leg than to return to Spain and face the tribunal of the Inquisition. Those who traded in sorcery had no place in Spain; the skull he carried with him was proof of that. Martinez hoped that it would have important uses: its magic, and his own, small as it was, would have to protect him in this strange land. He reached back again to fondle the cowhide sack, and the bone beneath it that had once encased the brain of the greatest wizard in Spain.

"What's that you're playing with?" asked Luis Garcia, his long face showing friendly curiosity.

"Tools of my trade," said Martinez, smirking at the small joke of deceiving this lout by telling him the truth.

"Good enough," said Garcia. "I'll wager there are a score of men in that city who need them. These heathens' swords are made of stone, not steel, and they make messy wounds. There will be work for you."

As he fell into step beside Garcia, Martinez attempted to adopt the swaggering attitude of a soldier of fortune. His muscles ached from the long march, and the tropical heat had sucked the strength from his bones, but he was determined to prove himself as tough as the next man.

"If there are wounded," he said, "then some will live and some will die. I will do what I can for them, but I am not here seeking sainthood."

Garcia looked at him with a narrowing of the eyes the alchemist could not interpret. "There are only two reasons for a man to come to this land of devils," said Garcia. "Gold or glory."

"You noticed yourself that I am no soldier."

"Gold, then. Well, there is plenty here for you. It's not hard to find, but it may not be so easy to carry away with you."

"Is there really so much?"

"More than you have ever dreamed of, physician."

"You have never seen my dreams."

"No. But I have seen the treasure in the palace of the king, and a man could hardly dream of more. And yet, great as it was, this king Montezuma seemed to think it a pittance. He gave us permission to construct a chapel in the palace, and we found the treasure hidden behind a wall. It was the fortune of his father, they say, and no man had ever bothered to look at it for years. There was a great hall hidden behind the plaster, piled with gold and silver and pots filled with jewels the way you might fill them with water. There were wheels of gold, and bars, and nuggets just scattered on the floor. And there were statues and ornaments made of it, but we melted most of them down when we came to divide it. They use gold as a white man might use wood or marble!"

"You've already divided it?" asked Martinez.

"Yes," answered Garcia. "I gambled it away in a week. But there will be more. These savages don't know the value of anything. Montezuma hardly seemed to care if we found the gold or not. I wonder if he even remembered it was there. It couldn't have meant much to him, for he gave it all to Cortez of his own free will."

"What kind of fool is king of this country?"

"So great a fool that he has lost his throne as well. And so great

4

a fool that he thinks Hernan Cortez is some sort of god."

Alfonso Martinez, stumbling down a mountain slope, had nothing to say. What he had heard made no sense to him. He broke his clumsy descent by falling against Garcia's solid back, instantly drawing himself up with a show of dusty bravado. "You are mocking me," he said. "They say Cortez is a good commander, but he is a long way from being a god!"

Garcia took a step back. "Cortez is lucky," he said, "and luck is worth more than skill or sanctity. Every soldier knows as much, and you will learn it too, if you live long enough. Look at that city! Do you think we took it by force of arms? There are not many of us now, and we were fewer still when we first arrived. But these Indians have a legend that one of their gods will return to them, and they have decided that Cortez is the very fellow they were waiting for. A white god, they say, and Cortez looks pale enough compared to these brown bastards. Of course it makes no sense. I have seen statues of the god they speak of, some sort of a dragon, but covered with feathers. How they could take Cortez for him I couldn't say, but it has kept us alive, and that's all I ask."

"Then they have more gods than one?"

"Hundreds, I suppose, and each more bloodthirsty than the next. Thousands die on their altars every year, and the congregations eat their flesh. Men, women, and children die; and men, women, and children devour them. They worship idols that look like devils. They know nothing of Christ. Whatever else a man comes here for, he learns soon enough it is his duty to wipe out these horrors."

"Is it black magic, then?" Martinez asked eagerly.

"Call it what you will, it is an abomination."

Martinez paused for a moment, then asked, as if he were changing the subject: "Where does the gold come from?"

"From mines, I suppose. Where else could it come from?"

"Well, these Aztecs sound like a race of wizards, and I thought they might have found the secret . . ." Martinez let his sentence trail off.

The two men had continued to trudge down the slope as they

spoke, but now Luis Garcia stopped and turned to look at Martinez with the enigmatic squint the alchemist had seen before.

"The secret of what?" asked Garcia. "The secret of making gold?"

Martinez said nothing, fearing that he had already said too much.

"I never thought of that," said Garcia. "Nobody has ever thought of it. There must be a reason why they have so much, and why they seem to care so little for it. And there must be a reason for all those sacrifices to their demons. You are a clever fellow, physician."

"It was just an idle fancy."

"Best to hope it's not true, then. If the gold comes from the ground, we will have it all. But if it comes from those gods, it will go with them, and we will be the poorer for it."

Martinez was dismayed. Could his comrades be such fanatical Christians that they would seal up an endless stream of riches for no other reason than to satisfy their scruples? What good was any god except for the gifts he gave his followers? If it was true, as he believed, that these demonic idols rewarded their followers with the gift of growing gold, then they would find an ardent devotee in Alfonso Martinez.

Like every other alchemist, he had labored for years to find the way to turn base metal into glittering riches, and had grown old before his time in the search. Years spent peering into smoking crucibles had left his back bent and his shoulders rounded; years spent with an ear cocked for the officers of the Inquisition had left him with shattered nerves and shifty eyes. At thirty-eight, his hair was gray, most of it gone. His beard was thin and scraggly, his high forehead creased by constant anxiety. He was a small man, and even he would have acknowledged that he was a wicked one. Yet he had a vision, and it made him brave and strong enough to cross an ocean that few men had dared.

The vision was simple enough: Alfonso Martinez, seated on a throne, surrounded by piles of gold and caressed by adoring women. The world was at his feet—a globe, as every sensible man had learned by now—and even the globe gleamed yellow. It was a pathetically simple picture, as Martinez himself admitted in his more cynical moments. But it pleased him, it drove him onward, and it made him something more than just a coward or a rogue. He knew there were those of his calling who claimed that the gold the alchemists sought was only the symbol of a purified spirit; but Martinez would have none of this. He was true to his dream.

Garcia's voice drew Martinez back out of his vision. "Listen, physician," said the soldier. "I'm going to leave you for a minute. Just keep your place in line and march along with the rest, and you'll be fine. You're surrounded by fighting men, and there's no enemy about. Even these savages you see here are our allies. They don't like this city any more than we do. There's nothing to worry about."

Martinez nodded, still half lost in his own thoughts, his eyes on the silent city.

Garcia was still anxious to excuse himself. "Did you see that canoe that came across the lake just now?"

Martinez had seen nothing, but pretended that he had.

"I think it was a messenger," said Garcia. "It can't hurt to find out what's going on, and I have a friend who's an aide to Cortez. Keep marching. I'll be back."

"Go," said Martinez irritably, reflecting that this Garcia must be a tenderhearted fellow to show so much concern for him. Either that, or he was afraid.

Martinez was anxious himself. He wondered what had happened to his countrymen in the city on the lake, and what would happen to him. His legs began to tremble. He had not forgotten Garcia's description of the room filled with forgotten treasure.

Yet there was little to protect him, or to lead him to a fortune, except the Aztecs' insane belief that Cortez was one of their gods. Garcia had forgotten the name, or was too sanctimonious to admit that he knew it, but the ugly word had been burned into Martinez's brain as soon as he heard it. Quetzalcoatl, the Feathered Serpent. How Cortez had acquired the identity might remain a mystery, but there was something to be learned from the

7

simple fact of the impersonation. Martinez knew more than a smattering of the ancient theologies, and of the numerous deities that had struggled for power in the world of the Romans or the Egyptians. Might there not be another god here, one who rivaled the Feathered Serpent and who might prevent Cortez from enshrining Christ in the name of Quetzalcoatl? Christ gave no gifts of gold, and he was no god for an alchemist. The Feathered Serpent had his uses, evidently, but the mind of Martinez raced forward to a day when some other demon of Tenochtitlan might make him rich.

He wished, not for the first time, that there was more of the divine in his own appearance. This seemed to be a land where any man of commanding presence might proclaim himself the incarnation of a supreme power, but Alfonso Martinez knew all too well that he did not look like a god. The fates conspired against a man from the moment of his birth, and the shape they gave him was no small part of his destiny. If Martinez had been a dark giant like the man whose skull he carried, things might have been different. Such a man had commanded fear, even before he had transcended death.

Martinez had never seen Don Sebastian de Villanueva, but he had heard stories about him, wild tales that were hardly to be believed. But Martinez had believed, and he had stolen the skull. He took it one night from the workshop of another magician, and betrayed the man to the Inquisition before there was time to investigate the robbery. Unfortunately, his contact with the dread tribunal had put Martinez himself in jeopardy, and he had been forced to flee to the New World before he had found time to test the powers of the skull. Yet he never doubted its merits as a totem of true magic, and had guarded it jealously throughout his travels. There was something in the shape of the skull, and in the configuration of its long sharp teeth, which convinced Martinez that it was the key to his destiny. Even the blackest periods of poverty had not tempted him to have it melted down, although careful observation had convinced him, against all logic, that it was made of solid silver.

Martinez had long pondered the question of what sort of man might leave such a relic behind. Don Sebastian had been a warrior and a wizard who had destroyed himself in flames rather than become a prisoner of the Inquisition. That had happened twenty-four years ago, in 1496, but it was said that Don Sebastian had died years earlier, and had given himself a life beyond death by invoking dark forces and imbibing the bright blood of living men and women. In short, Don Sebastian had been a vampire, a brooding monster who lurked among the towers of his ancestral castle. His brother, the Grand Inquisitor, ruled the frightened city of their birth.

An unholy pact had been made between the brothers, motivated by their shared fascination with the mysteries of black magic; but something had gone wrong. No one living knew the entire story, but the Grand Inquisitor had disappeared and Sebastian's burning body was discovered outside the black walls of his castle. Some time later his skull had been dredged up from the waters of the moat, passing from hand to hand for years before it fell into the clutches of Alfonso Martinez. And now it was in Mexico, with its owner cursing himself because he lacked the knowledge once contained in the hollow, fleshless head he carried with him. Martinez swore that he would unlock the secret of the thing, that somehow its power would become his own.

"I think we'll be all right," said Luis Garcia. He startled Martinez by lumbering breathlessly up the hill, but his message was reassuring. "Only seven dead, and more wounded, of course. They'll be glad to see you, physician. It's not quite clear what happened, but it seems our men attacked some of these barbarians at one of their festivals and killed a bunch of them. And they fought back, for a while. I guess you and your comrades are responsible."

"Me?"

"These natives learned that you and your expedition had come to take command from Cortez. They expected you to win, and that made them bold, but when they heard you lost, they stopped fighting and settled for a blockade of our garrison. No real harm

9

done, I suppose, except for a few poor devils who will have no tales to tell to their grandchildren."

A golden chord cut through the hot dry air.

"Trumpets," said Garcia. "Cortez ordered them, to signal the men in the city. You can see where they are, in Montezuma's palace—over there, to your left. He gave us quarters there, before we took him prisoner. The people and the priests may not like it much, but Montezuma knows who we are and what the future holds for his people. He knows that we were born to be his masters, and those who doubt it will learn soon enough."

Artillery fire echoed across the great salt lake, and along the nearer causeway, that led from the city of water toward the mountains.

"They've heard us," said Garcia. "They're answering as best they can, with gunfire. They're still alive, our brothers, and soon we'll be in command of the city again."

"With the help of the Feathered Serpent," mumbled Martinez. He shifted his pack on his weary shoulders, and followed the long line of conquistadors down the slope to the city.

2. The Palace

THE false physician had been sent to visit the casualties as soon as he reached the sprawling palace of red stone. Inside, he had been led through endless rooms and corridors until he reached the wounded. Stifling his awe at the alien surroundings, he had adopted an indifferent air and set himself to examining the stricken men. The charade had not taken long. Martinez had contemplated dozens of hideous injuries with apparent satisfaction, and had commended the makeshift work of the Spanish priest who had done what he could to bind up the stumps and gashes. Martinez himself treated only one man—and that because he could not stand the screaming. He hoped the fellow would die before the sleeping draught wore off.

As soon as he could safely claim his work was done, Martinez had demanded an escort back to the great hall where Luis Garcia waited. It was the only room of the palace that rose above one story, and it was big enough to house more than a hundred men. Beds of matting, each with its own canopy, lay in long rows on the floor, and braziers burned, filling the air with sweet, smoking incense. The Spaniards were anxious, and none more so than Martinez, who was driven into a suppressed frenzy by the strange splendor he saw all around him. Nothing he had seen in the New World had prepared him for the magnificence of Tenochtitlan, and he was more convinced than ever that magic had played a part in the growth of the city on the lake.

Without supernatural intervention, reasoned Martinez, it would have been impossible for this race of small, dark men to engineer the wonders he saw around him. The complex of palaces and temples that formed the heart of the city looked like the work of a giant; the low building in which he stood covered acres of ground. The architecture was inhuman to his eye: vast interlocking rectangles of some unrecognizable stone lying close to the ground, these interspersed with towering layered pyramids that seemed even stranger than the legendary monuments of Egypt. To a man who had never before left Spain, Tenochtitlan looked like the landscape of a fever dream. Far easier to imagine it the handiwork of some uncanny force than to believe that these pagans had constructed the three causeways, each miles long, that ran through the city and across the blue water to the shores beyond.

The lack of furnishing in the countless chambers of the palace confirmed his hypothesis that the Aztecs were merely the tenants of some dark god's domain. There were no beds; even the nobles slept on woven mats. The chairs were sorry things, so close to the ground that one sat upon them cross-legged. There were a few low tables and decorated screens, but in all it seemed a bare and empty edifice, one whose inhabitants might well be interlopers.

The bright murals on the walls, all the more vivid in contrast to their bleak surroundings, provided further evidence that this was a city built by spells. The walls were alive with monsters. Whatever artists worked here had seen horrors, and had delineated them in a style so unearthly that this thrilled Martinez more than the images themselves. The figures were outlined in bold strokes of black, the outlines filled with unshaded patches of violent color. The drawing was flat, without perspective, and Martinez was wise enough in the ways of magic to recognize that every image was a symbol of some unknown power. These were not portraits but portents, and Martinez struggled to grasp their significance.

There were men in the murals, but they were paltry beside the hideous demons they served. These devils announced themselves in lurid shades of red and yellow, blue and green. They were shaped like dwarfs, with outsized heads and shrunken bodies, striped faces and bared teeth; their eyes were cold. From head to foot they were enmeshed in strange designs whose meanings seemed as if they might be hidden in some forgotten corner of the mind. They tantalized Alfonso Martinez until he thought he would go mad.

"Garcia," he said. "Take me out of here. Show me the city."

"Too dangerous," said Garcia stolidly. "We're safer here."

"I would never have taken you for a coward, Garcia. Are you afraid to show your face to the sun?"

Martinez had his answer as Garcia's sunburned hand took him by the throat. He was lifted into the air, his feet barely scraping the floor.

"No man calls me coward," said Luis Garcia. Martinez felt the man's hot breath in his face. "I'll show you a few things, and then we'll see how brave you are, physician."

He lowered Martinez slowly, unaware of the fact that the alchemist no longer wished to go anywhere in the company of such a hot-blooded soldier.

"But you're not such a bad fellow at that," Garcia said, giving Martinez a slap on the back that nearly knocked him to the ground. "I'll bet there's not another man in this palace with the nerve to go outside. And you're not even on duty. Just want a look around, do you? You shall have it."

Martinez felt a heavy arm thrown about his shoulder and was half carried across the great hall to its entrance. The man on guard at the door was evidently a friend of Garcia's.

"Listen," Garcia said. "We have a scholar here. I want to show him the city. If things don't go well, this may be his last chance for a look at the place. He should see the temples, and Montezuma's menagerie. And the skulls. He's a little cocky, and that should calm him down. Let us pass, will you?"

Garcia winked broadly, and seemed on the verge of nudging

the man in his armored ribs. The short, stocky guard returned the wink and stood aside.

Martinez winced at the mention of the skulls, but nobody seemed to notice. He had no idea what they were talking about, but he was all too aware of the silver skull buried in the sack that had never left his side during the long voyage which had brought him to Mexico. In fact, he would have sworn that something had bumped against him when Garcia brought up the subject of skulls, but he was more than willing to attribute the thump to an imagination inflamed by heat, hunger, and the subtle horrors of Tenochtitlan.

"Lead on," he told Garcia. This was no time to lose face, especially now that he was aware of Garcia's mercurial temperament. Martinez might lose more than face if he tried to back out —the dangers in this strange land were not only those of the spirit. Yet everything he saw convinced Martinez that this was indeed a country of conjurers, where his own minor magic might work wonders and where the native necromancy had in fact revealed the secret of making gold.

Garcia worked his own more mundane magic on several other sentries until at last they reached the final portal of the palace. The afternoon sun beat down upon them.

"That's not really Montezuma's palace," said Garcia. "It's his father's, but it seems that each of their kings has to build his own. Anyway, it's been Montezuma's since we took him prisoner and brought him over to the place he appointed as our quarters. Now it looks like maybe nothing is his anymore. But at least you'll have a chance to see what he's lost."

Martinez blinked in the sudden brightness of the day and squinted down the long street that led into a causeway and toward the distant shore.

"It's a trap," said Garcia. "The whole place is a trap. But we've been hoping they won't have the sense to spring it. There are three ways out of this city, each one a line of bridges over the water. And each one of those bridges can be drawn up in a matter of minutes, leaving us stranded on an island in the middle of a lake. You may think you're tough because you're willing to come out here, and you may think I'm tougher. But only Hernan Cortez has the balls to march into a place like this, where we're outnumbered at least a hundred to one, and where a dozen idiots can cut off our retreat at a moment's notice. After you've seen what sort of barbarians they are, maybe you'll realize the kind of risks we're taking."

The two men stood in the great plaza near the center of Tenochtitlan. The square, paved with huge flagstones, was deserted save for a few Spanish sentries, yet Martinez felt the presence of the Aztecs everywhere. They were in the city, waiting.

"That red pile to the south is the palace where we kidnapped Montezuma," said Garcia. "I'll take you down that way so you can see his pleasure gardens. To the west, there, is the biggest of their pyramids. We'll circle around and come past it back to where we started. It's the temple of their war god, I think, and they make sacrifices there for his glory. You've heard of that, I suppose—how they cut the living hearts out and feed them to the flames? That's just one of the ways they have of killing people, and that's just one of the places where they do it. There are temples all over this city. In fact, there's another one right beside the one you're looking at, but you can't see it from here. Some black god with an unpronounceable name. I don't know what he stands for, but he's the ugliest one I've seen, and that's saying something."

They walked south as Luis Garcia continued his monologue. "This plaza," he said, "is the only part of the city where you can walk any distance without running into one of their damned canals. They use canals instead of streets, the way they do in Venice, I suppose. These Aztecs come and go in canoes, and they use barges for transporting goods. I guess boats seem like a sensible way to travel to men who've never seen a wheel or a horse. We won our share of battles on our way here because the fools scattered in panic at the sight of a stallion. But they have strange beasts of their own, and Montezuma has collected them. This is his menagerie."

They were in a garden, the most beautiful that Martinez had ever seen. It stretched out so far that he could not see the end of it, and it was filled with fruit trees, flowering shrubs, and beds of herbs and blossoms. Stone walks intersected the garden, running between the gleaming marble buildings arranged about the grounds. And from their white walls came ungodly screams.

"The animals must be hungry," said Garcia. "Their attendants seem to be busy elsewhere. You won't believe it, physician, but I swear to you that this Montezuma has hundreds of men who do nothing but look after his pets. I don't know what's happened to them all."

"There's one," Martinez said uneasily, as a figure stepped out from behind a distant stand of trees. The man saw the two Spaniards, stopped, and hurried off in the opposite direction. Martinez was glad to see him go, but cringed at the thought of furtive savages lurking in the shrubbery around him.

"Forget him," said Garcia. "Look at that." To the left of the walk was a sunken area, and in it was a large stone pool full of brightly colored fish. "He has dozens of pools like that, some for fish and some for fowl. And the pools are filled with fresh or salt water, whatever suits the creatures best. Whoever heard of such a thing? Montezuma's beasts are treated better than men, and what he feeds them every day would serve an army."

The soldier stopped at the entrance to one of the white buildings. "Let's go in here," he said. "I think these are some of the stranger animals."

A cacophony of howls and roars poured through the doorway. To Martinez, the place looked like a tomb, but he went in. He was so afraid the building might be filled with armed men that he could hardly spare a glance for the beasts. Nevertheless, he and Garcia were the only human beings there.

When he finally began to study the animals, Martinez was tantalized by their similarity to the creatures he had seen in Europe, yet his eye was keen enough to recognize the differences, even through the elaborate latticework that masked the roomy cages. Some of them seemed to be wolves, foxes, and lions—but they were not. Others looked like nothing he had ever imagined. In spite of his fear, he was fascinated.

"Look out for those," said Garcia, pointing.

"The ones that look like spotted lions? Why? Do they roam through the streets?"

"No. But if you see a man wearing one of those skins, keep away from him. They call those beasts 'jaguars,' and the men who bear those spots are their most dangerous warriors. They have two sorts of knights here: these jaguars, and the 'eagles,' who wear feathers. Each serves one of their gods. The eagle knights belong to that feathered serpent we spoke of before, and they are bad enough. But they are with Montezuma, and their god is the one whose mantle Cortez wears. The jaguar knights know no master but that black god whose temple stands beside the great pyramid. When you've seen their shrine, you'll know why I warned you."

One of the black-and-gold creatures clawed at the latticework cage. Its red mouth gaped, snarling. Martinez stepped back involuntarily; the fear he felt was something more than a dread of its bright fangs.

"Let's go," he said. "I've seen enough."

"I must show you the birds," said Garcia. "You've never seen anything like them. They're like rainbows. The Aztecs use their feathers for decorations."

"I can see birds enough to suit me from here," said Martinez as he stepped out into the sunlight. He began to wish that he had never left the palace.

"The serpents, then. There's a whole house full of them. There's one that's a marvel. His tail is covered with little bells, and he rings them before he strikes with his poison."

"No serpents," said Martinez.

"Getting jumpy, are you?" Garcia grinned. "Well, there's one more place here I have to show you before we visit the pyramid. This is sure to interest a man in your line of work. Come on, now. I insist."

He grasped Martinez by the arm and all but dragged him

forward. The alchemist knew that he was being mocked, but there was nothing he could do. He thought of running, then thought of himself lost in the city.

"They're a strange people," said Garcia, brutally, indifferent to his companion's protestations, "those knights I mentioned. When there is no war, they fight among themselves, the eagles against the jaguars. And I don't mean tourneys such as civilized men might have. They take the losers and sacrifice them to their gods. Their best men! They're crazy. And wait till you see what Montezuma keeps in here."

He stopped outside the white walls. Martinez heard strange cries from within, but he could hardly imagine what sort of animal might make such sounds.

"Look at those plants before we go in," said Garcia, obviously enjoying himself. "I've heard the herbs that Montezuma grows here make good medicine. Things we've never learned about. You should study them, physician. They might be of use to you."

Martinez stared stupidly at the ground and made a show of examining the leaves and flowers. For all he knew there was magic here, but now he could not bring himself to care. "Fascinating," he said at last.

"Come inside," said Garcia. "You'll love this."

"Are these buildings always left open? Shouldn't they be locked?"

"These people have no locks. It seems they have no thieves, either. I told you they weren't civilized. Look!"

For a moment Martinez could hardly see in the dim light of the menagerie. There were braziers and torches here but, unattended, they had gone out. The faint shapes he saw, and the jabbering and screaming he heard, convinced Martinez that this must be a house of monkeys. Then his eyes adjusted to the light.

It was a house of horrors.

"Montezuma keeps his monsters here," said Garcia, and he laughed.

A dwarf leaned his huge head against the latticework. He was unconscious, if not dead, but his head lolled back and forth as he was rocked in the arms of a wailing albino whose white eyes were wild. A naked hunchback groped out through the bars, speaking frantically in an unintelligible tongue.

Alfonso had seen misshapen men before, and their appearance had never disturbed him. He had known a dwarf who was a master magician. But he had never seen a collection of such people before, and he had never seen them caged like beasts. There were dozens of them.

"I think they're starving," said Garcia. "Nobody has time for them now."

A woman with no arms or legs squirmed like a snake in the corner.

"How do you like them?" asked Garcia. "I thought they would interest a man of science like you."

"Enough," said Martinez faintly. He pushed past his guide and staggered out into the fresh air. "They are human, Garcia. Can't something be done for them?"

"They were well kept, my friend, until this rebellion started. Now their keepers are in turmoil, like everyone else, and have other things to worry about. If they trouble you so much, you can feed them your next meal—if you can find one."

Martinez did not reply. He tried to blot the grotesque menagerie out of his mind, and to find consolation in the fact that he and Garcia were going back the way they had come. Their shadows were long in the afternoon light, and the palace loomed before them.

"Not so fast, physician. You're going the wrong way. The temples are over there, to your left."

"It's late, Garcia."

"They have no need of you in the palace. And you told me you wanted to see the city. I wouldn't want to disappoint you. Behold the great pyramid."

"I've seen it."

"Look again. This is the heart of the city, where the hearts of men are torn bloody from their ribs."

The white pyramid stood to the west of the palace, and its bulk blotted out the sinking sun. It rose in five stages, each taller than a house, but it did not reach a point. The top of the great pyramid was flat, and on the terrace at its summit stood twin shrines. A double staircase ran up the steep side of this imposing temple; the railings were twin serpents made of marble, whose fierce faces rested on the ground while their tails stretched toward the sky.

"How big is it?" Martinez asked at length.

"Who knows?" said Garcia. "It's the biggest thing in the city —that's for sure. There are a hundred and fourteen steps to the peak, and those two shrines at the top aren't small. Want to go up?"

"No," Martinez said nervously. "Have you been up there?"

"Montezuma took us once—me and Cortez, and some of the others—to show us the shrines and the view of the city. The second time was only with our men. Cortez took an iron bar and smashed the idols, and we rolled the blood-stained things down the steps and shattered them against the stones you're standing on."

"What did the Aztecs do?"

"Well, they didn't like it much, but Montezuma smoothed things over. For a while, anyway. I told you he thinks Cortez is a god, and the one who founded the city, at that! So he decided that if Cortez didn't like the sacrifices there must be something wrong with them, and he let us put the image of the Virgin up there. The priests wouldn't accept it, though, and they predicted that their god would punish us."

"And?"

"You and your accursed second expedition arrived. Since then, things have been going to hell. We had to leave the city to put your expedition in its place, and while we were gone this rebellion broke out. The Devil is no weakling."

"Which god dwells in this thing, Garcia? The jaguar or the eagle?"

"This is their war god. Everyone worships him without really caring one way or the other. It's the two below him who cause the trouble. One, the patron of the eagle knights, is that feathered serpent that Montezuma follows. He stands for peace or some such foolishness, but they think Cortez is his incarnation, so I suppose we should be grateful for him. It's the other who worries me. Come, I'll show you his temple. I don't know much about this, physician; you should ask our priest. He's studying their religion—he thinks it will help him to convert these savages."

Martinez felt his pulse quicken. He had pieced together his own version of Aztec theology from Garcia's ramblings, and he felt certain that this was the god he wanted. A god of darkness and mystery, who cared for neither war nor peace. A god of sorcery, and perhaps one who made gold.

"What is his name?"

"I don't remember. None of their names can be spoken by any Christian tongue. But it does have a meaning—something about a mirror. Not a looking glass, more like a crystal. They say he looks into it and sees the future. But see for yourself."

The temple stood south of the great pyramid and west of Montezuma's menagerie. Its central position alone gave a clue to its importance. Smaller than the sanctuary of the war god, it rose on three levels to a bare platform. There were none of the carvings that adorned the base and the summit of the larger pyramid. Stark and cold, the black stone structure stood in the twilight.

"I think it's bigger than it looks," said Garcia. "They say this is the only temple in the city that goes down into the ground farther than it rises toward the sun. You can see the door there; it's open. But not even Cortez wanted to go through it."

Carved on the side of the black pyramid was a gigantic face; its mouth was the entrance to the temple of the dark god, and it yawned open as though beckoning visitors to step between its jagged teeth. The face, Martinez suddenly saw, was really a gigantic skull. He stepped back from it and thought of the skull of the sorcerer Don Sebastian de Villanueva, buried in the sack that was still strapped to his back. A shiver ran up his spine.

"It's getting late," said Alfonso Martinez. "Let's go back, Garcia."

"I've one more thing to show you, physician. Tales don't mean much, and I doubt if you realize how evil these gods are. But this should convince you. Come into the shadows, here, between the pyramids."

Martinez felt himself forced onward, although he had no wish to go. He was relieved at first to see that the gathering darkness held nothing more than another pyramid, but before he could speak he realized that this one was composed entirely of human skulls.

"These are the relics of their gods," Garcia said. "This pyramid, and those two towers flanking it. One of the men sat here for a day, when times were better a few months ago, and he counted a hundred and thirty-six thousand skulls. How do you like the city now?"

Martinez stumbled out of the shadows and toward the square. "Look!" he gasped. "Someone's coming!"

"Our own men," said Garcia. "One of our patrols. Nothing to worry about, but we'd better get back to the palace just the same. You act like you've caught a fever."

A handful of armored men rushed past them. A few were on horseback, but most were on foot, and some of them moved as clumsily as Alfonso Martinez.

"Those men are hurt," said Garcia. "Something has happened. We'd better get back."

Wild shouts came from the twilight at the other end of the eastern causeway.

"They've risen again," Garcia said. "Come on, physician. We'd better run!"

3. The Jaguars

MARTINEZ kept to the palace. The whole city, led by Montezuma's brother, had risen against Cortez, and by the third day of fighting the alchemist would have sworn that he had treated every Spanish soldier for at least one wound. Even Cortez came to him with a gash in his left hand. Martinez thanked the fates that had protected him alone from injury. He realized that he had been spared because he stayed far from the battle, yet he could not suppress the conviction that he was also under the protection of the grisly talisman hidden in his pack. The skull had power, and he believed that it was saving him for some higher destiny than an encounter with an Aztec arrow.

For now, though, he wished it would teach him medicine. He feared that his disguise was slipping. The courage of the Spaniards and the stoicism of their Indian allies had helped to keep his secret safe, and the situation of the besieged palace was so desperate that none of the soldiers had any time to keep an eye on the activities of the company's physician. The men accepted his crude treatment and returned to battle. Only those who were too severely injured to fight on had a real chance to observe his incompetence, and those he drugged. They would either die or heal themselves. Many of them had died, but it had not always been the fault of Alfonso

Martinez. The Aztecs fought viciously for their city.

Martinez looked ruefully at his diminishing supply of sleeping powders and prayed to the silver skull for a change in his fortunes.

On the first day after the Aztecs attacked, Cortez had ordered four hundred men to move out of the palace and restore order; but the Spaniards soon found themselves attacked by a wave of warriors so numerous and ferocious that no progress was possible. Cortez had underestimated the city that had endured his orders so patiently for so many months. Neither armor nor guns were of any use against the onslaught of Tenochtitlan's rebellious population. Stones and spears poured down from every rooftop, and the Spaniards were forced to retreat to the palace with their attack scarcely launched.

The Aztec advance was heralded by thousands of voices crying wildly, by the sound of piercing whistles that signaled assault, and by the unearthly wailing of the conches that served as native trumpets. Spaniards fell under the cloud of missiles that flew over their defenses, while flaming arrows set fire to the palace and the timbers that shored up the wall around it. The flames and smoke created havoc, and the Spaniards were near panic. No one could hear orders, but everyone heard the ominous pounding of the great logs battering against the walls. Even Martinez heard it as he hid in the innermost recesses of the palace, finally having given up, in his terror, all pretense of offering aid to the wounded men.

Finally Cortez was forced to do what his enemies could not. The sole way to put out the flaming walls was to knock them down with cannon fire. The Aztecs poured through the breach, and only the coming of the night slowed their invasion. They drew back as the sun set, and left the starving Spaniards to spend the night repairing the broken wall and digging in the ground for water.

On the second day Cortez himself led an attack, but the Spanish onslaught was stopped completely when it reached the canals beyond the central plaza. All the bridges had been drawn up or broken down, so that it was impossible to move forward through the water. Canoes were everywhere, and Spanish riders who moved too close to the water's edge were gutted by upthrusting spears. The Spaniards took revenge for the previous day's disaster by burning several native houses, but the canals prevented the fires from spreading, and before the day ended Cortez was driven back to the palace. His own troops were decimated, but the ranks of the enemy seemed untouched. The entire population of the city was in arms, including the women, and reinforcements were pouring in from neighboring cities under the control of Tenochtitlan. The Aztecs numbered at least a hundred thousand, perhaps two or three times more. Cortez realized too late the consequences of releasing Montezuma's brother, Cuitlahuac; he had unleashed a demon, and there would be no calling him back.

That night, Cortez determined to begin the construction of towers that would protect his men when they ventured forth from the palace. But it would take time to construct these from the available timber, and he had no guarantee that they would serve their purpose. Still, it was an idea, and the exhausted men willingly fell to work.

By the morning of the third day Alfonso Martinez was close to madness. The hollow pain in his stomach was gone, but he felt a giddiness that was surely a symptom of starvation. He had not slept. He was exhausted, yet too nervous to rest, and in any case he had no time. During the day, the severely stricken were carried in to him, and at night their comrades staggered into his stronghold with what they thought were only minor injuries. Martinez had never seen so much blood in his life. From time to time he dozed against a wall, but these moments of unconsciousness brought him no peace, only enough strength to endure further tortures.

What worried Martinez most was the constant presence of the expedition's priest. He was the only man except the alchemist who spent all his time among the wounded, and his sturdy, resolute figure was too often beside Martinez when it was time to treat an especially urgent case. He asked difficult questions, and his eyes gleamed with a curiosity in which there was a growing measure of suspicion.

A party had gone out at dawn; shortly afterward they were back, bearing their fallen comrades. Some of these were easy enough to deal with. In fact, Martinez was surprised at and sometimes a little proud of the crude skill he had developed in two days of practice on helpless patients. But there was one man with a wound so terrible that it was impossible to believe he was still alive. His belly had been slashed open by a jagged stone sword, and over his legs poured yards of intestines, glistening except where they had dragged in the dust. Martinez turned away, sick to his stomach. He had never seen anything like this before, and he could not bear to look at the man, much less try to help him. His own face felt as white and cold as that of his patient.

The priest hurried up. He looked at Martinez and at the stricken man. "What's the matter?" he said. "Help him!"

He spun Martinez around to face the figure on the floor. Martinez spared the twitching, gasping man one glance, then averted his face again.

"Do something!" said the priest. "We can save him. I've seen them live through worse than this." He dropped to his knees, gathered up the soldier's spilled intestines in his hands, and began to stuff them back into the wound.

"He's yours, Father," said Martinez as he stumbled away. "Give him the last rites."

As he turned his back on the priest and his charge, he saw Luis Garcia among the men hurrying out to rejoin the battle. The tall soldier wore a dirty bandage under his helmet, and on his face was a wolfish grin. "Hello, physician," he roared. "My head's fine. And there's a good fight brewing. You should come and join us. They've got men on the great temple now, and we have to clear them off before they shoot down enough arrows to kill us all. Cortez is leading the next charge."

Martinez could imagine nothing that would appeal to him less, until he heard the voice of the priest in his ear: "That man is dead, and you could have saved him. At least you could have tried! What kind of a doctor are you? I've been watching you, Martinez. I don't think you know what you're doing!"

Martinez ran from the accusing voice. "Hold on a minute," he said, as he fell into step beside Garcia. "I'm going with you."

"Good enough," said Garcia. "I can't figure you out, physician, but I'll say one thing for you: you're game."

Martinez ignored the comment and hurried from the indignant priest. He snatched a helmet from a corpse and clapped it onto his own head, then stooped again to pick up a battered shield. At the door he turned for an instant and addressed the priest.

"You take care of them, Father," he said. "I've had all I can stand. There's a war to be won, and a man can only stand by for so long."

Bolstered by his own courageous claims, Martinez made it through the gates and into the plaza before he realized what he had done. His stone sanctuary was behind him. He was in the thick of the fighting, in the midst of a battle so fierce that he gasped at the sight of it. Rocks and arrows fell all around him. Not three feet away a man dropped, howling, to the ground.

Martinez ran back for the gate, but it shut in his face. He put his shield over his head and huddled beneath the wall of the palace, waiting to be killed.

He was surprised to realize, as the minutes passed, that he had been spared. In fact, it seemed that the missiles had ceased dropping around him. The sound of the conflict was distant now. Cautiously he lifted his shield and peered out from under it. What he saw amazed him. Hundreds of men, Spaniards and Aztecs alike, stood quietly in the plaza with their arms at their sides, their weapons trailing on the ground. Like Martinez, they had become observers. A truce had come into being without negotiations, as all those on the edges of the fray turned their attention toward the great pyramid, where the day's glory was to be won and lost. Martinez lowered his shield to the level of his nose and looked over its top toward the struggle for the towering temple.

Cortez himself led the attack, his injured left hand protected by a shield strapped to his arm. He and hundreds of his men charged the pyramid, the fire from cannon and musket cutting the way through the ranks of the defending Mexicans.

The pyramid was alive with Aztec warriors. They represented every rank, and seemed to be dispersed upon the five receding levels according to their status. At the base of the temple were hordes of common soldiers, wearing loincloths. Above them stood the proven warriors, their station indicated by the red bands around their heads, and by the quilted cotton armor that was sufficient to deflect almost any native weapon. On the third and fourth levels were the knights of the eagle and the jaguar. Their bodies were protected by plates of gleaming metal; on their heads they wore the insignia of their knighthood. The Knights of the Feathered Serpent were adorned with feathers, and their rivals, joined with them in the war against the invaders, were adorned with spotted skins, the heads of wild animals forming rude helmets that masked their warlike features. At the summit were the chiefs, bearing feathered cloaks of such ornate intricacy that they seemed utterly inappropriate for fighting—visible proof that these arrogant Aztecs never expected to meet their enemies in personal combat. Among the chiefs ran the priests of the native gods, their hair long and their beards wild, their black robes embroidered with skulls.

Cortez, followed by his own men and their Indian allies, stormed the steps. From the heights came a shower of missiles: arrows, spears, stones, and also timbers, some of them afire. Many men fell in the attack, but many more pressed onward. Continual blasts from the guns opened a path for them, and they struggled up the double stairway to the first level. Once they had reached it the battle was more than half won, for the Aztecs above them were obliged to stop the hail of weapons to avoid injuring their own troops. In hand-to-hand combat, the Aztecs were no match for the invaders. Spanish steel and Spanish armor had already forged a young empire in the New World, and the natives had nothing but courage to stand against the onslaught.

The higher the Spaniards went, the wilder the struggle grew.

The knights of the eagle and the jaguar fought with ferocity and skill that seemed inspired by the black-clad priests who raged above them at the peak of the pyramid. Since the Aztec knights wore armor too, here the contest seemed more equal. By now the battle was more than a hundred feet above the ground, and Martinez watched in sick horror as men on both sides dropped, wailing, from the temple to be shattered on the rocks below.

The distant rattle of muskets echoed through the plaza and another handful of Tenochtitlan's defenders tumbled down the steps. They could not fight the guns, and one by one they withdrew to the terrace atop the temple. There they waited for Cortez.

He was not long in coming. The broad pavement at the peak of the pyramid became a battleground from which there could be no retreat. A dozen Spaniards were thrown backward down the steps as they swarmed over the last step of the stairway. The guns on the ground grew silent; like their enemies, the Spaniards could no longer afford to send death rattling into a mass of men that was half friend and half foe. The fight for the pyramid would be decided by those who struggled on its summit.

Martinez watched the battle with an interest that was almost abstract. He knew as well as any man what was at stake, but there was something so bizarre in the spectacle of the small figures murdering each other atop the gigantic temple that he began to view it as a show designed for his own amusement. Not much time passed before he began to enjoy the beautiful symmetry of the arcs made by men falling from the terrace to meet death on the stones below. He noticed with some interest that more Aztecs than Spaniards were dropping, at least on the side that he could see; but then again, there were more Aztecs.

He spotted Cortez just once, recognizing the tiny man in the distance only by his armor and his shield. The commander teetered on the brink, an Indian clutching each of his arms. Martinez held his breath then, suddenly aware of his own vulnerability, and of how dim his chances of survival would be if this one man fell. Cortez dropped to one knee and twisted his body, and all at once the man on his right arm was hurled over the precipice, plummeting like a shot bird in a mass of feathers. His sword arm free, Cortez slashed at the man who held his other arm, and in an instant he was alone. He stood there for a heartbeat, then dashed back into the fray.

Martinez felt like applauding, and indeed he heard a cheer rise up from the throng gathered around the base of the pyramid. The alchemist felt a surge of power rush through him. He could not contain himself. He glanced around quickly, determined that he was unobserved, then rushed from the wall and slipped his sword through the naked back of a native near at hand. The man crumpled, and Martinez felt his weight on the blade; then the body slid off the sword and collapsed. No one had noticed. Feeling more of a soldier, Martinez stepped back behind his shield. It was his first kill.

Unexpectedly, he found himself shaking. Some part of this was excitement, but more of it was fear. He did not regret killing the man, but somehow it had reminded him of his own mortality. He sensed that he had been out of the palace for too long, and he wondered how many hours had passed since the gate had closed behind him. The sun was certainly lower, and while it seemed to Martinez that there was less activity now upon the high terrace, it was impossible to tell what that might mean. He could only see what was happening at the nearest edge, and that was next to nothing. He saw a great many corpses, but almost no one who was moving.

He looked toward the two shrines rising up from the top of the pyramid, then realized that his eye had been drawn to them because they were aflame. At the sight of the smoke, another roar ran through the ranks of the troops on the ground. A few Spanish soldiers moved warily down the highest steps, and more followed. The shouts around Martinez grew louder. Cortez had won. His men streamed down the double stairway, hundreds of them, almost as many as had fought their way to the top. They brought prisoners with them: bloodied knights, feathered chieftains, and two stiff, black-robed priests.

To retreat after this triumph seemed like insanity, but Alfonso Martinez knew that Cortez had no real choice. He had shamed the Aztecs, and the initial effect was strong enough to render them immobile, but it could not last. Better to return to the palace and hope that the battle for the pyramid would make the city of Tenochtitlan more malleable.

But would it? Martinez had a sinking feeling that nothing had really been accomplished, unless it were the loss of more precious Spanish blood. They had had a victory of sorts, but its ultimate result was that the forces of Cortez were weaker than ever before. The men who had survived were now marching away from the temple toward the palace, and no attempt was made to stop them. Martinez wondered how many of them had wounds for him to treat. Then he thought of the angry priest he had left not many hours ago, and wondered what his own life would be worth if he returned, to be denounced as a charlatan. Panic fell on him like a dead weight. The palace might be more dangerous than the plaza.

Someone touched him lightly on the shoulder. He whirled, expecting his uncouth companion, Luis Garcia, but saw instead the head of a jaguar. The man's eyes were shadowed by the black and gold, but his mouth was grim. Martinez moaned. "Not now," he said. "We've won."

He whirled and saw another jaguar knight behind him. Four hands reached out to hold him, and a third man dressed in jaguar skin caressed his throat with a black stone blade. One of them spoke, but Martinez could not understand.

"Open the gates!" screamed Martinez, but even as he spoke he knew that only the trumpets of Cortez could gain admittance to the palace, and that the heroes of the pyramid were still long minutes away.

"Open the gates!" he cried again, but nothing happened. He spoke to the masked men who held him. "You don't want me," he said. "They need me inside. Let me alone."

Gently but firmly the three jaguar knights pulled him away from the gate. They drew him toward the south, away from the palace. His feet dragged, but the blade beneath his chin was most persuasive. He tried to argue, but understood that his words meant nothing to the trio dressed in the skins of predatory beasts. He nearly wept when, just before they dragged him around a corner, he saw the gates of the palace swing open. Then he was in another street, and could not even see his sanctuary. These were the knights of the black temple. He knew where they were taking him.

4. The Skull

ALFONSO Martinez did not give up hope entirely until the three jaguar knights shoved him through the jaws of the skull that formed the entrance to the black pyramid; but when he stumbled into that dark hole, he knew that he was lost. There was no chance that the Spanish troops would find him here. He staggered down a shadowy inclined plane, his captors close behind him. The depths of the temple were honeycombed with passageways, and the men in the spotted skins hurried him through one after another. They were not so gentle with him now that there was no possibility of anyone noticing his abduction; more than once he lurched into walls or tumbled to the floor as he was driven through dim tunnels that seemed to lie at crazy angles to each other. His knees were scraped, his face was blood-ied, and he was delirious with terror.

When they finally stopped, he was grateful for a moment, then filled with an even greater fear as he realized how close to death he must be.

He stood in a black stone room. The walls and ceiling tilted grotesquely, but the floor was level. It was made of glistening, translucent mica. Flaming braziers stood in the corners, and five stiff figures waited in a row against the farthest wall. Before them stood an altar with a small statue on it, and a stone slab big enough to hold a man. Martinez looked at it and groaned. He tried to back away, but the warriors held him.

The little idol was made of obsidian, the same gleaming black stone that gave the Aztecs blades for their swords and knives. A golden band encircled its head, and in one hand was a dark shield, so highly polished that Martinez saw himself reflected in it. The black mirror was surrounded by feathers of blue and green. In its other hand the idol held four arrows.

Martinez peered beyond it to the silent figures waiting by the wall. One by one they moved toward him, and he knew them for the priests of the dark god. Their robes were black, the borders embroidered with white skulls, and below the hems were feet and ankles hideous with bloody scars. The lobes of their ears had been slashed too, and their long hair was matted with gore. Their coppery faces were almost as black as the robes they wore, for their features were smeared with dark, resinous pitch. Only their eyes were bright.

When the last of the five stepped toward him, Martinez saw to his amazement that it was a woman.

He saw no scars on her body, no pitch on her face, no dried blood in the black hair that flowed gleaming to her ankles. She wore the same costume as the others, but her face seemed less menacing than the craggy features of the four men who surrounded her. Her huge eyes gleamed, her nostrils flared, yet her full lips were twisted into something like a smile. She looked nothing like the pale women of Spain, but there was a dark beauty in her that kept Martinez entranced. He forgot his fear in the wonder of her face.

"I am Toci," she said. "This is the house of Tezcatlipoca, the Smoking Mirror."

"Toci . . ." echoed Martinez. "Tezcatlipoca." The alien words seemed suddenly important to him. The name of the priestess was simple enough, but the name of the god reverberated through his rattled brain. "Tezcatlipoca," he said again. "The Smoking Mirror." This was what he had sought, and he began to feel less frightened than fascinated. Then he realized what she had said to him.

"You speak Spanish," he said. "Do you know what I am saying?"

"Cortez has a woman," answered Toci. "She learned to talk for him. The Lady Marina. She talks for Cortez, and she talks for Montezuma. She talks for the Feathered Serpent, the god of Cortez and Montezuma. I heard, I learn, and I speak for Smoking Mirror, the god of this house. The great god."

She was no more than a foot away from him. He wanted to take hold of her, to shake her, to make her explain herself, but a glance at the men around her dissuaded him.

"What will you do with me?" asked Martinez. "Will you kill me?"

"You do not know me, but I know you, and Smoking Mirror knows you. You are here for him. He spoke of you."

"Of me?"

"You are Martinez, the magic man. Cortez has a priest, but he is like the priest of the Feathered Serpent. You are the priest we want. You bring Tezcatlipoca with you. Your name for him is Smoking Mirror."

Martinez thought of the skull in his pack and his knees quivered. He was too amazed to speak anything but the truth. "I am Martinez," he said. His words came simply; the last thing he wanted was to confuse this woman, especially since she was the only one in this distorted room who seemed to understand him. "I am the magic man. I came across the sea when I heard of you. I want to see your god." He wanted to ask about the gold, but he was still too afraid. His head spun. He was torn between fear for his life and the hope that this woman with the golden skin was the key to his destiny.

"This is Smoking Mirror," said Toci, and she pointed toward the black statue. "But he is more. You bring more, Martinez. You bring him."

"What do you want from me?" asked Martinez.

"You know," said Toci. "Smoking Mirror." Then she said something he could not understand. Her face betrayed neither anger nor impatience, but at her word the men in jaguar skins forced Martinez facedown on the floor. He felt his nose crushed against the stones and hands ripping at the pack on his back. Then he heard a chorus of shouts and gasps. Some of the weight fell away from him, but one hand was still on his neck, pressing his head down, and he did not resist it.

Something rolled across the flagstones and came to rest before his upturned eyes. It was the silver skull of Don Sebastian de Villanueva. Its empty sockets seemed to stare at him. The three jaguar knights drew back from it, and the four priests dropped to their knees. Martinez remained where he was. Only Toci stood erect. She crossed her brown hands on her breasts and chanted again and again the name of her dark god.

Martinez stared at the skull, and at the skulls embroidered on the hem of Toci's robe. He could only guess what was happening, but his instincts told him that this was a time for boldness. He snatched at the skull, and, struggling to his feet, held it out to the priestess. "Tezcatlipoca," he said, staring at her with all the strength of character he could muster. The skull seemed to quiver in his hands. Its cold vibrations numbed his fingers.

As he reached out to the priestess the seven men sprang up to surround him, but she stopped them with a word. She stretched out her arms to Martinez, and her fingers touched his as she took his offering. Her hands were warm, but his were icy.

Martinez tried to speak carefully. "This is the skull of the greatest wizard who ever lived in my land," he said. "I carried it across the waters because I know its power. But its power is too great for me. I give it to you, if you will give me my life."

The priestess cradled the silver skull in her arms while the four priests gathered silently around her. Their faces were masks of malice. The three warriors stood between Martinez and the door, but at least they no longer held him. At last Toci answered.

"Your life?" she said. "You have your life. I have Smoking Mirror. He said he would come. The stars said he would come.

And you bring him. I do not want your life. I want you to exchange for our great priest."

Martinez felt his heart sink.

"Cortez took him today," continued Toci, and Martinez remembered the sight of the sullen idolators who had been led away from the battle on the pyramid. "Cortez has the priest," said Toci. "I have you. I want the great priest of Smoking Mirror, and Cortez wants you. You have your life."

Martinez let out an involuntary sigh of relief. Suddenly the tilted black room and the red glow of the braziers lost some of their menace, but the reassurances of the mysterious woman who held the fleshless head of Don Sebastian only served to set his mind racing off in another direction. If there was to be an exchange of prisoners, then he was safe, but that meant he had only a short time to fathom the secrets of the Smoking Mirror cult. What did they want with the skull? And was there a way for him to use his knowledge of its origin for his own benefit? A risky game, thought Martinez, but one in which the rewards might include secrets for which any risk was justified. If the secret of the Aztec gold was anywhere, it was in the bowels of this black temple. He watched the priestess as she clutched the silver skull to her heart, and he thought of her as one of the countless beauties who would adorn his throne when he was master of the world's riches.

"Tell me of it," said Toci abruptly. She turned her back to Martinez and placed the skull carefully on the long stone slab. Her four pitch-smeared priests gathered before the slab and hid the death's head from Martinez.

Martinez tried to answer her but could not find the right words. He wondered what she would understand. He longed to concoct an ingenious lie, but was forced to settle for the simple truth.

"I said that he was the greatest magician of my land. He died in battle, but he lived after he died. He lived on blood; others died to make him live. Fire killed him again. This is all that is left of him. But few know of him even in Spain. His power is a secret. What do you know of him?"

37

"He is Smoking Mirror. He talks to me. Cortez came to be Quetzalcoatl, the Feathered Serpent, the god who fights in the sky with Smoking Mirror. The Feathered Serpent is a bad god for us. He talks peace and he makes Montezuma a woman. Now I have Smoking Mirror. He loves war and we want him. He is good for us, bad for Cortez. He comes from far and you are his servant. Smoking Mirror comes to fight for us."

Martinez surmised from her enigmatic remarks that there was a cult in the city ready to combat the influence of Cortez. The alchemist was happy enough to have his theory vindicated, but the enthusiasm of the priestess disturbed him. He knew that the skull was strong, but what could the relic of even so mighty a magician do that would satisfy her expectations? And what would she think of Martinez when she realized that she had hoped for too much?

"What will you do with it?" he asked nervously, gesturing toward the four grim priests and what lay concealed behind them.

"Watch," said Toci.

The four priests stepped away from the black slab, revealing the body of a man stretched out upon it. He had not been there a moment before, and Martinez thought at once of magic, but dismissed the idea as quickly as it came to him. The man was mortal, and he was alive. Martinez guessed there must be another entrance to this chamber, and his guess was confirmed when he saw that now five of Tezcatlipoca's dark priests were gathered around the idol. The fifth held a jagged knife of gleaming black, its hilt the head of a monster.

There could be no doubt of what they planned to do. Martinez had heard of these ceremonies before, but had no wish to see one. He stared at the victim, amazed that he made no struggle, then concluded from the uneven rise and fall of his chest that the man must be drugged. He was nearly naked, with only a bit of white cloth wrapped around his waist. As the color of the pathetic garment registered in his mind, Martinez suddenly realized what he should have noticed long before: the man was white, too—he could only be a Spanish prisoner.

The priests remained silent, but the priestess sidled up to Martinez and whispered proudly. "See," she said. "Smoking Mirror wants blood. Blood of his people. Blood of his land."

She held up a large bowl decorated in black and white. "And more," she said. "His land. Your land. The trees bring it."

Martinez saw to his bewilderment that the bowl was filled with ordinary dirt. He tried to piece together Toci's puzzling remarks, and began to remember something. There had been trees, Spanish trees, saplings that the priest of the second expedition had nursed throughout the voyage so that he could try growing them in Mexican soil. And on the first night in Tenochtitlan the trees had been torn out by their roots, the pots emptied. So the dirt in this bowl might have been dug from Spanish ground. It was possible, but it made no sense. What good was dirt?

Only one sort of creature could care so much for its native soil, thought Martinez, and that was one that could not survive without it. But how could the servants of Smoking Mirror have known that the silver skull was the relic of a vampire? And what good was a bowl of earth to a wizard who could never rise again for long enough to seek peace in the ground?

"Look," said the priestess, clutching the alchemist's arm.

Four priests took the captive by each of his arms and legs. The fifth stood at his head, holding the black knife aloft in both hands. The prisoner stirred. Toci moved away from Martinez. She reached into the bosom of her robe and pulled out some sort of dried flower, which she held beneath the nose of the man on the slab. He coughed and kicked, and his eyes opened.

"Help me," said the prisoner, looking straight at Martinez. "Stop them."

For an instant Martinez thought of doing something, but before he had a chance to make even a futile gesture the three jaguar knights stepped forward to surround him. He could only turn his head away.

He heard a scream, and against his will he looked back across the room. The flames from the braziers cast gigantic shadows on the wall, and the biggest of them was the image of the priest who

39

held the knife aloft in both his hands. The black blade dropped down and ripped into the body of the man, who writhed and squirmed in the grip of his captors. His gasp was cut off as the knife tore into the flesh below his ribcage, and he was nearly dead when the priest reached into his chest and pulled out his heart.

Martinez winced, but his fascination was greater than his fear. He watched as Toci stepped forward to scatter earth over the twitching corpse, and he even watched when the priest thrust the dripping heart between the jaws of the silver skull she held.

Something was wrong with the room. The walls began to shimmer, and at the sight Martinez realized how terrified he was.

One of the warriors stepped forward, and with a single blow of his obsidian sword lopped off the head of the body on the black slab. He dropped it into a flaming pot beside the idol of Tezcatlipoca. The brown hands of the priestess put the silver skull down where the head had been. Her hands were red, and the skull was red, and the walls were red. Blood was everywhere.

The five priests stepped back from the black stone. The young priestess remained beside the scene of sacrifice, and she held her hands over her eyes. The three warriors lowered their heads. Only Alfonso Martinez was fool enough to look.

The sloping ceiling slid downward; the flames that lit the room rose to meet it. There was a flash, and everything turned white and cold. The people in the pyramid were insubstantial shadows; the black idol turned to gold. Then it disappeared. There was nothing in the room, nothing in the universe, but a flat black stone awash in blood.

The skull grinned up at the sky while tendrils of red crept up its cheeks. It grew thick with gore while the body beneath it seemed to waste away. Blood traced crude features on the gleaming bone, it glistened in the hollow sockets where once eyes had shone. Black hair bristled on the silver brow, and the silver face turned white as death beneath the crawling crimson. The decapitated corpse grew long and thin, and its hands reached slowly up to claw at the face of a man dead for a generation. Pale fingers with black nails clutched at the head as if intent on claiming it, and when they slipped away they exposed dark, dead eyes. The horror on the slab raised itself and turned its gaze on Alfonso Martinez. A silver silence overwhelmed the temple of Tezcatlipoca, and finally Martinez turned away.

When he looked again, the room beneath the pyramid was as it had been before. The warriors were gone, though, and the five priests of Smoking Mirror lay facedown on the floor. Even the priestess Toci was kneeling, before the altar that held the small black idol. Beside her stood a tall, gaunt figure draped in robes of red and black and white. His dark hair hung to his shoulders, his long black mustache almost reached his chin. A pale scar ran down the left side of his face.

Martinez had never dared to imagine such a feat of necromancy, but he could scarcely doubt that this was Don Sebastian de Villanueva, the warrior, the wizard, the vampire, the man who had been destroyed in flames twenty-four years ago.

The dead man smiled at Martinez.

"See," said Toci. "Smoking Mirror."

Martinez tried to answer her, but darkness overwhelmed him. He was only a minor magician. He took one step forward and fell in a faint at the feet of the monster he had carried halfway around the world.

5. A Rain of Stones

MARTINEZ awoke to find himself being dragged through the twisting corridors of the black pyramid. Before he had time to realize where he had been, he was outside in the great plaza. The morning sun blinded him, and he realized that he had spent the entire night in the temple of Smoking Mirror.

As soon as he could see again, he began to squirm in the hands of his captors. Thousands of soldiers stood in the square, Aztecs and Spaniards alike, and their presence convinced Martinez that he was being thrown out to die. Then he realized that none of the men were fighting. In fact, he saw a narrow corridor between the silent ranks of the warriors, and it seemed to lead toward the palace of Montezuma. It looked like a road to freedom, and Martinez would have been glad enough to take it, especially when he remembered the horrors he had seen not many hours ago. Yet he had seen magic, and now no power on earth could persuade him that he had not left behind him the secret of making gold.

He twisted his head to look back. A pair of jaguar knights were holding him; they looked like two of the three who had taken him the night before. Behind them walked Toci, the priestess of Tezcatlipoca. Martinez almost expected to see the tall, pale ghost of Don Sebastian looming above her, but she was alone.

"Where are we going?" he asked her.

"Cortez," said Toci.

"They'll never let us through," protested Martinez. "They'll kill us."

The priestess did not bother to answer him. Martinez scrambled to his feet, but the men who held him were strong. There was no chance of running back into the pyramid. Martinez was a little shocked to realize that he was capable of considering such a move, but the dark secrets behind were less immediately frightening than the thousands of armed men who waited ahead. At least there were laws for magic; but who could predict the behavior of so many unruly mortals, any one of whom might strike him dead on a whim?

Deciding that resistance was impossible, Martinez pulled himself up as tall as possible and tried to walk as if he wanted to. His eyes darted right and left, searching the crowd for a man who might be ready to strike him down. He and his guards passed into the opening between the troops of Tenochtitlan, and Martinez felt a frantic pounding in his head which he knew came from the beating of his heart. The blistering white sunlight was intolerable. Martinez passed row upon row of dark faces, their expressions a strange mixture of passivity and hatred. He thought that Toci was still following him and hoped that her presence might guarantee his safety, but he was afraid to look back, since that would mean taking his eyes off the silent soldiers who surrounded him.

He reached the great pyramid of the war god. Beyond it was the palace of Montezuma. The feathers and skins of the Aztecs gradually gave way to Spanish armor, and Martinez began to believe that he might survive after all. But he still had a long way to go, and there was still an array of deadly weapons at his back. He put one foot in front of the other and tried not to think.

Sooner than he would have believed possible, he had a clear view of the palace walls, and then of the small group of men who stood before the gate. The metal plate armor they wore had lost its polish beneath a covering of dust and dents; some of them were bandaged; and all of them sagged with exhaustion. They were a sorry lot, but they were his countrymen, and that fact meant more to him than it ever had before. He would have hurried toward them, but now the jaguar knights beside him held him back.

An alien figure stood in the midst of the Spanish soldiers; by his black robe and matted hair Martinez recognized him as the captive high priest of the Smoking Mirror cult. He wore an elaborate headdress of bright feathers, bound in enough gold to keep a man alive for years. Hanging from his neck on a thick gold chain was a gleaming disc of black obsidian. Like Martinez he had a guard on either arm, but he did not seem to care. His predatory features were rigid with indifference, his head was thrown back proudly; he seemed to be gazing into the sun. Only when he came closer did Martinez realize what that fixed stare into the source of all light must mean. The high priest of the black pyramid was blind.

This revelation was lost upon Martinez when he recognized one of the men who stood beside the priest. Beneath a battered helmet loomed the long, flat face of Luis Garcia. Martinez was astounded by the strength of his emotion at the sight of this ungainly lout. The man might be a bully and a clown, but he was the closest thing to a friend that Martinez had found on this accursed continent.

"Garcia!" shouted Martinez.

The bearded soldier looked up and smiled a slow smile. "Hello, physician," he said. "I thought we'd lost you."

"If you'd seen what I've seen," Martinez began, then stopped himself. It would be stupid and even dangerous to describe the unholy resurrection of Don Sebastian de Villanueva, and nothing was worth discussing if it delayed his access to the safety of the palace. "Let's go inside, Garcia."

"Take it easy. You've nothing to fear. There's a truce on. Didn't they tell you? It's Montezuma's truce. He's going to talk to his people and see if he can get them to lay down their arms. You can thank him for calming things down enough so

44

that we could trade this blind idolator for you."

"Well, make the exchange, will you?"

"You know," said Garcia, "I think you're glad to see me."

"I'd be glad enough to see you inside. What are you waiting for?"

"These things are tricky, physician. Everyone has to move very carefully. You can run for the gate if you want to; it's only a few feet away. But I'll bet you don't make it."

Martinez decided to stand still. He watched Toci lean forward to whisper something to the high priest. Martinez thought she could be planning treachery, or even discussing him, but somehow he was sure that what she spoke of was the skull that had spawned a walking corpse.

Garcia nodded, and the blind priest was released. He walked unerringly toward the knights who served his god. At the same moment, Martinez felt his arms go free.

"Come to me, physician," grinned Garcia, and Martinez stepped cautiously across the few feet of open ground between them. He saw to his surprise that Toci still followed.

"This one is worth more than you and that heathen put together," said Garcia, leering at her. "But for some reason the natives insisted that we take her along with you. She's part of the deal, and we're supposed to deliver her to Montezuma as soon as he's finished his speech. I guess their black god wants to be sure he's got somebody to talk to the king, even though he's not really king anymore."

"Not really king?" said Martinez. "What do you mean?"

"I'll tell you later. They're opening the gates."

Martinez was the first man through, and the first person he saw was the Spanish priest.

Martinez winced at the sight of him, remembering what he had forgotten during the dangers outside the fortress. This was the man who had seen him for the fraud he was, and whose shouts had driven him out into the arms of the jaguar knights. He was as great a threat as any man in the city, and he was rushing toward Martinez.

The stocky priest's honest face was flushed. He reached out both hands to Martinez, who could not bear to look at him.

"Thank God and all the saints you're safe," said the priest. "I could never have forgiven myself if you'd been killed. I know it was my tongue that drove you out into the battle, and I beg your pardon. These wars make men mad, physician, and I lost my head. I had no right to speak to you the way I did. I've prayed for your return, and for your pardon."

Martinez was at once delighted and embarrassed by this unexpected apology. He smiled sheepishly. "I was not myself either," he murmured diplomatically. "These are difficult times for all of us."

"Worse than difficult," said the priest. "Our situation is impossible."

"And this Martinez is just the man for an impossible situation," roared Luis Garcia. "He's performed a miracle. Physician, you're the first man to be taken prisoner by these pagans who lived to tell about it. How do you account for that? You lead a charmed life, that's for sure."

"I owe my life to Cortez," said Martinez, "or to whoever took that blind priest. They wanted him more than me. It wasn't pleasant, however. They had plenty of other prisoners. I saw a man sacrificed, and I might have been next. There was no magic about my escape. Only luck—and maybe the prayers of a good priest."

Garcia turned to the priest. "You'd better take this woman," he said. "She speaks for Montezuma's god, or at least one of them, and you seem like the man to bring her to him. Martinez and I may be needed here if things don't work out."

The priest walked away, and Toci calmly followed him.

"She seems to know what we're saying," said Garcia. "Maybe he can convert her."

"I doubt it," said Martinez. "That's a dangerous woman. I'd feel better if she was back in her pyramid. I don't know why she's here, but she's up to something, you can be sure of that."

"Well, she won't see Montezuma for a while. He's going to be up on the walls in a minute or two, and if he says the right things

46

to his people we just might get out of here alive. She'll have to wait her turn if she's worried about the state of his soul."

Again Martinez was reminded that he was the only Spaniard in the city who knew what had happened last night, even though he could only guess what the ghastly resurrection might mean. And he did not dare to speak of it. Meanwhile, though, there were things for him to learn.

"What were you saying about Montezuma?" he asked Garcia. "What did you mean about him not being king?"

"More Aztec treachery," mumbled Garcia. "You remember the day you got here, when Cortez released Montezuma's brother, Cuitlahuac? He was supposed to be an emissary, but when he was freed the Aztecs took him for a new king. He's been leading this uprising, and by now there's no way to tell if anyone cares what Montezuma has to say. But he's been their king for years, and he should still be good for something. The important thing is that he's on our side. If he can calm them down, we might be all right. But if he can't, we'll have to fight our way out. And then God help us all!"

Martinez tried to decide what he hoped would happen. An end to the fighting would save his neck, and that was certainly desirable, but it would probably mean a retreat from the city, away from the black pyramid and its mysteries. He could hardly bear the thought of running away when he was so close to the secrets he had sought for years. The pale face of Don Sebastian de Villanueva haunted him. He was afraid to see it again, but almost more afraid that it might disappear forever, leaving Alfonso Martinez no wiser than before. But the worst of it was that it hardly mattered what he wanted: events would take their course with no concern for his wishes. The Aztec gold seemed very far away.

A blast of trumpets drew Martinez from these unhappy thoughts. Something was happening on the top of the wall, and there was a vast murmur from the crowd that stood outside it. Martinez gazed up and saw a small group of men moving to take a central position overlooking the plaza. Towering above the clustered Spanish helmets was a crown of eagle feathers.

47

"Montezuma," whispered Luis Garcia. "We might as well wait here and listen to him. Plenty of men inside need your help, physician, but if this doesn't go well it won't much matter what you do for them."

"Is there actually any chance that he can get them to let us stay?"

"Not much hope of that. In fact, that's not even what he's going to ask for. Our best hope is that they'll lay down their arms for a day and let us crawl out of here."

Martinez felt his heart sink. Could this be the end of the adventure, an ignominious retreat just when the technique of making gold was within his grasp? Had he carried the silver skull across the ocean only to abandon its magic to a race of dusky heathens?

"Here's your chance for a look at a king," said Garcia. "And maybe your last. They know how to dress them, that's for sure. You could buy a city with what he's wearing."

A hush had fallen over Tenochtitlan. The entourage of armed men stepped aside, and Montezuma stood on the parapet in solitary splendor. His heavy, pointed crown was wrought of solid gold, and Martinez was impressed to see how high he held his head beneath the weight of it. Feathers sprouted from the crown like rays of the sun, and a long, rich robe of intricate featherwork flowed down Montezuma's back. He looked something like a bird, something like an angel, and something like a god. The mantle he wore was blue and white, and in the clasp holding it together was a green stone as big as a fist. His robes were adorned with a multitude of gems that sparkled in the hot sun, and in his hand he held an ornate wand of gold and precious stones. Even his sandals were of gold.

Martinez tried to count the jewels, to estimate their worth, and to decide how many were emeralds or diamonds. The stones were too dazzling for any close calculation, however, and he was finally most impressed by the way in which Montezuma's costume duplicated the one he himself dreamed of wearing when he had mastered all the mysteries of alchemy.

Montezuma began to speak. Martinez guessed he was about

48

forty years old. He was tall and thin, paler than most of his race. His thick black hair was cut shorter than was customary among his people, and unlike many of them he had a beard, thin and wispy except at his determined chin. Martinez could not see the king's expression clearly, but there was dignity in his bearing, and an air of resignation. He did not gesture when he spoke. Something in his demeanor suggested a gaudily dressed puppet, moving stiffly at the insistence of some hidden master. Martinez wondered if Montezuma still believed that Cortez was a god, or if he spoke only to save his own life.

"What is he saying?" he asked Garcia.

"Who the hell knows? Do you think I speak their ugly tongue? Nobody does, except Marina, Cortez's native woman. I'm sure she's listening somewhere and telling Cortez what he says. But it better be the right thing. If we have to shut his mouth, we'll be worse off than before."

Someone in the crowd below Montezuma shouted. The deposed king continued his oration, but not before Martinez had seen him stiffen. The shout had not been a friendly one. The soldiers around Montezuma stirred nervously.

"It's not going to work," Garcia said.

As if inspired by his prediction, a series of angry cries rose up from beneath the walls around the palace. Montezuma was silent, but his head began to droop under the weight of his golden crown.

"Damn it," said Garcia.

Martinez stared upward at the splendid feathered figure on the battlements, and saw something arching through the sky from the multitude hidden behind the wall. It was a stone, and it struck Montezuma's arm. The king did not flinch as it hit him. His head was bowed. He did not move. Martinez saw a gleam that might have been another jewel below Montezuma's eye, then there was a sudden shower of stones.

Spanish soldiers rushed toward the king, their shields held high, but they were far too slow. Spears and arrows rattled off their armor, but they were better protected than the man they guarded. Rocks fell like hail on the abandoned king. He staggered as a black rock bounced off his temple, then dropped into the arms of a frantic Spaniard, and all at once there was a wall of shields around him.

"This is the end," Garcia said. "We're done for!"

A handful of steel-clad men stumbled down from the parapet like some ungainly beetle, carrying a drooping, weaving mass of feathers.

"Have they killed him?" asked Martinez.

"Don't ask me, physician. You'll be the one who gets a chance to look at whatever's left of him. But it doesn't much matter now. They didn't like his speech, and that's the end of it."

Martinez felt his stomach tighten and his mouth go dry. He realized that there were worse fates than the loss of a fortune. He remembered the dead smile of Don Sebastian, and now he perceived the mockery in it.

Men rushed back and forth chaotically within the confines of the fortress that had been Montezuma's palace. They shouted without any real purpose, but their anxious screams were nothing beside the wail of anguish that rose from the square outside. Too late the Aztecs sensed that they had killed their king. Their keening drifted away, and Martinez needed no sentry to tell him that the inhabitants of Tenochtitlan had fled from the enormity of their deed. For some reason, Martinez thought of the beautiful and enigmatic priestess Toci, and of the ghastly form of Don Sebastian de Villanueva, who had stood beside her in robes of red and black and white.

"We're all doomed," said Garcia. "Look at me, physician, and look well. I'll wager this is the last time you'll ever see a dead man walking."

6. The Dead King

MARTINEZ was soon summoned to treat Montezuma's wounds, and Garcia escorted him to the royal chambers. Once again Martinez found himself in an impossible situation; he felt the emptiness in his belly that was a fear too great for panic. He was groggy from too much tension and too little sleep. He could barely think of a way to keep his disguise intact, and was almost past caring. It was one thing to pass for a physician when the men he doctored were nonentities, but something else again to have a king under his care. Incompetence could hardly pass unnoticed here, and its punishment might well be death. Of course, he had little hope of surviving, no matter what he did—the hundreds of thousands of Aztecs surrounding the palace would see to that. Yet even an hour of life was precious, and there might be a small chance for escape from the Aztecs if he gave his own countrymen no reason to execute him. Martinez entered Montezuma's chambers hoping he would find the king dead.

The first thing he saw when he crossed the threshold was the black-clad figure of Toci. Her presence did not entirely surprise him, but it was disconcerting nonetheless. Memories of murdered men and the creatures that rose from their blood were the last things Martinez needed now, when all his concentration was necessary to preserve even the illusion that he knew what he was doing. And behind Toci stood the Spanish priest. The sight of these two together unnerved Martinez completely.

"I'm not well myself," he said, not daring to look at anyone in the room. "I've been a prisoner, you know. I haven't slept. There must be someone else who can do this. I won't be responsible in my condition. . . ." Martinez had intended that this speech would ring out with increasing forcefulness, but instead it tapered off into a whimper, and nobody took any notice of it except Garcia, who pounded Martinez on the back with rough affection.

"You can do it, physician," he said. "We all have to do the best we can." With that he turned and left Martinez alone with the king and his two comforters.

The room was not Montezuma's own, but one of those that had been assigned to him when he became the prisoner of Cortez. Still, the furnishings were rich. The low stools and tables were inlaid with gems and gold; the walls were bright with hangings of intricate featherwork.

Montezuma lay on a low straw mat, in itself no different from the bed of any man in the palace, although its canopy was beautifully woven. His robes had been stripped off, and his body was covered with bruises. These seemed to be minor injuries, but there was an ugly wound on his temple, black and oozing blood. Even from across the room Martinez did not like the look of it. The king was breathing raggedly, but was not nearly dead enough to suit his physician.

"Some of his women tried to bandage his head," the priest said to Martinez, "but he would have none of it. They did wash that spot on his temple, but you can see that it's still bleeding. And he won't take any food or water."

"Is he conscious?" asked Martinez, reluctantly approaching the royal bedside.

"He was, but I don't know what's happened to him since."

"I'll take a look," said Martinez.

The priest watched him with intense interest, while the woman

Toci remained indifferent, as still and stiff as one of the enigmatic figures on the wall.

Martinez reached gingerly across a low table covered with red earthenware dishes full of fresh fruit and stewed meats. The thick brew of chocolate and spices had grown cold in its golden cup. His hand hesitated over the wasted food; he could not remember when he had last eaten. Reluctantly he restrained himself, and his fingertips brushed the sleeping Montezuma's forehead in what was meant to be the delicate touch of a born healer.

For a moment there was no response. Then suddenly Martinez felt the grip of a strong hand on his wrist. Montezuma's eyes were open and fury was in them. Briefly Martinez felt the touch of a king, then he was unceremoniously hurled away. His foot caught the edge of the table as he fell and sent the bowls crashing to the floor. Martinez landed sitting down, his clothing covered with the food he had wanted so badly.

"He's awfully strong for an injured man," said Martinez petulantly. He stood up clumsily and tried to brush himself off. There was food on his fingers, and despite his best intentions he found himself licking them.

"He has refused all help," said the priest, "even my offer to pray for him. He seems to want to die. Not even Cortez could cheer him."

The king had sunk back on his bed again. He might have been asleep, or perhaps just waiting patiently.

"He is dead," Toci said abruptly. Martinez turned to look, but saw the king's chest still rising and falling unevenly. "He is dead soon," she continued. "Tonight."

"Is she right?" asked the priest.

"It's possible, Father. I hardly had a chance to look. He's badly hurt, and he should be treated, but it will do more harm than good if he fights like that every time someone goes near him. There is nothing I can do."

"You could drug his food, but that won't help if he won't eat any of it. There must be something you can do!"

"Listen, Father. These head wounds can be complicated. The most important thing is to keep him still. I can't make him eat, and I can't even go near him, without the risk of killing him at once. Anyway, if he lives, it will be a miracle."

"And if he dies," the priest said solemnly, "he will die without Christ. I must get his consent for baptism."

Toci stepped away from the wall to stand with folded arms between the priest and Montezuma. "The king has gods," she said firmly. "Not your gods. Not the Woman and the Boy. *They* have killed him."

The priest was stung at this insult to the Virgin and Child, but he answered as calmly as he could. "His own people tried to kill him," he said.

"He wants death, he waits for it. He waits for Smoking Mirror."

Martinez raised his eyes nervously at the sound of the name. The priest and the priestess looked at him, and he had the feeling that they expected him to settle their dispute.

"A man's soul is at stake," said the priest.

"Smoking Mirror wants blood," said the priestess softly.

Martinez did not really understand her argument, but there was something very persuasive about it nonetheless. She frightened him more than the priest, and he was more concerned with his own neck than Montezuma's soul.

"Perhaps what she says is true," he suggested. "He has his own gods, Father, and no reason to be grateful to ours, whose emissaries have brought him to this sorry state. She says he has refused you. Would you force him on his deathbed to become an apostate, and to suffer an eternity far more horrible than the one reserved for an innocent pagan?"

Martinez, startled by his own eloquence, discovered that his exhaustion had suddenly given way to a euphoric energy, as if he were a runner who had caught his second wind. The edges of everything he saw were unnaturally sharp and bright.

The face of the priest turned stolid and sullen. "Would you argue theology with me? You have not even wit enough to do your own job well."

54

Martinez felt giddy, at a loss for words, but Toci rescued him. "Marina," she said.

"Of course," said Martinez. "If you don't believe the priestess, then ask the Lady Marina. You said Cortez was here; she must have been with him, interpreting for him as she always does. Ask the Lady Marina. Cortez trusts her. Ask her what Montezuma wants."

"So be it. But I will not leave you and this evil woman alone with the king. I will ask Cortez to order guards for him."

Martinez saw a frantic gleam in Toci's eyes and interpreted it as best he could. "You will ask for no one," he said, with all the authority he could muster. "You have seen how the king reacts. Will you be accountable for his behavior if a troop of armed men rush into this room? Do it, and the responsibility will be on your head."

The priest stopped in the doorway, scowled, then left without answering. But Martinez thought that he had made his point. He turned to Toci for approval, and saw her squatting down to pick up a piece of fruit that had fallen to the floor.

She rose and offered it to him. "Eat," she said. "You want it."

Martinez did as he was told. He had no idea what he was eating, but it was good. He sat on a stool in a corner, as far as possible from both Toci and Montezuma. A bowl had rolled to the foot of the stool. He scraped out what was left in it with his fingers and stuffed it into his mouth. He was thinking that the Aztecs were more generous than his own people; he had returned from the pyramid as if from the dead, but no Spaniard had thought to offer him food. He looked at the king, apparently unconscious on his straw mat, then at the priestess, who had resumed her place by the wall near the entrance to the royal chambers.

"How did you become a priestess?" he asked her suddenly.

"How?"

"Don't you remember? How did you choose this god to serve?"

"Smoking Mirror chooses," Toci said. "All my life I am his."

"You mean since you were a child? What about your mother and father? Did they give you away to the priests?"

"I do not know. All my life is for Smoking Mirror. No mother, no father."

"Are they dead? Don't you want to know who they are?"

"No."

Martinez stared at Toci. "This is no life for a girl," he said. "You should have yourself a husband. Someone to love."

"I am bride to Smoking Mirror."

"Not much love in that." Martinez leered sleepily at her. "You should have a man you can hold in your arms."

Toci's gaze seemed utterly devoid of guile. "But Smoking Mirror is here," she said. "You have brought him to the temple. The story said he would come. All my life I dreamed of him. Now he is here for me."

Martinez gave up this line of questioning, with a mixture of confusion and dismay, but he soon embarked upon another. "What are you doing here in the palace?" he asked her. "It isn't safe, you know. It might cost you your life."

"I am here for Montezuma. I am here for Smoking Mirror."

"Smoking Mirror? Do you mean your god, or do you mean Don Sebastian? What is Montezuma to him? And what have you done with him?"

"Smoking Mirror sleeps," Toci said. "Montezuma sleeps. But Montezuma dies, and Smoking Mirror lives this night. Smoking Mirror wants blood."

Martinez at once rejected the idea that came to him, then stopped for a moment to consider it. Don Sebastian de Villanueva had been revived by Aztec sorcery, and he was still a vampire. Was it really possible that the cult of Tezcatlipoca planned to feed him with the blood of their deposed monarch? How could they hope to smuggle a living dead man past the walls and through the passages that would bring him to this apartment, a floor above the ground in the only part of the palace taller than one story?

Sunlight streamed through the open window, but Martinez was shuddering.

"So you believe that Don Sebastian is Smoking Mirror," he

said. "I suppose that makes a certain sort of sense, especially when you consider that Montezuma thought Cortez was this other god, the Feathered Serpent."

"Quetzalcoatl."

"Yes," said Martinez. "And he is the rival god of Tezcatlipoca, isn't he? So now you propose to teach Montezuma a lesson by feeding him to Don Sebastian."

He was talking to himself really, trying to piece together the intrigue that had enveloped him, but Toci answered.

"Montezuma knows," she said. "Montezuma knows Smoking Mirror."

This much, Martinez thought, was impossible. He himself had seen the resurrection of Don Sebastian, and he would have sworn that there had been no time for him to visit Montezuma. But what of the other Smoking Mirror, the one who had existed long before Spanish feet had ever touched this soil? Could it be that Cortez really was the Feathered Serpent, and that Don Sebastian really was the Smoking Mirror? The alchemist's mind was unnaturally bright but still far too exhausted to consider the implications. There was magic here, yet in what strange channels did it move? Was there some dark parallel between what happened here and what happened a hemisphere away? Or was it only that the Aztecs had the gift of prophecy, and that their attempt to explain auguries had created relationships where none had really existed?

"Montezuma told you, I suppose," he said sleepily.

"Montezuma said it, this day. Montezuma knows, for many, many days. Before Cortez comes here, Smoking Mirror tells him."

"How does he tell him?"

"A bird. Many days, Cortez not here, a bird comes here. A bird in the palace, not black, not white."

"A gray bird," said Martinez. "Long before Cortez came, Montezuma saw a gray bird in his palace. Well, what of it?"

"A black mirror on his head. Smoking Mirror. Mirror of sky, mirror of stars. Stars go. Mirror of men. Men in gray gold.

57

Cortez. Montezuma sees him. Montezuma knows. Smoking Mirror tells him."

"So Montezuma knew that Cortez would come," Martinez said slowly. "He should have paid more attention to this bird with the black mirror on its head. It showed him Cortez; no doubt it showed him everything. A remarkable bird. He told you this himself, did he?"

"This day."

"Well," said Martinez. "Your king should have paid more attention to his vision. If a man is lucky enough to know the future, he should have sense enough to act on it. Then again, if he's really seen what lies ahead, I suppose there's nothing he can do to change it. That's why oracles are always enigmatic, so you can't tell what they mean until it's too late. Visions. A bird bringing visions, reflections of Hernan Cortez in a smoking mirror."

He gave a quiet snort that had been intended for a laugh. His head lolled against the wall. His eyes closed. "Smoking Mirror," he said. "Smoking Mirror sleeps."

He sat up with a start. "I'm falling asleep," he said. "I can't do that now." The colors of the tapestries were so brilliant that it hurt to look at them.

"Sleep," said Toci, still standing by the wall.

"It's the food," said Martinez. He tried to get up, but his head swam, and he sank back down again on his stool. "The food was . . . drugged. Of course. I would have done the same thing myself. Even . . . the priest thought of it. And Montezuma wouldn't touch it. He knew they'd try to knock him out. But not Alfonso Martinez —he's a fool. . . ."

He smiled drowsily. "A fool," he mumbled. His head fell back.

"Sleep," said Toci.

Night had fallen by the time Martinez stirred. His neck was stiff and his head was throbbing; in fact, it was discomfort that awakened him. He had not dreamed. The room was dark as he looked around it, and for a moment he imagined that he might be back in a Spanish garret. Then he remembered, and winced at the recollection. He turned his head to peer around, and the slight motion sent a long, dull ache through his brain. Nothing had changed.

Montezuma still lay face up on his mat; his chest rose and fell. And Toci stood like a statue against the wall. Martinez would have sworn that she had never moved, although hours must have passed since he had last seen her. The only difference in the room was the light. The pale, cold rays of a dim and distant moon slanted through the window.

Martinez wondered if Toci had heard him move. Her rigid figure seemed hardly human in the shadows by the wall. He wished his head would clear, so that he could determine his position in the dark affairs of Tenochtitlan. He had cooperated with the priestess in keeping guards out of the royal apartment, but now he wondered why. He sensed that something would happen in this room soon, and considered calling for help. Toci had all but promised him that Montezuma would have a visitor tonight, and such a visit could have only one purpose. But would it help or hinder the fortunes of Alfonso Martinez? Did it even matter now what became of Montezuma? Was there anyone who cared about the king except the people of the black pyramid? And was Martinez one of them?

"He wants death," said the priestess suddenly.

Martinez jumped at the sound of her voice. She knew he was awake. Nothing escaped her, not even in the dark.

"What are you going to do?" he whispered. "Will you kill him? Don't do it. We'll be caught. We'll be punished. They'll blame us, no matter who kills him. What are you going to do?"

"See," said Toci.

Martinez glanced wildly around the chamber of the king. There was nothing to see, nothing moving. And then there was a flicker in the white light of the moon. Something had passed before the window. Martinez felt his scalp tighten and heard his own breathing drown out Montezuma's.

Martinez looked toward the window. He saw the purple sky, the cold shimmering of stars, and the flat white disc that cast its glow upon the floor. Then he saw the long fingers that groped over the sill. It was the upper sill. Something was crawling down the side of the palace and into the room, something that moved as no mortal man could ever move. Now there were two hands, each clutching one side of the window, and now there was a dark head silhouetted against the sky. The head hung down, and long black hair streamed toward the floor. Martinez burrowed into his corner as Montezuma's visitor slithered through the window like some gigantic snake.

Martinez could not bear to look, but he could not shut out the sound of sandals slapping down heavily on the stone floor. Don Sebastian was in the palace, and now Martinez was afraid not to look.

The dark form of the dead sorcerer from Spain stood at the foot of Montezuma's bed. His face was black against the moonlight that illuminated his Aztec robes of red and black and white. He turned slowly toward the dying king, and as he did so the left side of his face was illuminated. The long scar running down over his eye was almost glowing, but the right side of his face was lost in shadow. A disc of black obsidian dangled from the golden chain around his neck, and his naked forearms were bright with gold and jewels.

He stepped to the center of the room. He moved toward the priestess of Smoking Mirror, but only for long enough to acknowledge her presence with a stately bow. Then he turned toward the false physician.

"Do you know me?" he said.

Martinez gibbered.

"I hear that I have much to thank you for," said Don Sebastian de Villanueva. "You cherished my bones, or what was left of them, and you carried me across the sea to this New World, where I am to be a god. Tell me your name."

Martinez complied.

"Alfonso Martinez," said Don Sebastian. "Your reward will be what you deserve. You have done me a strange service, Martinez. You have drawn me back from a world you could not imagine, and set me down in a world that even I could not imagine. Were I more of a philosopher, I might resent your interference. But there are mysteries here for me, and I confess that I am intrigued. I never thought to see this earthly plane again, and I never thought to be a god. I have been on a long journey, and I never thought to see my home again. How long has it been, Martinez? What year is this?"

"Fifteen twenty," said Martinez.

"Twenty-four years. A generation. I am old enough to be dead, Martinez, and now I find that I am born again. And I have you to thank. It is a mixed blessing but I am not ungrateful, for my last stay on earth ended before I had achieved my goals. To make more time for myself I became one of the living dead, but still there were not nights enough."

"Enough for what?" asked Martinez.

"To learn, Martinez. To find a way out of this life that would be more than merely death. For years I studied, and wrote what I discovered in a book. My brother meant to publish it under his name, and thus gain favor with the Inquisition, but he proved treacherous and I was obliged to let him die. The book was burned. Only I know what was in it, but I need to know more, for my spirit is not yet free. Perhaps I shall find what I seek in this new land. In Spain I fed on the blood of criminals and outcasts, provided by my brother, the Grand Inquisitor. It was safer. But here I find magic such as I have never seen before, and I am offered the blood of a king."

Montezuma stirred uneasily, and Toci stepped from the shadows.

"If you kill him," said Martinez, "then you kill me. They think I am a doctor, and he is in my care."

"Be calm," said Don Sebastian. "I learned caution long before you were born. I shall not leave him dead, but only dying. I would leave him altogether but for the urging of this woman. She has plans for me, it seems, and a touch of royal blood will endear me to her."

"Drink," said Toci urgently, and at her words Martinez's mind began to race.

He had seen Toci and Don Sebastian as allies, himself as an expendable interloper, but now he thought again. Did he have any less to offer this exiled vampire than that brown woman? She might be beautiful, but she could hardly speak his tongue, and her magic was utterly alien. Alfonso Martinez and Don Sebastian de Villanueva, on the other hand, were countrymen and colleagues. They were versed in the same school of mysticism, and they spoke a common language. Toci's stilted speech was enough in itself to mark her as a heathen witch. If the Spanish occupation of Tenochtitlan was doomed to end in failure, then there was no reason why a man should not ingratiate himself with the one whose triumph might well prove to be his own.

"Yes, Don Sebastian," said Martinez. "Drink." He stood shakily over Montezuma. "If they want royal blood in your veins, why should you deny them? They think you are their god, and there is no reason to gainsay them."

"This woman has told me of the Smoking Mirror," said Sebastian, "and what it means to them. She says he is their primal god, and that the other gods are only masks he wears. I can hardly argue with her—and not only because she offers me shelter. The god of blood and war and sacrifice is always the first god, Martinez. And I am more than willing to be his incarnation."

"And may you be their king," said Martinez. He felt a weird exhilaration in speaking with a corpse. He had dreamed of necromancy; raising the dead was every wizard's dream, and Martinez felt an awesome power rising within him, even though the wizardry he saw was not his own. Two forces waited in this room with him: the dark sorcery that he knew, raised to unimagined heights in the person of Don Sebastian, and the black magic of an alien race, incarnated in the body of the dark and beautiful young woman who stood silent by the door. He thought of a scale, with two differents sorts of sorcery balanced in it. The weights were

Toci and Don Sebastian, but Martinez was the scale itself. If he could keep them in equilibrium, then both might be made to serve him.

"I am your servant," said Martinez, spreading his arms wide to embrace both the dusky priestess and the pale vampire. At his gesture they moved toward him. Each took one of his hands. His right hand felt warm soft flesh; his left hand felt cold hard fingers. The white moonlight streamed down upon them, and in its glow a pact was sealed. Martinez was enraptured.

Don Sebastian was the first to step away. "There is another here," he said. "We have a priestess, a magician, and a rogue. But what does the king say?"

Montezuma, emperor of the Aztecs, stirred uneasily. He rose halfway up from his bed, and then he spoke.

"Tezcatlipoca," he said.

"The god who warned him," said Sebastian. "The god I am to be."

For a moment Montezuma's eyes were bright; then he sank down upon his woven mat. His face turned toward the wall, exposing his strong brown throat.

"He has spoken," said Martinez.

Don Sebastian did not reply, but he drifted toward the bedside of the king. He knelt beside it, like a man paying homage, and then his head dipped lower.

Martinez stared. His hand gripped Toci's, and his nails dug into her palm. Yet she remained impassive. He looked into her eyes and saw that they were radiant, but he realized that the light in them was not for him.

Martinez was with his companions, and they had sworn fidelity to him; yet he was lonelier than he had ever been before as he listened to the sounds of a vampire feeding. Toci held Martinez's hand, but she was lost in an ecstasy he could not share. He looked to the walls and watched the woven images of gods he could not name.

7. The Bridge

AFTER Montezuma's body had been burned, the siege of the palace began again. Morning had found the king minutes from death, but still refusing the ministrations of both priest and physician. Cortez himself had stood at Montezuma's bedside, and when the king died he mourned sincerely, as did all the Spanish troops. Montezuma had been their only ally in Tenochtitlan; they had lost their one hope for a safe retreat. As soon as the corpse of the emperor had passed through the lines and into the hands of his people, his brother Cuitlahuac stormed the walls with unbridled ferocity.

The fury of the assault was inspired, at least in part, by the city's belief that the Spaniards had murdered Montezuma. The Spanish soldiers, who had seen the king fall under a rain of stones thrown by his own people, could only view this accusation as another symptom of Aztec madness. Just one man in Tenochtitlan knew the truth about the death of the king, and Alfonso Martinez thought it best to be discreet.

Toci was gone. As soon as he had pronounced Montezuma dead, Martinez had been hurried off to treat the wounded, leaving her behind in the royal chambers. His next glimpse of the priestess came hours later when he stood atop the palace walls with Garcia, watching the funeral procession move through the gates. Cortez had given up Montezuma's body as a mark of respect, and because he hoped the sight of it might sober the Aztecs. Cortez did not get what he wanted, but neither did Martinez.

"Look, there!" Garcia said. "Isn't that your sweetheart?"

Martinez, who had been regarding the spectacle with a combination of guilt and grogginess, followed the direction of Garcia's pointing finger. The sun was in his eyes, and he could hardly recognize the distant figures below him, but something in the bearing of the one Garcia indicated made him fear the worst. As he stared down in dismay the woman turned for an instant to look up at him, as if she had known all along that he was there. It was Toci.

Martinez wondered if there had been any expression on her normally impassive face in the glimpse that she had granted him. He would not have been surprised to see her laughing. As it was, Martinez was more than ready to laugh at himself. He had been betrayed. Of the three who had arranged the death of Montezuma, he was the only one left in the palace to face the wrath of Tenochtitlan. Don Sebastian had disappeared last night, sated with the blood of a king, and now the priestess of Smoking Mirror was marching out to safety as one of Montezuma's mourners. Martinez cursed himself for a fool, and his face flushed with anger and humiliation.

"Don't take it so hard, physician," Garcia said. "Nobody blames you. I'm sure you could have saved him if he'd let you near him, but as it was, what could you do? I'll admit things look black for us, but it's not your fault that Montezuma's dead."

"Idiot!" snapped Martinez, his frustration spilling over on the man next to him. "Do you think I care if he's dead or not?"

"It's the woman you're angry about, then. What were you up to in that pyramid?"

"We were raising . . ." Martinez began, but he stopped himself in time.

"I can guess what you were raising, physician," chuckled Garcia.

Martinez, flattered and furious at the same time, was still attempting to formulate a suitable reply when the first rock sailed past his head.

"Damn them!" roared Garcia. "They're at it again!" He threw up his shield and deflected an arrow with a casual gesture that amazed his companion. "Get down, physician." He knocked Martinez to his knees and covered him with his own huge body. "Start crawling," he said. "We've got to get off this wall."

Martinez could have sworn that he did not even breathe again until he stood beside Garcia in the comparative safety of the courtyard. "Don't go up there again," said Garcia. "I'd be in a hell of a lot of trouble if anything happened to you. I had a barrel of explaining to do when it looked like you'd been caught and sacrificed. We'll need you, physician, at least as long as there are any of us alive."

Garcia's talk was rough, but Martinez sensed a touch of sentiment beneath the bluster, and he was more moved than he would have cared to admit. "Isn't there any hope?" he asked.

"If I could predict the future, then I'd be a hell of a lot better gambler than I am."

Martinez looked across the courtyard. Work on new engines of war had begun days ago on the order of Cortez, who had apparently guessed that all would not go well with his plans to make peace. There were three of them, each almost as tall as the walls of the palace. The towers were wooden, two stories high. Each would hold two dozen men on its upper level, men with muskets. Loopholes studded the sides of the towers near their roofs, which were high enough to reach many of the terraces where the Aztecs stood to drop rocks on their enemies.

"Will they work?" asked Martinez.

"We'll know soon enough. We should be able to kill some of the bastards we couldn't reach before, but I don't know if it'll make any difference. There are just too many of them."

Martinez squinted at the towers, trying to create the impression that he was making an intelligent estimate of their chance for success. "I see the rollers at the bottom," he said at last, "and I see the ropes, but who's going to pull them?"

"Our noble native allies," replied Garcia sardonically.

"They'll be slaughtered."

"Maybe not. I admit it's not a job I'd like, but they're apparently impressed with the ingenuity of the thing. None of these heathens has ever seen a wheel before. Besides, they're not real men like us. They don't seem to care if they live or die."

"That might be their religion," ventured Martinez.

"Maybe so, but it doesn't seem like enough of a reason. Our own religion promises about as much as it can to a man who dies fighting for the faith, but you won't see any Christians pulling on those ropes. Still, they'll have some defense from our cavalry. If we don't protect them, those towers won't be going anywhere."

The shouts and whistles of the Aztecs made a roar outside the walls. "It's too damned hot," Garcia said. A stone the size of a fist fell out of the sky, and he sidestepped it nonchalantly.

Martinez began to watch the walls for signs of death dropping down. He was not in armor, like Garcia.

"Is there anything to eat in this accursed palace?" Martinez asked.

"Maybe," said Garcia. "Go ask the priest. You should be inside anyway. The wounded need you more than I do now. There's nothing for you to do out here but get killed. I'm going for a ride in one of those damned boxes."

Night was falling when Garcia shuffled back into the improvised hospital, followed by dozens of wounded men. He found Martinez stretched out on a pallet among the injured and the dying. The alchemist was asleep, and Garcia had trouble waking him.

"Come on, physician, there's work for you. It's lucky you had a rest, because you're going to need it."

Martinez felt himself hauled rudely from a beautiful dream. He whimpered at the touch of a strong hand on his shoulder and the sound of a rough voice in his ear.

67

"Go away, Garcia," he said, turning over onto his stomach and burrowing into his straw mat.

Garcia tried to smile, but it turned into a grimace when it reached the bruise on his cheek. "Get up," he said, sharply. "Soldiers have died to keep you safe for this little nap, and now it's your turn to do something for them. What's the matter with you, anyway? You act like you've taken one of your potions!"

He pulled Martinez to his feet and shook him. There was more truth than Garcia imagined in his guess that the physician had spent the day soothing himself with drugs, but Martinez still had a strong sense of self-preservation, and he managed to achieve a semblance of sobriety when he felt Garcia getting rough with him.

"I'm awake," he said. "Stop shaking me. What happened out there?

"Nothing good, physician."

"The towers?"

"Well, they worked, as far as they went, but they didn't go far enough."

"What do you mean?"

"It's the canals. You can't drag a tower through a canal, even with the best will in the world. Those bastards have torn down all the bridges on the causeways that run over the lake."

"And out of the city?"

"Yes. We couldn't go more than a few feet in any direction without running into a stretch of water. We're completely cut off."

Martinez stepped back against a wall and ran his hand over his mouth. "So we're really finished," he said. "I wasn't counting on that."

"Well, it's not so bad. We killed a lot of them. You should have seen us. They couldn't get near the towers at first; they didn't know what was going on. We rolled up to one rooftop after another, and it was heaven to watch the musket fire rip through the animals who've been dropping rocks on us for days. They must have thought they were pretty safe up there, I guess, or they wouldn't have had so many women and children doing the dirty work. You should have seen their faces when we opened fire! It's the first time I've felt right since we came back to this accursed city."

"So at least the roofs are cleared," Martinez said without enthusiasm.

"Only some of them. The towers weren't tall enough to reach the highest roofs, and one tower was just about smashed to pieces when it came too close to the great pyramid. The second one fell into one of the canals. Ours got through, though, or I should say it got back here to the palace. But what a fight it was, physician! There'll be ten of them in Hell tonight for every man of ours who died."

Martinez stepped away from the wall and thrust his face toward Garcia's. "What do I care how many you killed?" he screamed. "However many it was, it wasn't enough. They're still out there, aren't they? Who cares about those heathens? What I want to know is how many of us are going to die!"

"Quiet down," said Garcia. His voice was calm and cold. "I can't have you worrying the men." He moved deliberately toward Martinez, who backed away.

"Keep your distance," Martinez blustered. His voice was quieter. "It looks like I'll be dead soon enough without any help from you."

"Listen, physician. I like you. I don't want to hurt you. But I can't have you talking that way. There might be a chance, you know. There's always a chance."

"Tell me about that, then, and not about how many you killed." Martinez slumped down and sat on the floor, his head between his knees. Garcia squatted beside him.

"We're going to make a portable bridge," he whispered. "Out of the timbers from the tower we saved. One of the reasons we had to go out today was to see how big the gaps in the causeway are. If we can move the bridge across from one hole to the next, some of us will get away. We'll be setting out tomorrow night; they don't seem to like fighting at night. It's a chance."

"It sounds like a sorry night to come," said Martinez, but he

69

adopted Garcia's conspiratorial tone. "So that's it, is it? We're going to run. No gold, no empire, no magic. Some of us may survive, and that's it."

"Do you like it here so much?"

"I could have liked it," muttered Martinez, more to himself than his companion. "It could have been a paradise, if all the promises were kept. But you're right, Garcia. I don't like it here. I don't like it anywhere."

He pulled himself to his feet and looked toward the wounded. "All right, you men," he barked. "Who's hurt the worst here?" The men stirred, and two of them stepped forward, holding a third between them. His right foot was gone, the stump wrapped in a dirty shirt.

Martinez worked throughout the night, improvising the best treatment he could give his patients, and noting with surprised satisfaction that even a week's experience had given him some sort of skill in treating wounds. He had proceeded by trial and error until his successful cases had taught him what to do; his failures were buried. He dispensed most of his drugs, but saved some for himself in case the next night found him alive outside the city. The doses he gave were bigger than usual, since it seemed unlikely that he would have more patients in the future, and the men were sleepily grateful. For Martinez, it was satisfaction enough to know that they would not bother him again, at least not until morning.

Remarkably few men, though, spent the night in the hospital. Most of them, despite their injuries, were in the courtyard working to transform the last tower into a portable bridge. They had caught the enthusiasm that Cortez felt for the idea; Martinez alone thought they had caught a disease called madness. He sat in the sickroom and envied Cortez, whose will was so strong that men would follow him in any enterprise, however fantastic. Martinez had seen the commander infrequently, and spoken with him scarcely at all, but still he sensed the power in the man, and hated him for it. The fools building the bridge were not working out of panic, but out of faith in their leader. The sound of axes and hammers rang through the night, penetrating even the dark recess of the palace where Martinez sat alone among his dead and dreaming patients.

Yet he thought of Cortez less than he thought of another. Cortez might have let his ambition betray an entire army, but that hardly bothered the alchemist compared to the resentment he felt toward Don Sebastian de Villanueva for leaving him behind. He tried to remember exactly what the vampire had said to him. Still, it hardly mattered. Whether the promise had been stated or implied, it had been there. He should not be here now in this charnelhouse; he should be in the black pyramid, sitting at his ease between a living corpse and a warm brown woman, running his hands over great slabs of gold and laughing at the plight of Cortez. Instead, he was no more than an animal caught in the cage of Tenochtitlan. He had countenanced the slaughter of Montezuma, and now he had nothing to show for it but his own plight.

Martinez wandered through the empty halls until he found a window. He sat in the corridor across from it, searching the sky for a sign from Don Sebastian. Even now, there was nothing to prevent his rescue, if that was what the sorcerer he had carried across the sea intended. He looked for black wings, but saw only glittering white stars. His eyes began to sting from the strain of peering into the night, and he thought it would be safe to close them for a few seconds. He opened them once or twice without seeing what he wanted; then he drifted off.

When Garcia found him, it was late morning. Martinez woke reluctantly, the brightness of the day proof that he had been abandoned by his nocturnal allies. He stood quickly, nevertheless, if only to prevent Garcia from shaking him.

"The bridge is ready," said Garcia. "It looks pretty good. We'll be setting out in a few hours. There's something to do first, though, and I think you'll enjoy it."

"And what might that be?"

"Gold, physician. Free gold. All you can carry."

71

"What?" said Martinez. He was suddenly very much awake.
"You heard me."

"Impossible," said Martinez.

"It's true. Orders from Cortez. There's a room full of gold in this palace. I told you before that we got shares of it. But there's still more left than all of us can carry out of here. The officers have had their share, and Cortez of course, and the royal portion has been set aside; but nobody has taken more than a part of what he could have. We're going to be running for our lives, and it's too heavy. There's just too much gold and too many jewels. But the order is that every man shall have what he wants."

"Let's go," said Martinez.

"Wait a minute, physician. You're supposed to take the men in your charge, at least the ones who can get up, and bring them with you to the treasure room."

"To hell with them, Garcia! From what you tell me, nearly every man here has had his pick of this treasure while I've been asleep, and now you expect me to share the dregs with a bunch of cripples who won't even have the strength to walk out of the city! Are you my friend or aren't you? Take me there now, and then we'll see about the wounded."

"You would hide in this hallway," said Garcia, "and now you blame me because you were nowhere to be found. I looked for you. But it doesn't matter, physician. There's plenty left, and we'll be leaving more behind than we take with us."

Martinez refused to believe there was that much gold. Garcia, he thought again, had no imagination. "If there's so much left," he said, "then there's no reason why you shouldn't take me first. Let me have my share, Garcia, and then I'll see to the wounded."

"It's damned irregular," said Garcia. Then he laughed. "But what the hell, I can see you won't believe me till I show you. Come on."

Garcia led the alchemist through long passageways and empty apartments until they reached the room, near the center of the palace, where Montezuma's father had hidden his treasure.

"There's where we broke through the plaster when Montezuma said we could build our chapel," Garcia said. "And there's what he gave us. Is there enough for you?"

"Oh," said Alfonso Martinez. He could say nothing more.

"Somebody figured it at a million pesos. Maybe more, maybe less. Who can tell? I can count to ten, or twice that if I take off my boots, but a million! A lot of it is gone now, but you can't say you've been cheated, can you?"

Martinez stared. At one end of the long, low hall was a rough-hewn statue of the Virgin. Beside it was a pulpit, and a crucifix hanging on the wall. But Martinez hardly noticed them. At the other end of the room the wall was shattered, the hole in its plaster revealing the secret chamber hidden beyond. And below the hole, a fortune.

Gold was piled on the floor like kindling. Much of the Aztec treasure had been melted into small bars, which were stacked as high as a man and many times as wide. There was a great wheel of the yellow metal in one corner, elaborately engraved. Martinez lusted after it, but realized that he would never be able to lift the thing. Here was half of what he had dreamed of, yet more than fate would let him have. He saw pots full of shining stones, and wished that he knew more about them. Were they really precious, or just the baubles of a primitive tribe? They glittered, but so did the gold. And there were pieces that combined both gold and jewels. One of them was an ugly figure that reminded him of Smoking Mirror.

It was shaped like a skull, and was about the same size. It seemed to be made of beaten gold, but there was a wide band of blue stones around the eyes, and another around the mouth.

"I like this," Martinez said. He picked it up. The eye sockets were filled with gleaming black stone, but as he held it he recognized the teeth as unmistakably human. "It doesn't weigh much," he said, ignoring the uncomfortable fact that the thing was undoubtedly the head of a man, however embellished it might be.

"Might not be worth much for the space it takes," Garcia suggested.

Martinez shrugged and thrust it into his pack, into the same place where the skull of Don Sebastian had rested. "So you're a jeweler, Garcia," he said. "Show me what you took."

Garcia removed his battered helmet and pulled out a package wrapped in cloth. He unwrapped it modestly and displayed a dozen pale green stones.

"That's all? What are they?"

"I've been told the natives prize them. Gold doesn't seem to be worth much here. They only like it because it's soft, and it's easy to make toys from it. I'm thinking that if I make it out of the city, these green rocks may help me get back to the coast."

"You're a fool, Garcia. What if you make it back to Spain? Will you be happy with a few pretty rocks?"

"I'll be happy if I make it back at all."

"That's not enough for Alfonso Martinez. How many times do you think a man gets a chance at a prize like this?" Martinez picked up two heavy gold bars, one at a time, and dropped them into his pack. He did this gently, so as not to break the skull.

"Those things are too heavy, physician. Only an idiot would try to carry them. Gold isn't worth much if it costs a man his life."

"And a man's life isn't worth much if he has no gold," said Martinez. He looked Garcia squarely in the eye and took two more of the small gold bars. Then he took a handful of the green stones out of an earthenware pot. "Listen," he said. "If things get too rough, I can always throw away the gold. But to leave it here, without even trying! I'm not philosopher enough for that."

"You may be right," Garcia said. "Our men have been laughing at yours, the ones from the second expedition, because they were greedy and took too much. Still . . ." he said, and he picked up one of the gleaming ingots, "I guess we can always throw it away."

"Of course," said Martinez.

"Though I think it's easier to pick up gold than it is to let go of it," said Garcia. "Still," he added, selecting another heavy bar.

"Absolutely," said Alfonso Martinez. "If these savages are going to send us home again, the least they can do is pay our passage." He chuckled uneasily, but felt a little better when

Garcia joined him. Their laughter echoed through the empty chamber, and the sound of it silenced both of them.

"I can't see what you want with that skull," Garcia said. "It's too big."

"It reminds me of something. And it doesn't weigh much. It's hollow, like your head, or mine. I think it's an emblem of that god of theirs, the one who played host to me in the black pyramid. I wouldn't want to forget him, would I?"

"Whatever you say," replied Garcia, suddenly grim. "But I'd rather forget those gods now, and pray to our God to get us out of here." He walked slowly toward the crucifix and knelt before it.

"Garcia," said the alchemist. He tried to follow his companion, but something stopped him. Garcia's head was bowed and his lips were moving silently.

Martinez took another step forward. His burden was heavier than he had imagined. It was difficult to move. "Maybe I've taken too much," he said to himself. He wanted to stand beside his friend, but found that he could not.

"Christ," said Martinez, calling on a name he had all but forgotten. He could not cross the room. "It's the skull," he muttered to himself. "Maybe it really is Smoking Mirror. Or Don Sebastian."

Whatever the skull represented, its dead weight appeared to be dragging Martinez down. Perhaps there was nothing more to this sudden immobility than his own realization that joining Garcia would be an affront to the dark god of the Aztecs—the one whose power had brought a dead man back to life—but Martinez decided that he had no further business in the treasure room. While the soldier prayed, the alchemist crept quietly away.

8. City of Water

LIGHT rain began to fall shortly after sunset. To everyone else in the palace, the coming of the night meant that it was time for the escape from Tenochtitlan; but for Martinez the darkness meant that Don Sebastian had risen. If the vampire intended to rescue him, this was the time to do it. In a few hours it would be too late.

The alchemist was almost frantic as he watched the preparations for departure. Men moved swiftly and silently through the palace and the courtyard. The Aztecs had retired; the city was quiet. If everyone worked carefully enough, they would not betray their intention before the moment when the gates were thrown open. It was this that worried Martinez. No one outside the walls knew what was happening. Even if the Smoking Mirror cult did have plans for him, they had no way of knowing that this might be his last night in Tenochtitlan. More than once Martinez was tempted to cry out, to shout a warning that would rouse the city. It would be worthwhile if his scream for help reached the black pyramid, but by now he was not sure whether Smoking Mirror and his followers cared what became of Alfonso Martinez. Still, he might have tried it, even at the cost of every life in the palace, but he realized that he would be cut down as a traitor as soon as he opened his mouth.

As it was, he had no choice but to follow Hernan Cortez out of the city, risking his neck and leaving behind him all the wealth and power that could have come within his grasp.

"We don't have enough to worry about," Garcia said. "We have to get wet, too."

Martinez whirled. Lost in his own thoughts, he had not noticed the big soldier.

"Does it matter?" asked Martinez bitterly.

"It might be good, come to think of it. These savages usually don't like to fight at night, and the rain may be just the thing we need to send them all home to bed. Maybe Botello was right."

"Botello?"

"An astrologer, or so he says. Just a soldier, really, but he's made some good guesses before. Or maybe he actually knows something. Anyway, he predicted that this would be the best time for our retreat."

"There's no good time for a retreat," Martinez said, still full of regret, and angry with himself for not thinking to make his own reading of the stars.

"Spoken like a soldier," said Garcia, grinning. "But what else is there to do? We've got a whole city against us. We're not ancient heroes like the ones you read about in books."

"Horatio at the bridge," muttered Martinez, looking toward the wooden structure in the middle of the courtyard. "But we have to carry our own bridge with us."

"Well, it's solid enough. Nothing wrong with the way it's built. The hard part will be moving it."

"I'm not really looking forward to this, Garcia. What's the order of march to be?"

Garcia looked at him quizzically. "I never knew you were a strategist."

"I'm just trying to figure out the safest place to be when we march out of here. For the wounded, you understand."

"You've got me, physician. I can tell you how things are set up, but I'm damned if I can tell you the best place to be. It all depends on what happens. The advance is under Sandoval. They'll be the first out if things go well, but the first to fight if things don't. The rear is under Alvarado, and he's a good man, in spite of the way he messed things up when Cortez was gone. He might be in a good spot, if the advance has to fight its way through, but he might still be in the city when the Aztecs are aroused, and then he'll be in trouble. That's assuming they're not going to be waiting for us. It's hard to say."

"Where's Cortez?"

"In the middle. He has the king's share of the treasure, and Montezuma's son and daughters, and most of the artillery. That might be the best spot, but it might be the worst. I'm no astrologer. The middle won't have to break through, and they won't get stuck in the back, but they won't have the advantages of either. Your guess is as good as mine."

"I don't like the rear," Martinez said. "They might catch the brunt of the fighting if the city isn't ready now; and if the Aztecs are waiting for us beyond the city, they'll have no advantage except the chance to fall back to the palace and be killed a little later."

"True," said Garcia.

"And I don't like the front much. I'm not the man for charging into a rank of stone swords, and of course my patients won't be worth much in the vanguard. Then again, the front may be the only ones to get through. But I think I like the middle best of all. Moderation in all things, Garcia. Besides, that's where Cortez is, and he is where the gold is."

"You should have been a general, physician. I'll see if I can set it up. What are you going to do with the wounded who can't walk?"

"Somebody will have to carry them, I guess, but it won't be me."

"There are some horses, but I think they want them for the gold. I'll see what I can arrange for you."

"When are we leaving?"

"Midnight. You'd better get your men ready to travel, physician."

Garcia started off toward a group of officers standing in the courtyard, and Martinez ducked back into the doorway. The sound of the rain faded as he wandered with dragging feet toward his hospital and the dozens of men who waited there. He had no idea what to do with them; the only feeling he had for them was resentment.

When he entered the hall where the wounded lay, the first thing he did was to look to his own welfare. He gathered up all his possessions, sorry that it took no longer. His pack was on his back, and he was wearing all the armor he had been able to scavenge from the dead. He owned nothing else. The pack, which he had sewn himself, had been on his back for most of his adult life. He had walked the roads of Spain with it, but never before felt the weight of gold bars within it. He should have been happy, but he was too afraid of what lay before him and too sorry about what he left behind. He stood in the doorway and shouted to his broken army.

"Get up, you men! Get up, if you can, because we're getting out of here!"

The priest celebrated mass at midnight. Thousands of men stood in the courtyard to hear him, a comparative handful of Spaniards and a horde of their Indian allies who had no idea what the ceremony meant. The warm, thin rain fell on all of them.

Alfonso Martinez shuffled nervously back and forth. He was surrounded by the walking wounded, many of them standing only because they had another injured man to lean on. A few were on stretchers, accompanied by healthy soldiers who had volunteered to carry them, at least as long as seemed practical. Martinez doubted that any of them would get through, and he was not much more hopeful about himself.

"Everyone seems so cheerful," he whispered to Garcia. "Do they really think we'll just walk out without a fight?"

"They don't know what to think, and neither do I. Ask me again in an hour. Meanwhile, we might as well be cheerful. At least we're doing something, and not just waiting to be starved or slaughtered like pigs."

Martinez looked skeptically up and down the line. The center, where he stood, was the most congested section. The artillery, the ammunition wagons, and the carts filled with baggage were in front of him. Ahead of these was a company of selected officers, all mounted, with Cortez at their head. There were horses in this group that did not bear men, but gold for the king of Spain.

"I'd like to be on one of those horses," said Martinez.

"So would I, physician, and so would every man that's walking. But what would you have? They're carrying gold, and so are you and I. Admit the truth. That money is worth more to the crown than any one of us. Why do you think we came here in the first place?"

Martinez did not reply. Instead he peered off toward the distant head of the caravan, where the portable bridge stood, obscured by mist and drizzle. A squadron of bold cavaliers waited behind the bridge to lead the attack.

"There should be three bridges," said Martinez. "You told me yourself that there are three gaps in the causeway for us to cross."

"We've done all we can. Why don't you shut up?" Garcia turned away.

Martinez looked toward the rear. The priest was making his way along the line, blessing the men as they stood ready for action. The officers of the rear guard bowed their heads. Martinez felt his spine quiver. The raindrops falling on his helmet suddenly sounded like gunfire. The priest came closer, and his droning Latin cut through the rustle of the line of nervous soldiers. Martinez retreated rapidly into the shadows.

He waited against the wall until the priest had passed, then made his way back into the line. "Call of nature," he said to no one in particular.

"You all set now?" asked Garcia. "I swear you're the jumpiest man I ever saw. You must have a fever or something. I'd look after myself, if I were you."

"Tomorrow," said Martinez.

"Tomorrow, is it? Tomorrow. I've never known a man like you. Well, here's luck. They're opening the gates."

Horses stirred restlessly, their hooves echoing throughout the courtyard. The rain hissed down, and thousands of men drew their breath at once in a great gasp. From where Martinez stood, the gates made no sound, swinging inward like an image from a dream. Beyond them lay the silent city.

Martinez froze for an instant, waiting for a horde of savages to rush into the palace, but they did not materialize. The plaza was empty.

The bridge rolled out into the night, and the advance party followed it, moving like ghostly riders through the mist. They were lost from sight by the time there was room for Martinez to take his first step forward. His feet moved reluctantly, and he winced at every creak of wagon wheels, every cough from an injured man. Then he moved resolutely forward, his eyes fixed on the back of Hernan Cortez. He dared not stop to search the sky for dark messengers from Smoking Mirror.

As they passed through the gate, he glanced at Garcia, who grinned at him and winked. Martinez began to feel a conspiratorial glee. If they really did succeed in sneaking out of Tenochtitlan, it would be a triumph of guile and stealth, qualities that Martinez found much more to his liking than boldness or bravery. He crossed the plaza in an ecstasy of fear and pride.

The path of the Spanish army lay along the Tacuba causeway. It was not the way they had entered Tenochtitlan, but it was the shortest route to the shores of the lake that surrounded the city. The long line of soldiers turned west.

"We should have been in the front," whispered Martinez. "Where do you think they are by now?"

"On the causeway, probably," said Garcia.

Martinez followed him out of the great square and into a narrow street black with shadows. At the instant when he stepped into the darkness, the alchemist thought he saw something drift over his head. If he had been a little more certain, he would have screamed. As it was, he stopped dead in his tracks and looked anxiously upward until the man following ran into him.

"Get moving, will you? What are you waiting for?"

"I thought I saw something," Martinez said to the voice whispering behind him.

"I know, I've seen a million Aztecs since we left the palace. Forget it, you're imagining things. They won't sneak up on us."

Martinez moved ahead without answering, and finally passed through the street of shadows. The causeway stretched out before him, pale and faint in the misty downpour. Men were moving along it in dim rows; beneath them the waters of the lake gleamed like black obsidian.

Suddenly the line of soldiers stopped. As far ahead as Martinez could see, no one was moving. "What's going on?" he asked Garcia.

"They must have reached the first gap the Aztecs made," Garcia said. "They're putting the bridge into place."

Martinez waited while the minutes passed.

"Why don't they hurry?" he whispered frantically.

"I think they've done it, physician. Look. We're moving again."

Martinez went limp with relief. He looked around and saw smiles on the faces of even the most badly injured soldiers. There was a general rush forward. When Martinez stepped onto the causeway, he felt that he was halfway home. The feeling lasted only a moment.

"What's that?" he said to Garcia. "Are they crazy up there? Why are they shouting?" The unmistakable sound of men's voices drifted back across the lake.

"I don't think those are our men shouting, physician. I think we've been seen."

The wail of the conch shells the Aztecs used for horns cut through the falling mist. And from behind the Spaniards, deep in the heart of the city, came the echoing boom of a gigantic drum, the one that stood on the pyramid of the war god. Martinez cringed, anticipating an attack, but nothing happened.

"They've sounded the alarm," Garcia said, "but we might have a minute or two. We've got to get across that bridge." He cupped both hands around his mouth and shouted: "Move, you sons of snails! They're right behind us!"

All need for caution gone, the army of Cortez raced for their bridge. Thousands of rushing feet thudded on the stone of the causeway, yet hardly a man spoke, as if each hoped that silence might still save him. Martinez was in sight of the bridge when the crowd ahead forced him to stop. Instantly his patients bunched up behind him. Caught in a crush, he could scarcely move.

"Keep going!" he screamed to the men ahead of him, squirming up and down against the crowd to see the wooden planks that waited just out of his reach. "Run!"

"They can't," grunted Garcia, half embracing him. "Why do you think they've stopped? The advance has reached the second hole in the causeway, and the bridge is still back here."

Martinez, near panic, tried to force his way forward, and someone's flailing arm struck him in the face. He would have fallen, but there was no room. Slowly the mass of men struggled onward, less through their own power than the weight of the mob behind them. Martinez stumbled onto the bridge.

"They'll be here soon," Garcia said. "If we can get everyone across and pull up the bridge, they won't be able to follow us. Unless they take to their canoes . . ."

As the men struggled silently, Martinez heard a sound like the flapping of a hundred wings. He thought for an instant of a plague of vampire bats, then thought again, this time of paddles in the water of the lake. He looked from side to side, and saw a flotilla of Aztec canoes bearing down on the causeway. The sound of their progress was like the whisper of the warm rain, and so was the sound of the arrows that showered down upon the bridge.

"Garcia! Stay by me."

"Don't worry. I can't leave."

Martinez felt two arrows rattle off his helmet. Screams rang out all around him, but he ignored them and pushed on toward freedom as soon as he realized he had not been killed. The man he pushed against slumped backward unexpectedly, and Martinez found himself face to face with a corpse. He turned in terror, and saw the soldier with the missing foot forced off the bridge and into the water.

"Get me out of this!" Martinez wailed. The dead man in front of him dropped into an unexpected opening, and Martinez stumbled over the corpse without a second thought. He would have gladly slashed his way through the ranks of his comrades, but had no room to draw his sword. Someone thrust a shield above the crowd and Martinez grabbed it, holding it just above his head. The impact of arrows jolted his arm.

All around him men were slipping off the bridge. Some were slain, most forced off by the thrashing of the mob. Martinez kept to the middle. Thrown forward by a gigantic surge from the rear, he found himself beyond the bridge. The ranks of the Spanish forces were in chaos, and the order of the march was broken. Martinez felt himself smashed into a baggage cart that had started out a dozen yards ahead of him. Six arrows stuck out of it.

"Get over it!" roared Garcia. His huge hand grabbed the alchemist's arm and hauled him up. Martinez felt the arrows break as Garcia pushed past the obstacle. He fell on his knees and was almost trampled, but he fought his way to his feet with the help of the big soldier. A woman staggered past him, one of the prisoners. She might have been Montezuma's daughter. She had an arrow in her face.

"Nearly all across," shouted Garcia. Martinez risked a look back and saw the horsemen of the rear guard rushing across the bridge, trampling living and dead alike. And he heard the cry from one of the captains: "Bring up the bridge!"

The war canoes had reached the causeway. The fall of arrows was unceasing, but now it was augmented by the attack of long spears from the boats. Black stone blades shot up from below, slashing men and gutting horses. The silence of a few minutes before became a roar of agony.

Everyone was screaming for the bridge, and Martinez could see why. He was within sight of the second gap himself. Someone's

84

blood splashed across his face. There was no room to move, no room to hide. And there was no bridge to span the hole ahead of him.

"It's stuck," screamed somebody from the rear. He looked back and through the rain saw dozens of men working to free the bridge. He could hardly believe they were still there. Nothing on earth or anywhere else could have persuaded Martinez to stay behind. They were soldiers. But they could not dislodge the bridge. The weight of frantic thousands had driven it too far down. Heartsick, Martinez turned away from it, and realized that he could not find Garcia.

He had never been so frightened. Better the purposeful approach of a monster than this random slaughter that respected no one. He longed for the horse-faced veteran as a man might long for a lover.

"Garcia!" he cried. "Garcia!" An arrow glanced off his hand. It was a wound too small to consider, but it convinced Martinez that he was vulnerable. He was cold all over. He looked toward the gap ahead of him, and saw the officers of the advance leap into the lake. Their horses were tall enough to keep their heads above water, but the canoes were bearing down on them. Still, the officers had no choice. Their own men were driving them toward death.

A man in gleaming armor rode down into the water, and Martinez recognized him as Cortez. When he struggled up to the other side of the gap, a cheer went up from the ranks of the soldiers, and Martinez joined in it. Crossing the gap was not impossible, and Cortez had proved his worth again. Martinez was grateful for the lesson, since every second drove him closer to the edge of the precipice where the Aztecs had broken the stone ramp leading to the shore. Then again, Cortez had a horse. And there was a third gap still to come.

A big man careened toward him and broke his fall with his fingers in the alchemist's face. Martinez stumbled toward the edge of the causeway, but stopped his cursing when he recognized his unwilling assailant.

"Garcia! Luis! You're alive!"

"Just. I've been looking for you."

Feathered warriors streamed up from the lake, their black blades slashing. They were dangerously close. The causeway was already insufferably crowded, but somehow they found room to stand.

"Look out!" Martinez yelled. He clutched Garcia and spun him half around, right into the path of a stone sword. The black blade hacked at Garcia's shoulder, and he dropped to the gray rocks of the causeway.

"Sweet Jesus," said Garcia. His right arm flopped away from him, and someone kicked it into the lake.

Martinez dropped to his knees beside his friend. Red spattered everywhere, and was as quickly washed away by rain. Screaming soldiers would have trampled them, but Martinez fended them off with his stolen shield.

"Garcia!"

"Fix it, physician. I'm really hurt this time."

"I know, I know."

"Stop the blood! Do something!"

Someone kicked Martinez. "Listen, Luis," he said. "I'm no doctor. I'm a fraud. I don't know what to do."

"Really?" asked Garcia, offering up a caricature of the smile Martinez had so often seen before. "Damn you, Alfonso Martinez, you're more of a rogue than I suspected."

"What can I do?" wailed Martinez. Blood pumped out onto the feet of the soldiers rushing past.

"Nothing, physician," said Garcia. "You certainly fooled me."

Tears tore into the alchemist's eyes. He looked for something to stop the flow of blood. "I'm sorry, Luis."

"Forget it. A better man than you are couldn't do much now."

"I liked you," said Martinez.

"Yes . . ." said Garcia. He twitched spasmodically and rolled toward the edge of the causeway. Rain splashed into his upturned face.

A dozen men rushed by, kicking Garcia closer to the water.

Martinez drew his sword and slashed out at them hysterically. "Bastards!" he screamed. The thrust of the retreat was driving him away from Garcia. An Aztec warrior leaped up, and Martinez split his skull without a second thought.

"Well played, physician," Garcia said. He slipped closer toward the edge.

A careening horseman came between them for an instant, and when he passed, Garcia was gone. Martinez rushed to the edge of the causeway, and beyond it he saw his friend's face, no more than a pale blur against the black water. A canoe swept over the spot, and Luis Garcia was lost in the lake of Tenochtitlan.

"Garcia!" shouted Martinez. He felt a moment of overwhelming grief, then noticed all at once that he was hanging half over the brink, with the canoe and its warriors bearing down upon him. He forgot Garcia in the scramble to regain his footing while he dodged a barrage of arrows.

When he finally reached the gap, Martinez found it filled with broken wagons, upturned cannons, and dead horses. Corpses floated everywhere, and a strongbox, no doubt full of gold, was wedged between two shattered carts. Yet there was no clear path to the other side, only islands of debris emerging from the surface of the water. Martinez tried to estimate its depth in the seconds he spent poised miserably at the end of the causeway—until a spear flew past his head, reminding him that this was no time for speculation. He stepped gingerly onto the bottom of an upturned ammunition wagon.

The boards lurched ominously when his foot touched them. Martinez waved his arms frantically and jumped for the first shape he saw. He landed on the barrel of a cannon, the breath knocked out of him. His hands slipped on the wet iron, and he slithered down toward the waiting lake. Martinez caught the spokes of one of the cannon's wheels, but it spun around, dropping him up to his neck in dark water. He looked desperately from side to side, and screamed for help when he saw another Aztec canoe, filled with half-naked men dressed in spotted skins. Their paddles cut through the water with grim regularity.

If he held on to the wheel, they would reach him in a matter of seconds. He took the biggest breath he could and dropped down into the lake.

He heard a splash and a gurgle, then was overwhelmed by silence. As he sank into the depths of the lake, a dim and peaceful sanctuary, he watched the bottom of the canoe pass over him. He held his breath for as long as possible, then kicked upward for the surface.

He barely moved. Something was holding him back. His ears and nose were clogged with water; half his air rolled up in bubbles before he realized he was trapped. Then he remembered the gold. He had forgotten it for hours, but now it was dragging him down to the bottom of the lake. His feet touched mud; his hands worked hysterically.

He remembered his advice to Garcia. It had sounded so reasonable to say that the gold could always be thrown away if necessary, but now he was drowning and his fingers could hardly reach the fastenings of the deadly container on his back. Struggling to untie wet knots, Martinez felt his lungs exploding. The last of his air streamed out in glistening globes that rushed upward past his face. With one arm twisted behind him, he reached into the pack. His head was throbbing.

He grasped one of the golden bars and wrenched it through the opening. He kicked feebly, but he was still too heavy. He reached back again, his hand groping desperately in the layers of cloth. He was half unconscious when he yanked out the second gold bar, but he felt a little lighter. Suddenly inspired, he tore off his helmet, and then the shield still strapped to his left arm. He felt himself drift upward, but far too slowly.

His fingers scraped at the pack, then slipped inside once more. He felt something round and hard: the jewel-encrusted skull. On the brink of death, his senses were unnaturally acute. His fingers traced each blue-green stone, slipping over the surface and into the sockets where the eyes had gleamed. Alfonso Martinez was dying. His hand twitched and slipped down to the death's head's teeth. The teeth of Smoking Mirror and of Don Sebastian.

88

The touch of the thing shocked him, and his body reacted to the pain with a paroxysm that propelled him, flailing, to the surface of the lake.

He had time to inhale only once, then a strong brown hand caught him by the throat and dragged him up. More dead than alive, Martinez dimly sensed that he had been pulled into a war canoe. Someone had saved him from drowning; he wanted to know nothing more. He slumped into the bow, his head in someone's lap, and sensed dimly that the fighting was over. Strong strokes carried him toward one shore or the other.

The night was quieter, though distant shouts still drifted feebly across the lake. The light rain fell on his face, and Martinez opened his eyes. He was cradled in the arms of someone whose face he dimly recognized. He was too weak for fear. He looked at the face, but it was upside down. Its eyes betrayed it, finally, for they were blind. The man who held Martinez was the high priest of Smoking Mirror.

All the men in the canoe wore the spotted black and gold of the jaguar. Martinez stirred, and tried to raise himself. The canoe bumped against something. It was not the distant shore, but rather the stone side of a canal. He was back in Tenochtitlan.

The spotted knights lifted him from the boat. A woman walked toward him. Her face was grave; her skin was golden. Martinez longed to embrace her, but hardly had the strength to take a single step. She gazed on him with a thoughtfulness that touched him more than the playful looks of many women he had known.

And then she stepped aside. Behind her was a tall, dark man. His face was white, and he was dressed in robes of black and white and red. His hair hung to his shoulders; a disc of obsidian hung from his neck by a golden chain.

"You need not have run," said Don Sebastian de Villanueva.

The false physician slumped in the arms of the men who held him. The fighting was finished, and Alfonso Martinez had found a new home.

9. The Black Knife

S IT, Alfonso Martinez. And tell me what you know of Smoking Mirror."

Don Sebastian de Villanueva stood in the same room in which
he had been revived less than a week before. His long, pale
fingers stroked the miniature idol of the Aztec god as it sat upon
its pedestal in the depths of the black pyramid. He smiled, but it
only made him look more sinister.

"Sit, Martinez. You have nothing to fear from me."

Martinez had his doubts about the promise, but he obeyed. His
stool was the only piece of furniture in the room, unless he
counted the stone slab where he had watched one man die so that
another could be reborn. The slanting walls and ceiling still
disturbed him, but he was glad to see that at least his armed
guards had been dismissed. Nonetheless, he found it disconcerting to be alone with a man who had died two dozen years ago.

"Longer than that," said Don Sebastian. "I left the earth then,
but I met what men call death nine years before, at the siege of
Malaga."

Martinez nearly knocked over the stool when he realized that
Don Sebastian could read his thoughts, but he managed to catch
himself before he tumbled to the floor. "Clairvoyance," he said
in an undertone. He had learned as a boy that things were less

threatening when he had a name for them, and understood that it would not do to appear untutored in the ways of wizardry. "Can you always do that?"

"Not always. But when I am alone with a man, and waiting for his answer, sometimes I do not have to wait. Such a gift is doubly welcome in a city like this one, where the inhabitants all speak an alien tongue."

"All but the priestess," answered Martinez. "Do you understand her?"

"I hear more than she tells me."

"I wish I did. She sounds like she's making sense, but I can't be sure."

"We have much to learn from her, Martinez. But I confess that it is a pleasure to converse with a man who knows my own language. You would have been worth saving for that alone, though I hope to find other uses for you."

"I am conscious of the honor," Martinez said uneasily. "I am happier here than at the bottom of the lake. And a man with my interests could hardly hope for a wiser teacher than you. It took me years to get your skull, and even then I thought it no more than a talisman. I never dreamed that I would speak with you. Well, perhaps I did dream it, but nothing more."

"And perhaps I dreamed that you would be the cause of my resurrection. I hardly remember. But tell me. How did you acquire this . . . What did you call it? A talisman?"

"I stole the skull from a dwarf. He was a master magician, the greatest I had found in Spain. And you were legendary as the source of his power."

"Did you kill him?"

"Not really. I hit him a few times, but I don't think he died. I robbed him and fled to the New World, masquerading as a physician."

"Then you know nothing of medicine?"

"I knew enough to fool Cortez."

"I wish you knew more. There is a sickness among these people; the Spaniards brought it with them. The pox. I fear it will kill many, and I hoped that you might work against it."

"I might do something," offered Martinez, suddenly fearful that he had been tested and found wanting.

"No matter. I am less concerned with the health of these people than with their knowledge. The magic that brought me here exceeds anything I have ever experienced, and I would know more of it. I understand you witnessed the ceremony."

"I did," said Martinez.

"You must tell me of it. This woman Toci has done what no witch in Europe could do. It is one thing to raise the dead, but quite another to raise the dead who have died a second death. There is magic here, Martinez, such magic as you and I have never encountered. And I mean to master it."

"To what end? Those who study the supernatural do so most often for some purpose. They want wealth, or fame, or power. Some even do it for love. What do you want?" Martinez was suddenly abashed. "I only ask, you understand, so that I may help you."

"It would be pleasant, certainly, to rule this city," said Don Sebastian. "That should be motive enough for you, Martinez. I see that you are still very much of the earth. There are pleasures here, to be sure, and I would not place myself above them. But the greatest pleasure of all is knowledge. There are secrets in this city that I have yet to fathom."

"I believe that they have found the philosopher's stone," said Martinez. A second later he wished he had kept silent, for fear that his motives might seem too mercenary.

"Do you think so?" asked Don Sebastian.

"Where else does all this gold come from? They have so much that they scarcely value it. Montezuma gave Cortez a king's ransom. Tons of it—more than an army could carry!"

"And you lost your share," said Don Sebastian. His tone was unsympathetic, but his gesture was generous. He stripped a thick gold bracelet from his arm and offered it to Martinez. "Take this. I will find you more."

Martinez reached out eagerly. He was conscious of a certain

shame, intensified by a reluctance to touch dead flesh, but the gold was irresistible.

"So you think they make the gold," said Don Sebastian.

"Is it true?"

"I had not thought to ask. It hardly matters, Martinez, for they do not value it as we did in Spain. Power is the coin of the realm in Tenochtitlan, and it can only be won in warfare or witchcraft. There is no way to steal it."

Don Sebastian stepped away from the idol and moved toward Martinez. His white hand crept into his robe to withdraw an Aztec dagger, and Martinez cringed involuntarily at the sight of it.

"Look at this," said the wizard. "Look at the blade. Obsidian is worth more than gold in this land. The people call it 'tezcat' —from Tezcatlipoca, Smoking Mirror, the god whose incarnation I am destined to achieve. The black stone makes the mirrors, too, like this one I wear. The knife and the mirror, Martinez. These are the keys to power. Forget the gold."

Martinez did not forget, but did his best to think as though he had. It would not be easy to deal with a man who could read his mind. Yet Martinez was enough of a magician to have learned that one of the first secrets of sorcery was the technique of creating a vivid mental image. He filled his mind with the picture of the sacrificial dagger, confident that only this would be transmitted to his interrogator. Don Sebastian looked at him intently, his pale face devoid of all expression. Then he handed Martinez the knife.

"Is this . . . the one?" asked Martinez.

"It is. The woman Toci gave it to me—a small gift compared to the life that it restored. Examine it."

Martinez held the knife gingerly in both hands. The blade was short, with ragged edges, as if it had been hacked out, stone against stone, centuries before human hands had learned to work in metal. The hilt might well have been made of the same black stone, but there was no way to tell, since it was covered with a mosaic of jewels and precious stones. The handle took the form of a kneeling figure, bent over double with its hands reaching toward the blade. The head was crude, and thick with brilliant colors, but it looked like a skull to Martinez. He ran his right hand nervously along the edges of the figure, and the knife slipped suddenly, scraping his fingers against jagged blade.

The cut was small, yet it bled profusely. Martinez rubbed the blood away with his sleeve, but more welled up at once. He looked up at Don Sebastian and saw the dead eyes staring down. "Blood," said Martinez, wishing at once that he was mute.

The vampire spoke. "Have no fear," he said. "I am well provided for, and have no need to feed on you. I am not a wild beast, Alfonso Martinez. Blood sustains me, but it is not the reason for my being. Think of me not as a monster, but as a fellow magician."

The argument was persuasive, at least as long as Martinez kept his gaze averted from the lean, pale face, the lank black hair, the dull and dark eyes, the long bright teeth. As if to prove himself, the vampire turned his back and walked away.

Martinez was more grateful for the gesture than he would readily admit. He would have gladly been alone. He wanted time to decide whether he had found a wonderful opportunity or a terrible dilemma. What good was Aztec gold to him in a city where it counted for nothing? And how far could he advance himself in a world where wisdom and courage were the only virtues? He knew he was not much of a sorcerer, and no hero at all.

"You have a place here," said Don Sebastian, speaking to the farthest wall of the dark, angled room. "I have need of you. I am a creature of the night, Martinez, and this is a world awash in sun. You will be my eyes. There is much to learn here, more than I can learn in the hours of darkness. I depend on you to witness that which I cannot see, and to report it to me faithfully. You will be my colleague, and between us we shall master the magic of Mexico. I ask you to trust me. I have never betrayed one who was true to me."

"What would you have me say?" Martinez asked boldly, hoping that his cynicism would work to good effect.

"You have no choice, of course," said Don Sebastian de Villanueva, "as the only Spaniard left alive in the city, I believe, and here only by the sufferance of a walking corpse and a band of bloodthirsty savages. Remember that your isolation makes you unique. The rewards your position might bring are incalculable, and you are invaluable to me, at least for now."

"I am yours. But I am not such a fool as to imagine that my welfare is your principal concern."

"Of course. I like a man who worries. To do less is to confess stupidity. Be cautious, Martinez, if it pleases you, but remember that too much caution is another sort of folly. Believe in me, and you will find me a generous master."

"And me a devoted servant," said Martinez, making a bow that turned into a nervous stumble when the vampire turned again to face him.

"It must be as you say," replied Sebastian, "for these people believe I am a god."

"And you?" Martinez asked despite his fear. "What do you believe? Are you a god?"

"What is a god?" asked Don Sebastian, seating himself on the stone slab where he had found another incarnation. "Only a being with more power than its followers. And one who gains strength from their devotion. In short, a creature much like a vampire."

"Of course, of course. The powers are inside us and outside us, and they grow stronger from the correspondence. But much of this is sophistry. I ask you outright: Are you the Smoking Mirror they have waited for?"

"I like it that you are rash enough to challenge me."

"Not a moment ago you promised me your patronage. Am I to begin by doubting you?"

"If I am to answer your question, you must answer mine. Let me ask again. What do you know of Smoking Mirror?"

"Precious little. These people are like the ancients; they have many gods. And Smoking Mirror is their dark god, the power of evil, the source of black magic."

"Nothing you say is wrong, Martinez, but you do not say enough. Smoking Mirror is more than just another name for Satan. The Aztecs are more sophisticated than Europeans; they see the virtue in the powers of darkness. The priestess, Toci, told me a story about this god; let me tell it to you."

Martinez doubted that the tale would answer his question, but he listened nonetheless.

"The gods of this country are said to walk among the people," explained Sebastian. "Of course; how else could they accept me? It is said that Smoking Mirror, if he is seen at all, will be seen at night, and with that I cannot argue. And he is most likely to be encountered along a lonely road, near a forest.

"Imagine yourself walking outside the city at midnight. If Smoking Mirror is near, you will hear the sound of a man chopping wood. That sound alone, known for what it is, would send cowards into flight; but if you are brave, and ambitious, you will step off the road into the woods. There is a threat, but there is a temptation too, and even a promise such as I have made to you. A man with the courage to face the god may hope to gain from the encounter."

"And what may he gain?"

"Much. But only after he has faced the Smoking Mirror. If you follow the sound of chopping wood into the forest, you will see a dim glowing in the darkness. And if you do not run from it, you will meet the god face to face. You will see him standing among the trees, a gleaming skeleton, with eyes afire and a long tongue lolling between his gaping jaws. And he will challenge you, not with words or actions, but by his very presence. The sound you hear is not an ax, but the noise of the god's ribs, swinging open and shut like a door caught in a vagrant breeze. Behind those banging ribs is the living heart of Smoking Mirror. If you have the strength to reach out and clutch that throbbing heart in your bare hands, then this god of bones and blood will reward you with riches and glory. But if you turn away from him, then you will be blighted forever."

"What do you suppose they mean by it?"

"Probably they mean nothing, Martinez, for they do not see it as a piece of fancy, but as the simple truth."

Nonplussed, Martinez looked down and noticed that he still held the black knife in his left hand. He offered it to Don Sebastian.

"Another way of reaching hearts," said the vampire, as he took the weapon. "No less effective, but suitable only for a priest. Yet Smoking Mirror is willing to appear to any common man and give him the chance to grasp pulsating power in his naked fingers. You may never be a priest, Martinez. But tell me: What would you do if you met the god in the forest?"

Martinez considered for a moment. "Easy enough," he said, "to swear that I would be bold and resolute. Such boasts cost a man nothing. Yet I will not proclaim myself a coward in advance of the evidence. How can I know what I will do until the challenge confronts me?"

"I can put you to the test. What say you, Alfonso Martinez? This room is not a forest, to be sure, yet it is certainly a setting in which the god might appear. Are you ready to face him?"

Martinez stood, suddenly afraid that he had pushed his luck too far, and dropped his eyes. "My hand," he said. "I have hurt my hand. You can hardly expect me to reach between the clashing ribs of a skeleton when I can barely hold a coin in my fingers."

He kept his gaze averted from the figure across the room, but he could not block out the short, sharp noise that came from the shadows. It might have been the blade of an ax chopping into the trunk of a tree, or it might have been the sound of a trap springing shut.

"This is not the test!" shouted Martinez. "I will not look! I have not seen the god!"

He stared resolutely at the mica floor and concentrated on the way in which its gleaming surface both absorbed and reflected the light from the burning braziers. He strove to hold the shifting images in his brain and think of nothing else.

"So be it," said the voice of Don Sebastian. "You have not entered the forest, Martinez. Remember, though, that such a chance comes seldom. Still, you are not compromised. Come, have faith in me. Raise your eyes. You need not spend the rest of your life in contemplation of a floor."

Reluctantly, Martinez did as he was told, and saw to his relief that his companion looked no more uncanny than before. Yet once more the pale face wore its mocking smile.

"You need not be embarrassed, Martinez. A man should have the right to choose his moment, although in truth the world is not always so generous. But let it pass. For the moment you have eluded the god in the forest. Perhaps you will never face him."

"When I am ready."

"Even so. But you have not answered my question, and so you have denied yourself an answer to your own. Unless you are willing to take the god's heart in your hands, I fear that you will never learn whether I am Smoking Mirror."

Martinez sat again. "You might have answered me directly," he said sullenly.

"Gods seldom do."

10. The Temples

IN the months that followed, Alfonso Martinez became a student of Aztec theology. It was an uncomfortable education.

His schoolroom was the city of Tenochtitlan, and his teacher was Toci, the priestess of Smoking Mirror. He did not learn from books or lectures, even though Toci's Spanish improved with remarkable speed; instead, he learned from demonstrations. She showed him the rites of the gods of Mexico, an apparently endless series of lavish displays that would have delighted the eyes of any observer if they had not so frequently ended in death.

By day Martinez stood under the white sun and watched innumerable wretches sacrificed in ceremonies of blood and fire; by night he reported his observations to a living corpse. Don Sebastian had an insatiable appetite for detail; he was evidently engaged in a systematic analysis of the countless cults that controlled every aspect of life among the Aztecs. He brooded over manuscripts filled with the strange, flat drawings that Martinez found so disquieting, and he fingered the huge circular stones covered with apparently indecipherable hieroglyphics that represented the Mexican calendar.

"These people are fools," Martinez told him. "Look at that thing you're studying. Look at the shape of it. It's a wheel, isn't it? They have skill enough to make such a thing, but they don't have sense enough to know what to do with it. They still drag their burdens through the streets, and cover the only wheels they have with those meaningless scrawls."

"This may well be the most useful wheel ever invented," said Don Sebastian, but he would say no more.

Martinez grew increasingly impatient as the days passed. In his mind there was only one secret in the city worth uncovering, and that was the source of its gold. Yet whenever he mentioned the subject to Don Sebastian, he found himself turned away with an enigmatic remark, which was often accompanied by another gift of the precious metal. It was not long before the alchemist possessed a fortune. But he was still a virtual prisoner in an alien environment, one where his constantly increasing hoard was all but worthless.

The irony of the situation did not escape Martinez. He was not humorless, and more than once he laughed as he accepted another ring, bracelet, or necklace from his master, each ornament cold from contact with the flesh of a vampire. Yet the laughter was bitter. For years he had dreamed of accumulating such a fortune; its image had haunted him, and he had never doubted that somehow it would be his. But he had concentrated so intently on the mere accumulation of wealth that his mental projections had included nothing of the surrounding circumstances. He was certain that the intensity of his visions had produced the desired result, but equally certain that his failure to imagine sufficiently detailed conditions had caused his present predicament. The worst of it was that Don Sebastian seemed to know; the dead smile with which he bestowed the trinkets was proof enough. And indeed there might be a lesson in all this. The vanity of riches was an old sermon, but not one that Martinez wished to hear.

Still, he could not ignore the simple sensual pleasure that his new wealth provided. In his room in the palace, away from Toci and Don Sebastian, he found his principal diversion in playing with his golden toys. The mere touch of the objects was a promise of power; it only remained for Martinez to fulfill that tantalizing promise. Apart from this, his life was as empty as an alchemist's purse. The priestess and the undead wizard were his only companions, except for the servants who brought him the food he could not name and spoke to him in words he could not comprehend. Sleep on a straw mat under pictures of the hideous Aztec gods became a luxury, one that his keepers allowed him too infrequently. He began to think with nostalgia of the days when he had served in the Spanish army.

Cortez had fled the city in the early morning of July 1, and somehow his ragged army had fought its way through the outlying territory held by allies of the Aztecs. On July 2, while his former comrades struggled to save themselves, Martinez observed the first day of the festival of Xilonen, the goddess of young corn.

As the new corn ripened, the chiefs of each district gave freely of the food stored from the last harvest. The people feasted and danced in the streets. Martinez could not help reflecting that their recent victory gave them more to celebrate than the coming of a new crop.

Toci pointed out a young woman, one whom Martinez had already noticed for himself. She was dressed entirely in flowers. Her body was covered in white and yellow blossoms, and he found the effect so delightful that he was willing to overlook the red paint smeared on her face. More forbidding were the three ancient crones who accompanied her everywhere. Robed in black, their gray hair streaming in the dust, they seemed to have no other purpose than to feed her and to keep her dancing.

For days Martinez watched this lovely creature, enjoying both her presence and the images she inspired in his mind. He all but convinced himself that Toci had singled her out for his attention because she was to be a gift. But when he finally asked about her, he was disappointed. "She is the goddess," Toci said.

A charming custom, thought Martinez, still hopeful that the end of the celebration would leave this surrogate divinity free for earthly pleasures. Toci also drew his attention to a young man who was dressed with uncommon splendor, but the alchemist found him considerably less interesting. He preferred to direct his gaze toward the flowered image of the goddess, especially on the final day of the festival.

On that day, the goddess and her withered handmaidens mounted the steps of the temple, and there the object of the alchemist's desire began a frenzied dance.

In an ecstasy she tore the blossoms from her body until she was half naked, whirling on a carpet of yellow and white. Her torso gleamed with perspiration, her brown back arched, her pointed breasts thrust toward the sun. Martinez, who had often regretted the civilized garb of these savages, stared with undisguised delight. Not even the grave countenance of the priestess beside him could dampen his enthusiasm.

He was still staring when the three old women dragged his goddess down and hacked a hole in her chest with a blade of black obsidian. One of them held something up above her head, her hands dripping.

Martinez heard the voice of the crowd raised in a tremendous shout, but it seemed to come from a great distance. His lust gave way at once to horror, but there was an unforgettable instant where the two were mixed, and a lingering sensation that the tragedy he had witnessed was somehow ennobling. His feelings terrified him far more than what he had seen.

"The corn is ripe," said Toci.

He turned to her, half expecting to see in her eyes the mockery so characteristic of Don Sebastian. Instead, her face was sweetly serious, her eyes shining with unshed tears. "Xilonen is dead," she told him, "but she will rise again. The corn will rise again. It is good."

That night, a troubled Martinez spoke to Don Sebastian. He would have preferred to be reassured by Toci, but her acceptance of the ceremony was so complete that he could hardly expect her to discuss it rationally. And so Martinez, half ashamed of his own squeamishness, sought comfort from a being whose very existence was dependent on bloodshed.

Sebastian put aside his manuscripts and looked at Martinez

thoughtfully. "We are born to die," he said. "You have seen death before."

"But not like this," protested Martinez, sensing as he spoke that the creature before him had cast its cold eyes upon his inmost thoughts.

"You desired her, but death cares nothing for that, Martinez. The beautiful must die, as must the brave. Nor are the weak and ugly spared. All die."

"But the manner of her death!"

"All deaths are cruel; but I see that you mean something more."

"I almost think she chose it willingly. And the city cheered her slaughter. This is something I have never seen before—a nation that rejoices to see its daughters slain."

"Surely you know of such things, though you have never been a witness to them? Consider the creed of our native land, and the worship of its martyrs. It is a glory everywhere to die for a cause, to die for the gods and thus receive their favor. And there is a certain logic in it, since death is inevitable in any case. Would you not sacrifice yourself for a guarantee of endless bliss?"

"I might, if I believed in it."

"I strongly advise you to believe in something, Martinez. You are wise enough in the ways of the world to know the importance of faith. Years ago in Spain, my studies convinced me that the afterlife a man envisions is the one he will experience. I learned it from a woman. She was a vampire, like me, but her fate was not like mine. She expected only oblivion, and now she is no more. But somehow I have survived."

Martinez squirmed on his stool. "Then did you know that you would awaken in Mexico?"

"Perhaps. I knew, at least, that there was more before me. It seemed expedient to abandon this world temporarily, lest others should wreak their will upon my spirit. The secret of my undead existence had been discovered and I would no doubt be destroyed when the sun rose. My plans had gone awry; there seemed to be no escape. And so I set myself aflame before the walls of my black castle. But I never doubted that I would return someday."

"Return from what?" asked Martinez eagerly.

"I cannot easily tell you. And I wonder if I should. But I see that you have been chastened by this sacrifice, and I would show you what I can while you are still less worldly than you were. I dreamed in a sort of limbo—one of my own devising. I had peace there, and a beautiful darkness. But it was not enough. Not enough for eternity."

"Then you hope to find more here?"

"I must, Martinez. Why do you suppose I became the creature that you see before you? To revel in murder? To seek pleasure in a bed of earth? There may be some strange delights in it—such as the moment of madness you experienced when you saw the heart torn from the maiden you coveted, but there are more of shame and sorrow. If I endure these, then I must.

"Time, Martinez! I need more time. That black-and-silver world I constructed for my soul was not enough. I must have more. I will not spend the ages there alone."

Sebastian's face was contorted with emotions that Martinez never expected to see there, and he felt a pity for the lost soul that stood before him, mingled with a terror he had never known before. His own world was much simpler, but he felt to his dismay that it was shattering around him. He had always thought of himself as a young man, with time enough to worry about the state of his spirit.

"I have much to learn from you," he said.

"That is why we showed you the ceremony. It is easy enough to talk of mortality, but such a demonstration is worth more than words. It was Toci who guessed that it would change you. Dozens have died during this festival, but she knew that this one life meant more to you than most. Do not forget it, Martinez."

For a while Martinez did not forget. Yet the next festival, celebrating the birth of the flowers, was more pleasant. It followed immediately after the celebration in honor of the young corn, and Martinez began to understand that the life of the city was an endless cycle of religious rites, a pattern of continuous devotion that might dismay even the most devout Catholics of Spain.

"There are eighteen of these ceremonies," said Don Sebastian, "each lasting twenty days. They are something like our months."

"But they have forgotten five days," said Martinez. "That makes only three hundred and sixty. Or can't they calculate the length of a year?"

"Their calendar is exquisitely calculated, Martinez, and so complex that it will require months of study. Each day has its significance. I will show you when I know more. The five days you mentioned are not forgotten. They are called the five days of misfortune, and anyone born then is considered to be cursed. They fall in February, during those short, dark days when it seems that winter will never end."

"But does it all make sense?" protested Martinez. "Take this current celebration. Toci tells me that it honors Huitzilopochtli, their war god, the one whose temple dwarfs all the rest. But there are no blood sacrifices, and not even a mockery of warfare. There is only joy, and such abandon as I have never known here. The men and women even hold each other when they dance, something I have never seen before. And there is drunkenness. I had guessed that their strict morals were part of the discipline that produced warriors, yet they honor war by forgoing all decorum. They are mad."

"Perhaps they believe that Huitzilopochtli sees enough of killing, and can easily be spared more. That may be the nature of his holiday. Yet discipline is not altogether lost. Observe, and you will notice that only the old people are granted the gift of drunkenness. For all others, it remains a capital offense. Yet I grant you the paradox. Their beliefs are so complicated, so full of contradictions, that sometimes I despair of ever mastering them. And yet, if I can correlate them with the European systems, with our Zodiac, I believe that I will have the key to more power than any man has known before."

The thought intrigued Martinez. Time enough had passed, however, so that he was once again less concerned with his afterlife than with what he could acquire while still a man.

"Old habits die hard," Sebastian said, and by now Martinez was so accustomed to this mind reading that it disturbed him little more than the fact that he was conversing with a living corpse.

"The incongruities are intriguing," said Sebastian. "Tell me. What strikes you as the most appropriate time for the festival of Smoking Mirror?"

"I don't know. Scorpio, I suppose—the sign of death and transformation."

"And the time of All Hallow's Eve? The sign under which I was born. I would have guessed the same. Yet the feast of Smoking Mirror falls a full month earlier, when Libra rules the heavens— the sign of grace and balance, and the one ruled by Venus. But the Aztecs call Venus the star of the Feathered Serpent, the god whose mantle your Cortez assumed, the god who stands in opposition to Smoking Mirror. What do you make of that?"

"Nothing," replied Martinez. "This is superstition, not science. I suggest that you forget it all, and turn your efforts toward the conquest of these savages. To celebrate the spirit of the unknown so early in the year is against all precedent. Libra!"

"There is more. The constellation they ascribe to Smoking Mirror is not the Balance, but rather the Great Bear."

Martinez thought for a moment. "Ursa Major. . . . There is some sense in that, I suppose. But there's no system to it. You are embarked on the study of an illusion."

"I might agree with you, yet the mere fact that I am here argues against you. Their magic is potent, and there must be a methodology behind it. They say their gods come from the stars, from stars so far away that we can scarcely see them. Perhaps we are too much concerned with the lumps of stone and fire that spin around our own sun. There is an infinite universe beyond them, Martinez, with powers we have never dreamed of, much less summoned. You must forget your gold, and look to the glittering lights in the sky."

Martinez rarely saw the stars. He spent his days witnessing the rites of the Aztecs and his nights in the bowels of the black pyramid with Don Sebastian. And his discontent grew. Both Toci and Sebastian considered it sufficient to hint at their secrets; he was not really one with them, and he felt with some resentment that they considered him a novice in the quest for mystery.

The middle of August brought the celebration of the falling fruits. Martinez at once forgot the name of the god it honored, but he could not forget its rituals. The god was a god of fire, and the sacrifice was multiple. The greatest soldiers of the nation appeared, each bringing with him a prisoner of war. The pairs of men danced together, the captives no less dedicated to the ritual than their captors. In fact, Martinez found it necessary to ask Toci which were which. After a day of dancing, the prisoners were dragged up the steps of the god's temple, to its summit. A bed of coals burned there, and one by one the men were thrown into it. Toci assured Martinez that the victims were drugged to the point of insensibility, but still it came as a relief when the priests of the fire god dragged the half-roasted captives out of the flames with hooked poles and cut out their hearts.

The next ritual began on the last day of August. By now Martinez was sick of these gruesome celebrations, but he saw no way to escape them. And he had not yet lost all hope that there was a meaning to them. He asked Don Sebastian the name of the next god to be honored.

"Toci," said Sebastian.

"Toci!" cried Martinez. "You can't mean it? She is a priestess. They can't mean to kill her!"

"Toci is a goddess, who gave our Toci her name. There is no more significance in it than when a Spaniard is named in honor of some saint. She tells me that the name means 'Heart of the Earth.' Another fertility rite, now that the harvest is so near. Our Toci will not die. There is another woman who will assume the role of the goddess, and I understand that she will not be so lucky. Or perhaps she will be luckier, if she believes."

"I should have known," said Martinez. "You would not let your woman die, even if she had been chosen."

"You mistake me, Martinez. Toci is no woman of mine, whatever you may think or I may wish. She is a virgin, sworn to Smoking Mirror."

"Then you are not Smoking Mirror."

"That is as may be. Toci revived me and she sheltered me. She believes in me, and serves me in every way but one. Perhaps Smoking Mirror is beyond desire."

"But not Don Sebastian, eh?"

A twisted grin crossed the vampire's pale, scarred countenance. "Are you lonely, Martinez? There are maidens here for you to wed."

"I want no bride. I will not be tied to a savage. I am a Spaniard!"

"The city is not so ascetic as it seems. I understand that there are harlots here, though I know little of them. Ask Toci. Perhaps she will help you."

Now there was no doubt about the meaning of Sebastian's smile. He knew well enough that Martinez would never ask the august Toci to procure a savage slut for him. Martinez had some consolation in the thought that the great sorcerer was as lovelorn as the lowly alchemist, but no real satisfaction.

"Are they feeding you, at least?" asked Martinez.

"I am as you see me."

Martinez surveyed the gaunt figure standing between two flaming braziers at the foot of the black slab where he had been reborn. The face was white, and split by the old scar that ran down over the left eye; but the long hair was still black, and the dead flesh was firm. In his robes of red and white and black, adorned with ornaments of gold, Don Sebastian de Villanueva still possessed an unholy strength.

"You don't look starved," said Martinez.

The festival of the earth mother was the most elaborate Martinez had yet witnessed. It was called the Month of Brooms, and began with a ritual sweeping of the entire city, which made a bit more sense to Martinez when he learned that one of the titles of the goddess Toci was a term indicating she was a grandmother. In another manifestation of the goddess her name was Tlazolteotl, which meant "Eater of Filth"; she consumed sins, and pardoned them. The city's prostitutes were her wards, but the entire population exposed their failings to her in a ceremony Martinez could only regard as a parody of the Catholic confession. Somehow the goddess and the priestess who stood beside him were mixed up in his mind; he was tempted to confess to her and find redemption in her shining eyes, but he was too embarrassed, and hardly knew what she would regard as a sin.

Her beauty subdued him as much as her air of severity, and he was fascinated by the thought that she was still a virgin. He tried to guess her age, but could do no more than guess. The women of Tenochtitlan did not show their years, but he would have sworn that she was closer to twenty than thirty. Too young, certainly, to hear the sort of story Martinez had to tell. In any case, there seemed no profit to be gained from making sordid confessions to a creature who functioned more and more in his mind as a temptation. Martinez looked at her and longed for purity.

The ceremonies continued. The young man in the gaudy robes was there again, this time accompanied by four lovely young maidens who clustered around him as eagerly as brides; but Martinez was much more interested in the woman who played the role of the goddess.

She was a handsome woman, with strong features, but much older than the one whose death had shocked the alchemist. She had the air of a matron, which was further emphasized by the role she assumed. Dressed in white, like the image of the goddess in the temple, she sat amid a throng of dancers and worked on her weaving.

Four gigantic poles had been constructed in the courtyard before the pyramid, each of them so tall that they seemed to tower over the temple. Martinez could only guess their length, but they were certainly well over a hundred feet high, and close enough together that each set of two could be connected by numerous cross beams, so that they looked like two ladders reaching toward the sky.

On the last day of the festival, the mock goddess passed between these ladders, borne on the back of a black-clad priest. He carried her up the steps to the summit of the pyramid while the citizens of Tenochtitlan gathered at its base. As they reached the top—the woman in white with her face to the sun—another priest stepped forward, a black sword in his hand. The sword fell, and the woman's head fell with it. Blood spilled over the man who held the decapitated corpse.

Martinez had expected something like this, and tried to tell himself that he was past caring. But he was not prepared for what came next.

The priests bent over the body, their knives busy. They stripped off the woman's clothes, and then proceeded to remove her skin. Martinez felt his stomach lurch. The crowd was silent, and the sun shone down unmercifully. A naked man appeared, and stood motionless while the priests dressed him. His coat was the skin of a woman, peeled off her corpse from throat to thigh.

"She is born again," said Toci.

Martinez was nauseous, choking back his vomit as he turned away. When he had the strength to look again, he saw that the priests had covered the man's abominable garment with the white clothes that the woman had woven in the days before she died. Blotches of her blood were seeping through the cloth.

He made an effort to collect himself, remembering his duty to Don Sebastian. "Why is she a man?" he asked halfheartedly.

"She will fight," said Toci. "Now men will die."

Her remarks made Martinez expect something further from the hideous man-woman, but instead the creature disappeared into the depths of the temple, and two new priests took the stage as they crawled up the gigantic ladders in front of the pyramid. When they reached the top, they lashed themselves into place with ropes.

Captives were herded into the square formed by the four poles, and one by one were forced to climb upward toward the waiting priests. There was a brief flurry of arms and legs as each man reached the summit, then the captives dropped, shattering like ripe fruit on the flagstones below. A priest was waiting for them;

he cut off their heads and collected their blood in a golden bowl.

When it was finally over, the man in the woman's skin stepped forward from the crowd. He leaned over the bowl, dipped one finger into the blood, and licked it.

The gesture was a signal to every man, woman, and child in the great plaza. They bent down, touching their fingers to the ground, and then tasted the earth. Martinez stood erect while countless thousands stooped toward the ground. The goddess, he remembered, was an eater of filth, but he had hardly expected the populace of Tenochtitlan to follow her example. And certainly he was not prepared for what came next. Later, he tried to convince himself that it was an illusion, induced by horror and the heat of the sun. For what he felt was nothing less than an earthquake.

The ground he stood on shook; the long poles before the pyramid swayed dizzily. A vast rumbling rolled through the city, jolting Martinez so that finally he fell to his knees. He looked at Toci, and saw her slender figure thrown back and forth by the cataclysm. Her eyes were closed, her face ecstatic. The heart of the earth was throbbing, and Martinez clutched the ground to save himself.

Abruptly, everything was still. Martinez lay outstretched for a moment, then guiltily put a dirt-streaked finger to his mouth. He looked up, and saw the white-clad goddess surrogate advancing into the plaza, followed by a small army of soldiers dressed in golden skins spotted with black. They were the knights of Smoking Mirror.

More warriors rushed out from the mob to meet them: the Knights of the Feathered Serpent. This was the mock combat Martinez had heard about, though what it had to do with an earth goddess was more than he could guess. The enthusiasm of the fight appalled him—this was more than ritual. Men fell bleeding, and the air was filled with stones.

Martinez swore as a club flew past his head. He clutched at Toci. The city was in chaos. "Do they mean to kill each other?"

"Some die," said Toci. She took his hand and led him along

with the crowd toward the small shrine of the goddess with her name. Martinez saw that the battle was working its way toward the same objective. The twilight rang with shouts.

Night fell before the knights of Smoking Mirror and the Feathered Serpent reached their goal. On the edge of the city, with the shore in view, the fighting stopped. The man in the guise of the goddess, face streaming from a dozen wounds, struggled to the top of a black building where a straw dummy waited. He pulled off his woman's clothes, and then the woman's skin. He stood naked for a moment while the people streamed through the street to witness his abdication. He put the skin on the straw figure, then the white blouse and skirt. Devoid of his finery, he jumped down and disappeared into the ranks of battered warriors.

A ladder led to the rooftop. A young man in glittering robes stepped forward and pulled it to the ground. Four young women stood beside him; together they lifted the ladder and cast it into the nearby canal.

"It's him again," said Martinez, now totally bewildered. "Who is he?"

"He is Smoking Mirror," said Toci.

The alchemist felt something snap inside his head. "Smoking Mirror, is he? Then what of Don Sebastian?"

"The god has many faces," said a voice behind him.

Martinez whirled. The sky was dark, but he had never thought to see his teacher in the streets of the city. Martinez could not speak.

"There is another name for Smoking Mirror," said Don Sebastian. "He is the dark part of every soul, and sometimes they call him 'He Who Stands at the Shoulder.' "

"You deserve the title," said Martinez. "You haunt me like the horror that you are, and I have seen enough of horrors."

"Then perhaps you are ready, Martinez. For tomorrow begins the feast of Smoking Mirror."

11. A Box of Earth

THE festival that began near the end of September was called the Return of the Gods, and the first to return was Smoking Mirror.

Although Martinez was unnerved by the appearance of Don Sebastian at the conclusion of the festival for Toci, he could not suppress the fascination he felt at the news about the next celebration. He held his peace as he followed Sebastian to the black pyramid, speaking only when he was again seated in the subterranean chamber with the tilted walls.

"I suppose they'll be killing that boy."

"He will die in time, but not yet," replied Sebastian. "Tezcatlipoca is a god of such great importance that he is given two feasts. His representative is chosen a year in advance, but is not to be killed until the celebration marking the end of the drought, in May. Until then he is treated like a king. He does no work; all his wishes are granted. Those four young women with him are his brides—until the spring."

"I can wait."

"The death of Smoking Mirror is a ceremony worth waiting for. But this will be more than public spectacle—something that takes place late at night atop this very pyramid, with only the priests of this cult to witness it, something worth more to me than the slaughter of a thousand pampered boys. On that night the gods return from their journeying among the stars, and Smoking Mirror manifests himself."

"Exposing you as a fraud."

"Then you have decided against me, Martinez?"

"Should I acknowledge you as the god of a race you never dreamed of?"

"You have never seen my dreams," said Don Sebastian, and Martinez peered at him intently. "You would be well advised to trust me, Martinez. I will assume that the sacrifice today disturbed you. You know that without my protection you would not live long in Tenochtitlan. And you know that I offer you an opportunity few magicians of your rank will ever have. What more could you want of me?"

"The truth. I know you saved me, but for what? I live an endless round of horrors and frustrations. I have no friends, no position, no home, and no women. No one even speaks to me, except a woman made of ice and a man who should be dust. It's like living on some distant planet. And don't tell me how many magicians would be grateful for just such a chance. I've had the chance, and I know what it's worth. This city is no more to me than a dunghill covered with flies. What I want from you is not promises but the truth!"

"In your present state of mind, you would hardly be receptive to great truths. I almost think you mean to make me angry, though what you hope to gain from that I cannot guess. I am disappointed in you, Martinez. Ask your questions, and I will answer them if I can."

"Tell me about the gold," said the alchemist.

Sebastian moved across the room and stopped beside the idol of Tezcatlipoca. "Not the question I had hoped to hear," he said.

"You know what I mean. I came to this accursed continent in search of gold. And more than that, the secret of its source. They have so much, and prize it so little, that I guessed they might have found the philosopher's stone."

"I think not, alchemist," Sebastian said, and Martinez sat as if he had been turned to stone.

"It might not be beyond their powers," continued Sebastian, "but they would call a man mad for wasting his efforts on such an endeavor. It is pretty stuff, I grant you, and it gleams with a yellow like the sun. But what use is it? A soft metal, most valued here because it can be fashioned into ornaments. The art of the jeweler gives it what worth it has. It comes from mines, Martinez. It is a toy, a trifle. It answers no need. Any man in this city would tell you that a good blade of Spanish steel is worth its weight in gold, and more."

"I suppose you knew this all along," Martinez muttered. "You knew what I wanted, and you knew it wasn't here."

"I hoped that you would grow wiser. You already have gold enough to satisfy a man of your class. What would it matter if you could learn to manufacture it?"

"In this stinking city, not much. In the real world it would make me someone to be reckoned with. If I could return to Spain with the secret, I would be the wonder of the age!"

"I doubt if you will see Spain again, Martinez. Yet I won't deny you. Will you take this ring?"

"You think I will refuse it—you think you have taught me a lesson. But all the seers say that no man can predict his own future, however great his skill. Perhaps I will get out of here somehow; and if I do, I will be rich." Martinez took the ring.

"The last time you tried to carry a treasure out of this city, it all but killed you."

"Then I will have to be more careful."

"Let me show you something else, Martinez."

"Another sacrifice? Another magic trick?"

"I think it may impress you. I show it to you with the warning that it is guarded through the day by more jaguar knights than you would care to meet."

Sebastian led the alchemist across the crooked room to the wall that slanted over the sacrificial slab. His pale fingers ran along the dull black wall, and suddenly a portion of it dropped away. Martinez had seen panels hidden in other buildings, some of them counterbalanced so that they would spring open soundlessly at the slightest touch, yet this concealed chamber was like no other he had seen. Perhaps it was the oblique angle of the ceiling that made the long and narrow niche seem strange, but he could not shake off the notion that it was the entrance to another dimension —the work of a sorcerer, not an architect. Yet what it held was commonplace enough, no more than an open wooden box half filled with dirt.

"Your coffin," said Martinez.

"Mark it well. Whatever your ambitions, Alfonso Martinez, they will all end in a box like this."

Martinez turned away from the coffin and the dizzying crevice that contained it. "Your very presence shows me that death need not be the end," he said.

"It is not death that should concern you, but what comes after it. If you should die tonight, what would become of you? I have died twice, and twice returned to life, and still I am searching for a way to meet eternity. Your life should be a preparation for what will come."

"But who are you to tell me? You admit that you still know nothing, and you are in your third life. It would be wonderful if you could show me how to guarantee myself eternal bliss. What formula should I recite? Which incense should I burn? But for all I know, the path you want me to take leads to the void. I'll admit your way might be best, but only when there's proof that it goes somewhere. Meanwhile, I'll settle for the pleasures of the earth and let my soul fend for itself!"

"Come, Martinez. Every alchemist's apprentice knows that faith must come before the fact. I admit it is a difficult doctrine; indeed, it is devilish. If you believe in nothing, you cannot expect much else. Which leads us to your next question. Ask it."

Martinez sat on his stool and looked at the gold ring in his hand. "I can't believe that you will give me a good answer," he said. "I have asked before. And for this question I hardly know the answer that I want. I don't even know what the question means anymore."

"Can it hurt so much to ask?"

"You know I am a coward in many ways, and I confess that you can frighten me. That's what you've always done when I've asked questions. You are a magus, and you are undead. But are you Smoking Mirror?"

Sebastian touched the tilted wall, and watched the black stone swallow up his coffin. "Then you have not entirely renounced me, Martinez. I am grateful for what belief remains."

"What do you care what I think? Why don't you just kill me and be done with it?"

"I might have, years ago," Sebastian admitted. "But you have been of help to me. And for some reason I want to help you. Your skepticism is a rock to hone my thoughts. Your doubt strengthens my belief. And you are not such a fool as you make yourself sound. You are something like me, Martinez, and I will not kill you unless you drive me to it. And I will continue to protect you from the Aztecs. I will even try to answer your question."

Martinez stirred uncomfortably, then stood and paced across the mica floor. "Now you would shame me," he protested. "I don't know what to say."

"Then I will say it. Admit this: I am as much Tezcatlipoca as Cortez is Quetzalcoatl."

"Granted." Martinez stopped his pacing and stood against a distant wall. "But the comparison is instructive. Where is Cortez now?"

Sebastian glided from behind the black slab to stand again beside the obsidian idol. "I fear we have not seen the last of him. He fought his way out of the city, and now there are reports that he is active in the countryside. One by one, he is subverting cities that are chafing under Aztec rule. I believe he means to rise against Tenochtitlan again. He is still a god to many."

Martinez's mind was racing feverishly, but he tried to keep his thoughts from Don Sebastian.

"It has a bearing on our argument," Sebastian went on. "An

upheaval of the kind that I envision will interfere with my quest. I am fighting time, Martinez, and now I must fight you as well."

"Then you really do believe that you are this Aztec god?"

"What is the nature of these gods? The stories say that they are tangible beings, creatures who have appeared here before. The Aztecs have been waiting for us, Cortez and me, and their belief in us is unquestionably a source of strength. Cortez employs that strength strategically, as you would have me do. Perhaps I am mistaken in my hope that such strength can affect the spirit, but I shall stand by my judgment. Could it be true that these gods once walked the earth? And might their incarnations reappear?"

"I don't know," admitted Martinez. "But I ask you again: How can you cling to the hope that you are Smoking Mirror, and at the same time hope to see him in this ceremony that you spoke about? If he appears, then you will be discredited."

"Theology is subtle, Martinez. Think of Spain and its religion. What they worship is threefold, a trinity of power, each part separate and yet inseparable. Learned men debate such paradoxes, but I am willing to accept them. And when Smoking Mirror comes, I hope that he will not expose me but embrace me, and that his power will be mine."

Martinez rubbed his hand across his mouth. "There is a risk, even if your premises are sound. You hope to absorb the power of this god. It seems more logical to expect that he will absorb you. You might be lost forever, leaving me alone among these savages."

"We shall be obliged to take our chances," said Sebastian. "I choose to believe in their gods, and to assume that what they have of value here comes from the stars."

"Then you think these gods came from the stars?"

"The documents suggest it. And the idea makes more sense than the story we were told as boys, of one force in the clouds and another buried in the bowels of the earth. The universe is infinite, Martinez. Dimensions beyond dreaming lie around us. Who knows what powers career through the vast gulfs that spin around this ball of earth we stand on? You could speed among the stars for eternity, Alfonso Martinez, and never reach your journey's end. Somewhere in those endless reaches there must dwell forces of such magnitude that they would shatter our poor human visions. Perhaps all the gods of men are such—titanic entities that pass us on their travels through unknown realms. Gods beyond good and evil, gods who long to find strong souls to join them in their cosmic dance. Gods like Smoking Mirror."

"Perhaps," said Martinez.

For days Martinez watched the preparations for the return of the gods of Tenochtitlan. There was merrymaking in the streets; the ban against drunkenness seemed to be forgotten. Young men and women carried leafy branches, using them to decorate the shrines and temples of every god and goddess in the city. There were no sacrifices.

Each night Martinez reported on the day's events to Don Sebastian, and on the eighteenth night Toci followed him into the crooked room where the vampire waited.

"Smoking Mirror comes tonight," said Toci.

Martinez, who had done his best to forget Sebastian's ravings about monsters from infinity, felt a sudden chill.

"There will be four of us," Sebastian told him, "we three, and the blind high priest. And if things happen as they have been written, there will be a fifth."

"You really expect something?" Martinez asked, apprehensively.

"I have studied the stars and find them propitious. I might have chosen a later night, but this is the one that is prescribed. If we find less than I anticipate, I have another plan, based on my own calculations. Yet the Aztecs have studied their god for generations, and I will not challenge their traditions."

"What will happen?"

"What they expect is a small thing, though not without significance. But I expect much more. I may be disappointed, but I think the presence of a creature such as I am may encourage further manifestations."

"Just tell me what the small thing is," Martinez said.

"A footprint."

"A footprint?"

"The legends say that he has only one foot. He lost the other when the gods battled for possession of the universe. Four of us will wait at the summit of the pyramid, seated around a bowl filled with flour. And in the darkest hour of the night, Tezcatlipoca will stream down from the stars and leave his footprint there."

"Then he is invisible?"

"On this night he is, unless he honors us with more than he has granted before."

"A footprint," said Martinez. "I know a dozen men in Spain who could do more. I could do it myself, with the right equipment. Have I come across the ocean for a footprint? You should turn yourself into a bat for them, and they would make you king of all their continent."

"I am here to learn, Martinez, not to put on pageants. This is not magic as we know it. The priest will not impose his will upon the world of matter, but wait receptively until the great god comes."

"Then he won't gain much by it," said Martinez.

"He may not, but we might."

Martinez had forgotten Toci, but she stepped from the shadows to offer him a golden cup.

"More bribes?" he asked Sebastian.

"She is not offering you the cup, but its contents."

"What is it?" asked Martinez, trying to ignore the solemn gaze of the priestess, whose face was only inches from his own.

"A sacred potion," said Sebastian. "You should be flattered to receive it."

"Drink," said Toci.

"What is it for?" asked Martinez. He looked at the dark liquid below the golden brim, but turned away from Toci's shining eyes.

"It brings visions. Toci has told me it liberates the spirit, and sets the mind vibrating with the music of the spheres. Most of the ingredients are native plants. The seeds of the flower we call the morning glory, the essences of several mushrooms, and the buds of a plant called peyote."

"Have you tasted it?"

"Experiments years ago convinced me that it is unwise for me to consume anything but human blood. You are more fortunate."

"If you won't take it, then I won't," said Martinez. "I prefer to be sober while I await the coming of a god." He shook his head at Toci, then turned his back.

"You need not hide from it," Sebastian said, and when Martinez looked over his shoulder he saw Toci draining the golden cup. He watched for some spasm to run through her, but he was disappointed. She stood quite still, holding the empty cup between her breasts.

"You have lost an opportunity," said Sebastian.

"How will we reach the top?" asked Martinez. "By the stairs outside?"

"Toci knows the way," Sebastian said. "Follow her."

The path to the top of the pyramid ran through dark passages, lying at crazy angles but leading inexorably upward. Some of the rough-hewn ceilings were so low that Martinez had to stoop to pass beneath them. He sensed rather than saw that Toci walked somewhere ahead of him, but he was all too aware that the cold form of Don Sebastian was at his heels. It was a relief finally to step out into the night.

The blind priest sat alone on the bare summit; before him was a golden bowl. Martinez stopped beside the black trapdoor and watched Sebastian crawl out into the night. The peak of the pyramid was nothing but a bare black platform. Martinez found that no matter where he stood, he felt uncomfortably close to the edge. The city spread out before him; he stood above both pyramids and palaces. Only the great temple of the war god blocked his view. Canals reflected the dull light of the waning moon. Beyond them lay the dark lake, its surface masked by wisps of fog.

Here and there a light shone, but most of Tenochtitlan was dark. A few stars glimmered, but the night was cloudy, and the scene above him was much like the one below. Martinez felt as though he was standing on a mirror—a tiny mirror drifting through a sea of stars. In this setting, even the footprint of a god was not a matter to be taken lightly.

As he looked at his three companions, he was suddenly aware of an isolation he had not known before. Their garments were an outward symbol of some more subtle truth. Martinez alone wore Spanish clothing. The priest and priestess were draped in the black robes of their cult, with white skulls embroidered on the hems, and Sebastian was resplendent in his raiment of red, white, and black.

Sebastian and Toci sank to their knees on either side of the high priest; like him, they faced the golden bowl. It was left for Martinez to complete the square, which put him opposite the blind and clouded eyes of Smoking Mirror's priest.

They sat in silence while the stars moved slowly overhead. Sebastian kneeled, and the priest and priestess sat cross-legged. The others stayed quite still while the night crawled past; each of them seemed lost in a trance. Martinez squirmed with boredom and discomfort. He began to wish that he had taken the drug, and he would have asked for the golden cup if he had not suspected that silence was expected of him.

He tried to watch the bowl, but there was nothing there to interest him. At length, for lack of anything else to hold his attention, he began to stare at Toci. He wondered, not for the first time, how she would look without the grim black robe that covered her from throat to ankle. He guessed that her body would be slim and girlish, with smooth skin like polished gold. He dreamed of slight, exquisite breasts and strong, supple thighs. She seemed completely unaware of his relentless gaze, and her indifference was hardly encouraging, but it gave him a chance to study the woman as he never had before. Her huge brown eyes were radiant, and the high, wide bones of her cheeks looked like the work of a sculptor. Martinez was filled with melancholy, squatting beside a goddess, knowing he would never possess her. Yet somehow he was soothed and almost ennobled by her very presence.

And then he noticed what any sensible man would have noticed hours earlier. If his rapt inventory of her charms did not distract the priestess, it was because she was lost in contemplation of Don Sebastian. The brown woman and the pale man were caught in a communion, an exchange of souls so evident that it almost shamed Martinez. He was embarrassed by his own desire, and embarrassed to be witness to a rapture he had never known. He would not have been surprised to see light streaming between the dead and living eyes.

And what was he to do? Stare deliriously into the clouded cataracts that blocked the vision of the old high priest? Caught for an instant between jealousy and reverence, between lust and distaste, Martinez unexpectedly felt the presence of the god called Smoking Mirror.

There was no change in what he saw, and yet everything had changed. No monster roared down from the skies, but every detail Martinez looked at was thrown into some strange relief, as if the universe had dropped ten feet away. Both light and shadow seemed more vivid, and the faces of his three companions were like flickering hallucinations. Their faces spun around him: the dark forbidding beauty of the priestess, the wrinkled wisdom of the old high priest, the unmoving ivory features of the dead magician. And then the three merged into one, a misty creature with six eyes, part blind, part living, and part dead. The stars were bright as suns.

Martinez felt his scalp crawl. He lowered his gaze to the golden bowl, a solid presence in the midst of so much instability. He glared at the object as if it were all that kept him anchored to the earth. He was so dizzy that he would not dare to shut his eyes. He watched as the grains of flour in the bowl began to move. One by one they dropped away, some pushed toward the sides, some pressed down. A pattern formed in the smooth surface of the flour. It might have been a footprint; perhaps it would have been, if Martinez had waited. But when he realized what was happening, he jumped up.

His legs were stiff and clumsy; his left foot caught the golden bowl and sent it rattling over the peak of the black pyramid. He heard it crashing down the layered sides of stone until it reached the ground.

"It's here!" Martinez screamed. "It's here! I saw the footprint!"

Whatever spell existed had drifted away. The world looked right again, but Martinez was past caring. He stumbled back and forth upon the summit of the pyramid until he felt cold fingers grip him by the throat.

"Fool!" said Don Sebastian.

The strong right hand of the vampire lifted Martinez off his feet. Martinez tried to speak, but found that he could only gasp and choke. Sebastian strode to the edge of the small platform and held the alchemist aloft. Martinez felt himself suspended more than a hundred feet above the ground. He struggled for a second, then realized that breaking free would mean his death. The grasp that strangled him was all that kept him from smashing onto the stones below. He looked down, then wished that he had not. His pleas for mercy were unintelligible, and he was half unconscious.

Dimly he sensed two black-clad figures rushing toward him. He heard the old man speak in the language he had never understood.

"Stop!" said Toci. "Do not kill him. He has seen the god."

"And driven him away," Sebastian said.

"Did you see Smoking Mirror? We saw only one another. The priest saw only darkness. But the little man knows Tezcatlipoca. Do not kill him."

More dead than alive, Martinez loved Toci as he had never loved another woman. He hung in the air for another moment, then felt himself released. He started to scream, then stopped abruptly when he realized that he had fallen only a few feet. He lay crumpled on the summit of the temple of Tezcatlipoca.

"True," Sebastian said. "Too true, and my disgrace. You and I saw only one another. Martinez alone saw the footprint."

Toci hung her head.

"What does the high priest say?" Sebastian asked Toci. There was a brief exchange in the language of Tenochtitlan.

"He says that we are four, and four are needed."

"So," Sebastian said, "you are spared, Martinez. I am not happy with you, but there is much I do not understand. Get below, and sleep while you can. Tomorrow we set out for Texcoco."

"Texcoco?" whined Martinez. "What is that?"

"It is the city sacred to Smoking Mirror. There, the legends say, he first appeared, and there his temple towers above all others. We must reach the city before this festival is done."

"But how will you travel?"

"You have seen my box of earth. The jaguar knights will carry it. Now go below."

"I'll lose my way."

"We shall follow you, and we shall find you."

Martinez crawled to the trapdoor and disappeared into the depths of the pyramid.

Toci looked again at Don Sebastian. "I saw you," she said again. "I did not see Smoking Mirror."

"You have seen him," said Sebastian, his voice not as sure as it had been. "What passed between us made a road for him. Together we are the god. Believe me, Toci."

He reached out his hand, and it was shame rather than reluctance that prevented her from taking it. "Ask the priest," Sebastian said.

A few words passed between the servants of the god, then Toci took a step forward. "You are the god," she said.

She had never touched Sebastian before, but now her hand held his. She peered into his eyes, then twisted her head away, but her body moved toward his. And all at once she held him fast. He felt her soft, strong body pressed against his own. His dead flesh tingled.

"We go to Texcoco," Toci said. "You are Smoking Mirror."

12. City of Ghosts

THE city of Texcoco lay to the east, beyond the borders of the gigantic lake of which Tenochtitlan occupied the southwest corner. As their expedition started out in the bright morning, Martinez learned from Toci that the lake itself was called Texcoco.

He was surprised to hear that this lake and the second city shared the same name, yet there was certainly some logic in it, especially since Texcoco was a community sacred to Smoking Mirror. And Martinez could no longer doubt the importance of the god, not after what he had seen the night before. The footprint in itself was next to nothing, but the atmosphere in which it had appeared was something he could not forget. For an instant he had felt that a hole had been torn in the cosmos so that a solitary footprint could drop through. Martinez had seen the living die, and the dead live again, but neither sight had prepared him for the overpowering otherworldliness of the night atop the temple. Don Sebastian might not be Smoking Mirror, but something was.

The alchemist was subdued enough to keep silent during the preparations for the pilgrimage. He watched a squad of jaguar knights assemble, heavily armed and dressed in spotted skins. There were eighteen of them. Six carried Sebastian's coffin, six marched before it, and six behind. The high priest, blind as he was, seemed to direct their operations. Finally Toci stepped out of the dark doorway that was hidden in the mouth of the black skull at the base of the pyramid. She led Martinez to a position at the rear of the coffin, and waited there beside him until the march began.

The alchemist's pack, heavy with treasure, was strapped to his back. He might have moved more easily without it, but he could not bear to leave his gold behind him.

"Where is Texcoco?" he asked Toci.

"There," said the priestess, extending a brown hand toward the east. The day was clear, and Martinez thought that he could almost see the distant shore.

"But we're going south," protested Martinez. "Must we walk all the way around the lake? Why not take boats and cross the water?"

"Smoking Mirror says no."

"He does, does he?" Martinez lapsed into silence. He shifted his pack and took another step. Already, only a few paces from the temple, he felt that he had been transformed into a foot soldier again. His months in Tenochtitlan had brought him only another forced march, and one that did not promise wealth, just further horrors. He knew who had given the order to take the long route, and was irritated to hear Toci speak of Sebastian as if he were undoubtedly Smoking Mirror. He wondered at Sebastian's decision, then recalled something he had heard about a vampire's fear of running water. A legend said the undead could not bear to cross a stream or river. The lake was not really running water, but apparently Sebastian wished to take no chances, even if his skull had already crossed an all but endless sea. And Martinez understood the dangers. A canoe might well capsize; and if the waters of Lake Texcoco did not destroy Sebastian, they would surely wash away the precious bit of Spanish soil in the box, the dirt that was said to keep the living dead alive during the hours of daylight.

Martinez cursed the ignorance of the Aztecs, whose civilization had no place for either wheels or horses. "How long will this little walk take?" he asked.

"Two days," said Toci.

"Wonderful," said Martinez bitterly. "Just enough time to reach Texcoco before the festival of Smoking Mirror ends. Smoking Mirror!" He spoke the name as if it were an oath. "Tell me, priestess, do you really believe that Don Sebastian is Smoking Mirror?"

Toci smiled. She gave no other answer, but it was enough for Martinez. He had never seen her smile before.

Trudging down the southern causeway beside her, Martinez decided that the priestess had become Sebastian's lover. The vampire might not have lied to him; it could have happened as recently as last night, but Martinez was certain the expression on Toci's face could have only one meaning. Fuming with jealousy, he peered at her throat for telltale signs while she walked placidly along. He could not find the two small wounds he searched for, but their absence did not alter his conviction.

He did not speak to the priestess for the rest of the day. His silence seemed to have no effect on her at all. It bothered Martinez, though, and as the march wore on his thoughts turned inward. The evident understanding between Sebastian and Toci made him feel more isolated than ever before. His stay in Tenochtitlan had been a disappointment; the trembling sense of expectation with which he had greeted the revival of the magus had come to naught. Without Alfonso Martinez, Don Sebastian would still be a silver skull grinning on the shelf of a sorcerer's den somewhere in the back alleys of Madrid. Yet last night the vampire had almost killed him, for nothing more than a small display of nervousness. Toci had saved him, of course, but that was not exactly flattering. The two of them might have been parents bickering over the education of their child, and Martinez was not happy with that role. He was sick of being patronized, especially since he had been the only one to see the footprint.

Sebastian might talk of the search for Smoking Mirror, he might have his coffin hauled around the shores of Lake Texcoco, but it was clear to Martinez that the vampire cared less for the god than for the slim girl whose hair hung to her ankles. It was easy for Martinez to envision the future. There would be more invocations, more failures, more threats. In time Sebastian would tire of his quest, take Toci as his bride, and make himself immortal emperor of all the Aztecs, sustained by freely offered sacrifices. Martinez would become a sullen court jester, denied the doubtful gift of living death, then grow old and die among barbarians.

It would not do.

For some reason Martinez found himself thinking of Luis Garcia. Perhaps it was the long trek through the unremitting sunshine that reminded him of the battered veteran. They had marched together down causeways like this one, and a rough companionship had sprung up between them. Some of this feeling was nostalgia, no doubt; Garcia was a bully and a clown, and frequently Martinez had feared or hated him. Still, Garcia was human. He had joked, bragged, and blustered, but Martinez could deal with that. Garcia had been easier to comprehend than this clandestine couple, this pair of austere and sinister stepparents whose very whims meant life or death. Garcia had almost been a friend, certainly more of one than Martinez had known since that sad night when the rain fell and the bridge failed.

The alchemist, who loved to think of unearned miracles, tried to guess what he would do if an angel or a devil suddenly appeared before him and offered him a choice. The decision was surprisingly easy. He would pick the army of Cortez, with all its risks and hardships, over an exile's life in Mexico. With Cortez, who lurked somewhere in the hinterlands, there might still be a chance to see Spain again.

Martinez thought of Spain. He might return with gold, if not the secret of its origin. And even if he returned empty-handed, he would have tales to tell. He pictured himself, a grizzled adventurer, sitting safely in a tavern among his awestruck colleagues, regaling them with tales of Mexico. He would tell the story of the wizard resurrected from the skull that he himself had carried from the Old World to the New, and of the beautiful native priestess who had loved Martinez with most of her heart and all of her body. He would speak of her streaming eyes when he abandoned her; perhaps he would make her a princess. He would talk about the women he had seen skinned and disemboweled; and the whores would giggle and shiver and draw closer to him. And he would save at least one relic, a bit of stone or jewelry to prove that everything he said was true. It was a brighter picture than the one he had imagined for himself a moment ago: Martinez as the lackey of a monster and his mate.

But it was only a dream. Or was it? Martinez thought again of what Don Sebastian had offered him, and tried to decide what it was worth. If everything the sorcerer said was true, Martinez might be abandoning eternal ecstasy. But what were the odds? It was easy to believe that a man might have a pleasant life, and horribly difficult to think that an omniscient god might sweep out of the skies to gather him up and grant him unhuman bliss.

Martinez cursed himself as a man of little faith. He knew what he wanted—he wanted everything. But what could he expect to get? He felt little prepared for the gifts of Smoking Mirror, however much he might desire them. And he wondered if they were real. Perhaps in a later incarnation, Martinez would know more. There were levels of spirit, and a soul could only go so far in one lifetime. He was out of his depth. Still, he would give the god one more chance. Tomorrow night, in Texcoco, the destiny of Alfonso Martinez, an aging alchemist, would be determined.

The route to Texcoco took the expedition for several miles down the southern causeway, then east until they reached solid ground. There it was necessary to turn south again, following a narrow strip of land that ran between Lake Texcoco and the adjoining Lake Chalco. The jaguar knights kept close to the shore of Texcoco, and gradually they turned northeast. Slowly the cultivated fields and forests gave way to wilderness, confirming the alchemist's guess that sensible travelers approached Texcoco by the shorter route across the salt lake. The path along the water's edge was narrow, sometimes overgrown. The woods, when they appeared, were vaguely menacing, but somehow Martinez liked them more than the long stretches of arid wasteland, the sandy stretches where nothing grew and the trees in the distance looked like hiding places for tribes of savages. It was hellishly hot in these little deserts. Martinez felt the sun searing his armor, and wished he had not worn it, nor the sword that slapped against his leg. The Spanish steel was heavy, but Martinez did not feel safe without it.

He waited for the jaguar knights to stop for rest and food, but waited in vain. A brief pause came about midday, which lasted only long enough for Sebastian's six pallbearers to be replaced by six fresh men. He wondered what the coffin weighed.

His stomach rumbled, and he cursed himself for neglecting to bring food. At least he had a skin of water. He drank from it incessantly and finally, against his better judgment, he offered some to Toci. She accepted it, and Martinez was furious when he realized how touched he was by her generosity in deigning to notice him. Nonetheless he drank after she did, feeling for a moment as if he had stolen a kiss.

At last the sun began to fall. Martinez watched his shadow lengthen, eagerly anticipating the moment when darkness would put an end to his suffering. Weak and weary, he was amazed by the stolidity of the warriors who carried the coffin on their sweating shoulders.

At sunset the expedition stopped abruptly. No one spoke, and yet the knights of Smoking Mirror seemed to know when they reached the place: a clearing by the shore, surrounded by tall trees. Martinez did not question the decision; he dropped to the ground. He tossed his helmet and his sword away, and then eased off his pack, but stayed close beside it. He shut his eyes and tried to forget the trees. All day, even though he had feared a hostile ambush, he had hoped that Spanish soldiers might break through some patch of woods, kill all his companions, and rescue him. Now it was enough to rest. Cortez was evidently elsewhere.

He almost slept. He heard people moving, and smelled a campfire burning, but he ignored it all as best he could. He was lost in a dreamless trance, more free from fear than he had been for a long while. He thought of nothing—until some unidentified disturbance jolted him back into awareness. He sat up all at once, his eyes wide. The night was black, relieved only by the orange flicker of the nearby fire. At his feet stood the figure of Don Sebastian.

"There is food for you," Sebastian said.

Martinez sat where he was. He rubbed his eyes, then looked up thoughtfully at Don Sebastian.

"What will you do if nothing happens in Texcoco?" asked Martinez.

"I shall try again."

"And so on," said Martinez. "Where is the food?"

Toci slipped from the group of men around the fire and silently handed Martinez an earthenware plate.

"You gave her water," said Sebastian.

Martinez grunted. He looked at the steaming stew on the plate, picked out a piece of meat with his fingers, and put it in his mouth. It was probably dog, but he was used to it. Sebastian and Toci watched him eat, but Martinez never raised his eyes.

"What are you staring at?" he finally asked. He set his empty plate aside, and at once the priestess snatched it up and carried it away.

"I have been thinking about you," Sebastian said.

"And I have been thinking about you."

"What have you determined, Martinez?"

The cries of animals drifted out of the distant trees, echoing across the lake. "I don't know," said Martinez. "I wonder if you will ever succeed in your efforts, and I'm not even sure what you're trying to do. That footprint last night is as much as anyone expects to see of Smoking Mirror, and I can't see that it was any use. Yet you noticed that it was enough to frighten me. I don't know if we can ever find this god, and I don't know if I want to."

Sebastian sank down to his knees beside the alchemist and spoke to him earnestly. "Remember what I told you, Martinez, about those who meet Smoking Mirror but are afraid to reach out to him. It may be only a parable, but there is truth in it. My own studies have convinced me that belief in these powers is demanded of those who would receive them. Perhaps they grow from human thoughts, or perhaps such thoughts attract and nourish them. But surely they will never summon one who doubts."

"Even if it's true," protested Martinez, "what can I do about it? How can I make myself believe? How can I concentrate my will on something I cannot imagine and am afraid to see? I'm not like you. I'm just an ordinary man with ordinary dreams. The most I ever hoped for, even with the aid of alchemy, was to have a life of pleasure. I might have thought of death later, but not now. I'm afraid of Smoking Mirror. And I'm afraid of you."

"I know," Sebastian said. "I am a horror. Why do you think I seek to solve these mysteries? Because I must. There is no other hope for me. I can never turn back, and never be human again. I must go forward, wherever it takes me. This god, this force, this power may be the one thing in the universe with strength enough to lift me out of this decaying shell and set me free."

Martinez shifted his position to look into the shadowed face of his companion. Sebastian's dead eyes were as dark as his streaming hair, as dark as the gleaming mirror that hung from the golden chain around his neck.

"Maybe tomorrow," said Martinez.

"Tomorrow," said Sebastian, rising. "You must sleep now, Martinez. Everyone must sleep but me. I stand guard. Good night."

Martinez rolled over on his side and clutched his pack as if it were a pillow. It was hard and heavy, stuffed with gold and the last few vials of the potions he had brought from Spain. He shut his eyes, hoping he would not dream.

On the last evening of the twenty-day feast of Smoking Mirror, nineteen men, a woman, and a corpse reached the outskirts of Texcoco. There they waited for the sun to set. The eighteen jaguar knights sat quietly, their burden on the ground, while a restless Martinez peered anxiously toward the city.

"It's getting dark," he said. "You'd think there would be lights to be seen. What are they up to? Are they keeping the city black to honor the approach of the god?"

"They do not know we come," answered Toci, but she would say no more. She leaned over a small fire. Above it was suspended a small stone bowl filled with salt water from Lake Texcoco. When it began to boil, she dropped things into the water. Martinez watched her carefully, trying to keep track of the ingredients she put into her brew. He noticed flowers and seeds, roots and mushrooms, and small brown buds.

"It's that same stuff again, is it?" he asked, but the priestess did not answer him. Instead, she chanted to herself in an unnerving undertone.

"Maybe I'll try some of it tonight," offered Martinez, but when Toci continued to ignore him he turned away. He walked toward Sebastian's coffin and looked down at it speculatively. "Think you can do it?" he asked the wooden box. He was suddenly surrounded by half a dozen Aztec warriors. Two of them took him gently by the shoulders and pulled him back from the coffin.

"It's all right!" protested Martinez. "Do you think I'm going to kill your god? I was only looking." Despite his explanations he was dragged away, and not released until a contingent of armed guards had stationed themselves around Sebastian.

Spurned by Toci and Sebastian, threatened by the jaguar knights, the alchemist stood alone in the growing darkness and cast resentful eyes on his companions. Steam rose from Toci's potion, drifting on a breeze until it reached Martinez with an odor that was at once sweet and sickening.

And then Martinez saw another sort of smoke. Green and glowing, it poured from Don Sebastian's coffin. The men surrounding it dispersed before they were enveloped in the luminescent mist, and as they stepped into the shadows they bowed before the billowing cloud. Martinez watched as the cloud coalesced into a pillar of pulsating fog. He guessed what was happening, and wondered if the others did. Even Toci was transfixed by the unearthly sight, and Martinez had to remind himself that this was merely a more dignified way for a vampire to leave his coffin than crawling out.

The smoke drew in upon itself until it formed a grotesque parody of the human form. Wisps of haze turned into locks of hair, and gaps in the mist transformed themselves into a pair of dark, hollow eyes. Fog became flesh, and Don Sebastian stood at the edge of Texcoco.

The thing that might be Smoking Mirror looked around. "A dark city," he said. "Let us proceed."

They were more than a mile from the lake by now. The sun was gone, and when the fire had been extinguished Martinez found that he could barely see. The city they approached was a gloomy mass of indistinguishable buildings. One landmark rose above the rest against the purple sky: the pyramid of Smoking Mirror.

The formation of the march was much as before, except that now Sebastian walked with Toci and Martinez behind the empty box which six warriors carried on their shoulders. Six others walked before it, and six more behind. Martinez was more grateful than ever for their presence. "Something's wrong here," he said. "Where are the people?"

"There may be none," Sebastian said.

"What do you mean?"

"There are only rumors. Yet Cortez had the king of this city executed months ago for inciting a rebellion against the Spanish occupation. And when Cortez was driven from Tenochtitlan, the army of Texcoco stood against him in his flight. But Cortez broke through, with horses and guns. Since then, there has been little word from Texcoco. Some say the people fled in fear of Cortez, convinced he was the Feathered Serpent, the ancient enemy of Smoking Mirror. Some say they fled to join him, wherever he may be. But it matters not at all to us, Martinez. We are here not for the city, but for its god."

The humble buildings they were passing were utterly devoid of life. Martinez felt his skin crawl. "There's nobody here," he said. "A whole city, and it's been abandoned. Did you know this?"

"I feared it," said Sebastian. "It matters little for this night's work, but it bodes ill for the future. There was an alliance between Tenochtitlan and Texcoco, and even an apportionment of interests. Tenochtitlan was the military capital and Texcoco the center of culture. The most revered of the poets and priests were here. It was a more civilized city, but also weaker. And now it seems that there is nothing left of it."

"But surely Smoking Mirror is the god of blood, and the Feathered Serpent the god of art and learning . . ."

"Another paradox, Martinez, and one that I cannot explain. Yet what has happened is beyond doubt. This is a city of ghosts, and one haunted by the image of Hernan Cortez."

At Sebastian's words, a dim shape raced across the street in front of them. Toci gave a sharp command that Martinez could not interpret, and three soldiers rushed off in pursuit of the phantom.

A moment later they were back, a prisoner within their grasp. By the faint light of the sliver of moon, Martinez saw that it was an old woman. The shadows made her wrinkles look like black war paint.

"Question her, Toci," said Sebastian.

A terse exchange followed, and if Martinez could not understand the words, he understood something from the tone of the old woman's voice. They were well into the city and she was the only human being they had found.

"She is alone," said Toci finally. "Texcoco is gone. All are gone. She says Texcoco is her home. She stays. Where can she go?"

"She is mad," Sebastian said, and Martinez thought he saw his mouth twist in the moonlight. "Let her go."

The old woman scurried off into the darkness.

"There may be others," said Sebastian, "more dangerous than this one. Watch carefully, Martinez. Watch the shadows."

Martinez looked anxiously around. There was only light

enough to frighten him. "Perhaps we should turn back," he said. "Who knows what powers rule here now? An empty city. There will be scavengers. Perhaps entire tribes of savages, armed with spears and arrows. Weapons made of wood."

"If that wood strikes my heart," Sebastian said, "I will be no worse off than before you brought my skull across the seas. We must press on. This may be our last chance. Cortez is still in Mexico, and stronger than before. His strategy is clear. One by one, he will subvert both tribes and cities, until he has an army even Tenochtitlan cannot withstand. Our time is running short. Tonight we have the opportunity to meet with Smoking Mirror. We may never have another."

13. The Pyramid

THE pyramid of Smoking Mirror blotted out the waning moon, and its gigantic shadow fell upon the twenty-one pilgrims who waited at its base. To Martinez its black bulk seemed much more imposing than the temple of the god back in Tenochtitlan; he would have sworn that it was higher than the great pyramid of the war god. An all but endless row of steps led up one side to the distant peak, bordered by carvings whose details were obscured by darkness. The shrine looked as dead as the empty city that huddled around it.

"We should build a fire," suggested Martinez.

"I think not," Sebastian replied. "As you said, there may be scavengers about. Not beasts—who fear the flames—but hungry men, who might be drawn to them. If our presence here remains a secret, we will be the better for it."

"Then tell me what is to be done. You have said nothing of your plans. Only that you hope to raise the god."

Sebastian stared at him steadily but did not reply.

"I thought I might take some of that brew tonight," continued Martinez uneasily, "the seeds and buds and mushrooms. Perhaps it will show me something I cannot deny."

"No, Martinez."

"No? What would you have of me? Two days ago you all but

ordered me to take it, and now you deny me! Don't you want your apprentice to meet this fabled god? Are you ashamed of me?"

"Too late, Martinez. You are too late."

"Too late for what? I am here and I am ready. I will do what you say."

"Precisely. And I say that you will wait here with these warriors while Toci and I ascend the pyramid."

The alchemist looked wide-eyed at Sebastian, and then at Toci. Neither of them spoke, but Martinez began to sputter incoherently. "You can't mean to leave me behind," he finally blurted out. "Why did you bring me all this way?"

"You would not be safe alone in Tenochtitlan. You know that. And in truth, I did not decide what would be done with you until last night, when we camped by the shores of Lake Texcoco."

"Last night? Why?"

"Remember your own words. You told me once again that you could not believe, and that you were afraid to try. You have no faith, Martinez, and your will is set against the god, when faith and will are all we have to draw him down to us. The presence of an unbeliever is too great a risk. We must succeed tonight, regardless of the cost. I am sorry, Martinez. I did not hope for this."

Martinez shook with indignation. "Was it for this I took your side? Was it for this I carried your accursed skull halfway around the world? I was good enough to be your brother then, but now that you stand on the verge of triumph, you find you have no need of me. Just you and the woman, is it? Up there alone in the dark, with her drugged past caring? I doubt she will come down alive, and I pray your thrice-accursed Smoking Mirror will carry off the pair of you!"

He turned away in fury, but before he had taken a step he felt Sebastian's strong hand fall on his shoulder.

"Take care, Martinez," Sebastian said. "I have no wish to make an enemy of you, and you would be wise to feel the same for me. This decision is your doing as much as mine, and it is only for tonight. If we find Smoking Mirror, you will share his blessings.

And for now, you are spared the dangers of courting him. Do not cross me, Martinez."

The face the alchemist presented to Sebastian was empty of all expression. "So be it," he said.

Sebastian gazed at the blank countenance for a moment, then he stepped back toward Toci. He stood protectively beside her as she raised a small flask to her lips, then put an arm around her shoulders and led her to the first step of the pyramid.

"Just a little fire?" begged Martinez. "Only for a minute. I want to brew some chocolate. It will help to keep these men awake."

The two devotees of Smoking Mirror ignored him and moved slowly up the narrow stairs. Martinez watched them carefully until they reached the summit and, stepping onto it, were lost from sight.

The shadow of the pyramid dropped behind Sebastian when he reached the peak; the square platform that he saw was lit by the weak rays of the low crescent moon. He helped the priestess up the last step, more out of gallantry than any need, then stepped away from her to pace the perimeter of the stone terrace. He surveyed the darkened city on all sides, but the dim and distant buildings were no more to him than the lonely landscape that might surround an isolated mountain. And at its top stood two small figures who were utterly alone. Somehow the dead city pleased Sebastian, yet he was troubled by the feeling that there might be an omen in its desolation. An image of Texcoco's sister city swam before his eyes and disappeared.

"The potion," he said. "Is it working?"

"No," said Toci. "Soon." She walked across the broad platform to stand beside him.

"You know what I must do," Sebastian said. "There is no other way. I can drink nothing but blood."

"I said yes," Toci replied. There was no recrimination in her tone.

"I have seen the priests do as much," Sebastian continued, "bleeding themselves as penance to placate the gods. Smoking

140

Mirror needs blood. And only when his drugs run through your veins may I taste of them."

"Soon," said Toci soothingly. She touched his arm and led him to the center of the terrace. There she sat cross-legged as she had two nights before in Tenochtitlan. Sebastian kneeled before her.

"I shall not kill you," said Sebastian.

"I know."

They waited together while the stars wheeled slowly overhead. Sebastian saw a change come over his companion. Her face turned pale, and a delicate film of perspiration gleamed on her brow. Her eyes grew huge, and they began to shine. Her breathing grew more rapid; Sebastian could see her breasts and shoulders rise and fall beneath the black robe. He found himself thinking too much about the priestess and too little of the god; but then, he had not yet tasted the god's potion.

Toci stretched out her arms behind her and leaned back. Her beautiful small head turned gracefully, and her long bright hair cascaded over the black stones. "I took more," she said, "for you."

Her golden throat throbbed, and Sebastian knew that it was time. He slid toward her, his anticipation tinged with an unexpected melancholy. Something in her willing youth and innocence called out to him for mercy, and he wished for a moment to be an uncorrupted Aztec boy who would offer this lovely woman nothing but affection.

He took her face in his hands and looked into her shining eyes. His fingers stroked her cheeks and slipped through her bright black hair. He kissed her lips gently, and when her mouth opened under his he felt her warm, sweet breath flow into him.

A mixture of regret and gratitude welled up in him when Toci pulled back from his kiss to offer him her throat, but he could not resist the offering. He kissed her there, and put his arms around her. The two of them sank down. Gently, carefully, his teeth slipped into the pulsating vein. Her blood was sweet.

She lay beneath him quietly at first, a sacrificial victim, but when his bite sank deeper, he felt her respond by digging her long, pale fingernails into his shoulders. Rapture overtook Sebastian.

He doubted that the drugs could act so quickly. Rather, it was Toci that intoxicated him—her bright blood, her unquestioning acceptance. Knowing he could never drink enough, he stopped himself and drew away from her.

She lay very still, and for an instant he feared that he had been too greedy. But she was still breathing, though now her gasps were deeper and more regular, as if she were asleep. She stirred, and he gathered her up in his arms. Two dark wounds glistened in her throat. He lapped the trickling blood away, and waited for her eyes to open. "Toci," he whispered.

Slowly she regained possession of herself, until finally she could sit opposite him again, trembling but erect. "The god will come," she said.

Sebastian wondered, but only for a moment. He felt a touch of giddiness, something draughts of blood had never brought to him before. The weight of his dead flesh began to drop away, as if his body were no more than a shell housing his spirit. This was something he had always believed, but he had never experienced it so vividly. He lifted his head toward the heavens. With no fires to obscure the sky, the stars seemed very close. They began to spin before his startled eyes, leaving glittering streaks of multicolored flame against the darkness. He felt as light and insubstantial as a ghost, and yet uncannily aware of every nerve and muscle he possessed.

His gaze dropped down to the small black mirror hanging from his neck. He recollected dimly that a vampire could never hope to see his own reflection, but nonetheless he raised the dark disk to his face. At first he saw nothing in its shining surface. Then, gradually, a glowing mist began to drift up from the black obsidian. He stared at it for centuries, or so it seemed, until the mist parted to reveal a bright unblinking eye.

"The Smoking Mirror," said Don Sebastian, hearing his voice echo from afar.

His very words took shape in gleaming arcs of molten metal;

he was seeing sounds and tasting colors. He closed his eyes in momentary weariness, but the pictures on his eyelids were more than he could bear. He looked into the smoking mirror once again, and there he saw the face of Toci carved in gold. He studied it intently, forgetting the living woman who sat a few feet away, only to see the gold slip down her face in rivulets, exposing the naked skull. He wanted to weep, so great was his sense of love inexorably lost, but then the skull transformed itself into a sad-eyed silver mask alive with fire. It was still her face, yet it was his own as well, and as he stared, it dissolved into a blast of pure white light so blinding that he let go of the illusive disc.

And there before him sat the priestess of his visions, her huge brown eyes absorbing him. A cool breeze slipped across the pyramid; it caught her long black hair and spread it out across the stars.

Almost aghast at her ethereal loveliness, Sebastian attempted to compose himself. "The food of the gods," he said. "And you have tasted it before. But it was never so ennobling, I venture, for it was never filtered through your precious blood." His voice cut glowing swaths across the air that kept Toci's face hidden from him, but when the silence came again she was still there, her lips parted, her face raised expectantly.

She moved her head, and he saw a thousand images of her embossed against the sky, each one a small part of that graceful motion, each one a frozen instant of perfection.

"Toci," he said. "You are more beautiful than the moon." He wanted nothing more than to reach out to her, yet he would not. Some small resolute part of him still held the hope of seeing Smoking Mirror, and he doubted that the god would come to them if they were lost in passion, however exalted it might be.

"I dare not touch you," said Sebastian, "but surely you can speak?"

"You are the god," said Toci. "I see it. Wait. Wait for the light in the sky."

"How long have we been here?"

"I know not. Wait for the god." Her words were low and clear, like distant bells. Each syllable surrounded Sebastian with luminescent rings. He felt an exultation rise within him, streaming up from his heart into a rush of raw energy exploding in his head. He reeled backward, a million galaxies away from Texcoco, and yet still close to Toci. His face fell toward the black stone terrace, and every speck of dust he saw became a universe.

Flat on his back, he watched the moon dance past him. Patterns danced in the streaming stars, cold white pictures of the god Tezcatlipoca. He saw the pale skeleton that rattled in the forest, and the dark idol that squatted in the temple, and the brightly colored image that adorned the walls of Montezuma's palace. He felt the huge bulk of the pyramid straining up beneath him, its massive stones extending upward to the cosmos through the small terrace where he and Toci worshipped. The few square feet of stone became an interface between the tiny earth and the infinities surrounding it.

"Toci," said Sebastian. "The god is here." He sat up suddenly, his head reeling, and as he did so his hand stretched out to take his dark companion's wrist.

The slightest touch of her was overwhelming. Deliriously, he felt her naked flesh and sensed the vibrant flow of rich red blood that coursed through her. His eyes caught hers, and they were locked together in a communion he could not undo. All thoughts of Smoking Mirror were lost in her. A still, small voice chastised him, but he chose to ignore it. If he was a god, then the privileges of a god were his.

He took the priestess by the shoulders and pulled her to her feet. She rose to meet him in a series of fragmented pictures, each more exquisite than any painting he had ever seen. "I have waited for the light," he said, "but you are the light. You are the god, and I am the god. Together we are Smoking Mirror."

"Yes," said Toci, and the word generated silver flames around them.

Tenderly, Sebastian kissed her glistening eyes. He had no thought of blood, no thought of domination. His only wish was to become one with her. He took her black robe in his hands and

144

lifted it. Toci flowed toward him, her head bent low, and suddenly he held her only garment in his quivering hands.

The golden goddess stood before him, naked and unashamed. Her body shone like some forgotten antique statue in the moonlight, except that it was real. She was not marble, but rather an awesome amalgam of black and bronze. Her dark hair streamed behind her like a cloak; her frank and open gaze suspended him somewhere between the earth and sky. Her figure was exquisite. Plump thighs, slim hips, and gently swelling breasts chastened his lust while they inflamed it. For a moment he was afraid to touch her, but then he ran hands along her perfect cheekbones and stroked her full lips. His fingertips were afire. He ran his right hand down her throat, past the cruel wounds he had demanded of her, and traced a path between her small dark nipples. Her belly was firm and flat; as he sank down upon his knees before her, his pale fingers reached up to sink into the softness of her breasts. She was half a dream and half a woman, a vision sent by Smoking Mirror and yet a victim, too. He felt a love for her that he had never known before, as if she were part of himself that he had lost and then miraculously regained. His hand slipped down between her thighs and sought the crevice waiting for him there. He had no wish to hurt her, for she was not another, but himself. He caressed smooth round buttocks, and he kissed her tenderly. A white light roared around him, and he heard her moan.

Toci collapsed upon him in an ecstasy. Then the blinding light was everywhere. The night was gone, and the first rays of the morning sun streamed brilliantly across the surface of the pyramid.

"The light!" Sebastian screamed. The sun!"

He pushed the priestess from him frantically and pulled himself along the terrace toward its edge. The bright rays of the dawn seared his pale skin, and his howls of agony careened through the abandoned city. Toci rose to her feet in drugged bewilderment, watching her lover all but throw himself down the long stairway.

She stood at the brink and stared in horror as he crawled, head first, erratically down the narrow steps like some exotic insect.

His robes of red and white and black were steaming. Toci forgot her stunned surprise and raced naked down the pyramid behind him. Below her, she could see the bodies of the jaguar knights stretched out in sleep. Neither the sun nor Sebastian's anguished cries awakened them.

By the time the vampire had reached the ground, the shadow of the pyramid was long, but his coffin lay beyond it in the sunlight. He leaped out of the shade to grasp the wooden box, and his titanic wails seemed loud enough to shatter the sky. Toci screamed at him to wait, but he was past all reasoning. Limbs flailing, he dragged the coffin toward the shadow of the temple. In her rush to reach him, the priestess tripped over the bottom step and fell flat on her face upon the pavement. Gasping for breath, she raised her eyes and saw Sebastian creep tortuously toward the darkness, pulling the box of Spanish soil along with him.

The wind had been knocked from her, and her body felt like one long bruise, but she staggered to her feet in time to see Sebastian achieve his goal. He gave one final heave and fell into the shadow. And still the men around him did not move.

Toci called on them to wake, then ran to Sebastian's side. He was as immobile as all the others, but she knew that each dawn brought him death. When she reached him, however, she saw that he had not entirely escaped the sun. He lay sprawled on his back, but his sandaled right foot had fallen out of the shade into the blazing beams of dawn. The foot was gray and withered, and as she stared at it the flesh began to boil. Horrified, she grasped the vampire by his hair and heaved him out of the sun entirely. The foot was a blackened, blistered stump, but Sebastian was saved. Calling up all her strength, she dragged the dead weight of her lover to his coffin and rolled him into it.

For a moment she stood panting, a naked woman alone in a city of ghosts. Then she began to walk among the jaguar knights. All of them were dead.

They lay where they had fallen, their eyes staring, their faces white against the spotted skins they wore. The flower of Tezcatlipoca's warriors were here, and each one had been murdered. The lips of some of them were covered with a fine froth; it did not take a physician to see that they had all been poisoned.

"The little man," said Toci. Alfonso Martinez was nowhere to be found.

The naked priestess shivered in the sunlight. She was alone in Texcoco, far from home. Her knees were bleeding from her fall, her chin was bruised, and her head ached. Slowly she ascended the steps of the pyramid, and there retrieved her long black robe. She winced as she put it on, and yet the wearing of it gave her comfort. She was not just a frightened woman, she was the representative of a great god. She thought of the vampire's hideous foot, and felt a thrill run through her body that was something more than terror.

"He is lame," she said. "Smoking Mirror."

The god had come after all. The legends said that the gods had battled in the skies to gain possession of the earth when it was new, and that the struggle for supremacy had cost Smoking Mirror a foot. Now Sebastian bore his mark.

She walked slowly down the steps of Smoking Mirror's temple, her head bowed, her mind obsessed by visions. She dragged the coffin to the base of the pyramid and threw herself full length upon it. There, alone, she waited for the darkness.

14. The Bats

THE god mocks us," Sebastian said. He sat on his own coffin below the pyramid, and Toci sat beside him. The night was only a few minutes old, but he had been awake for long enough to comprehend the plight in which Alfonso Martinez had left them.

"Martinez," said Sebastian bitterly, looking out at the dim, unburied forms of eighteen warriors of Tezcatlipoca. "I shall see Martinez again and I shall relish the encounter. I wish I were as sure of Smoking Mirror."

"But Smoking Mirror came!" protested Toci. "You said it, in the night."

"I thought for a moment that there was something, but what has come of it? Our escort has been destroyed and we are trapped in this abandoned city. The alchemist has turned against us, and the sun has crippled me."

He contemplated his withered right foot. "But I am to blame," he said. "More than the sun, more than Martinez, and more than Smoking Mirror. Perhaps the god might have appeared, had I not been intent on you to the exclusion of all else. I have betrayed myself."

Toci stared at the ground, her eyes averted from Sebastian.

"Smoking Mirror makes men want women," she murmured. "There is magic in it."

Sebastian stood up suddenly. He nearly fell, but slowly regained his balance and began to pace back and forth, at once expressing his frustration and testing his ruined limb. At least he was walking, however much more sinister his limp made him appear. Half sick with sorrow, Toci nonetheless felt a tenderness for Sebastian that she had never known before.

"Look," she said. "Look at you. You must believe the god has come. He left his mark on you."

Sebastian stopped. "The lame foot," he said. "I never thought of that, though you told me the story, and I told it to Martinez. So you think this new monstrosity I bear is a sign from the stars that I am chosen? I would have been content with less than this."

"Who knows the gods?" Toci replied. "I see you, and you are Smoking Mirror."

Sebastian sat down again. "A god of tricks and treachery," he said. "A god who tests his followers, who lures them on with dreams of love and power. It might be true. Perhaps this is his way of greeting me, for all that it is not a welcome one. I suspect that what I feel for Smoking Mirror now is what Martinez felt for us when he poisoned his guards and ran away. I will try to be more of a philosopher than he was, however grim our present plight may be. And it is grim enough."

Toci had nothing to say.

"I might have tried to carry the coffin myself," Sebastian continued, "but now I can hardly walk, and there would have been much risk in it, we two traveling alone through wilderness at night—especially when every man we met might be our enemy. There's no way of telling where Cortez may be, no guarantee that any Mexican is not his ally. Apparently Martinez was certain that the Spaniards are nearby; certainly he did not flee to find a new home in the jungle."

"Then will we go?" asked Toci.

"There must be a way. I thought of flying, by transforming

myself into a bat. It is a long way to Tenochtitlan, even if I fly across the lake, and I must have the coffin to take me every morning; without it I cannot survive. I would have to fly to Tenochtitlan, alert the high priest to our predicament, and then return again by sunrise. It would be unwise to risk it, and I cannot leave you here alone at night."

"You love me?"

"Suppose that I do," Sebastian said. "Or suppose that I care nothing for you. Suppose I want you only for your strength, for that firm purity of purpose that's born of your virginity."

Toci gazed at him earnestly. "What is this 'suppose'?" she asked.

"A word," Sebastian answered. "Only a word. Pretend you never heard it."

"And what is this 'pretend'?"

"Nothing," Sebastian said. "Forget I said it." He took her head in his hands and pulled it down upon his shoulder. "You were right the first time. I love you, and I would not leave you here, even if I could." Toci embraced him eagerly.

Despite himself, Sebastian summoned up the ghost of a smile, a mixture of derision and delight that Toci did not see. "Are you so eager to sacrifice your innocence?" he asked. "Remember, you are sworn to Smoking Mirror."

"I am sworn to you, then."

"There are more ways than one of showing love," Sebastian said. "Nothing would please me more than the chance to take you —to steal away your blood and your purity. And yet I need your life, and your maidenhead, because you are my only link to the god."

"I am here for you," Toci said simply. "Do what is best."

He kissed her fiercely and then drew back.

"You tempt me, Toci, more than I can say. But this is not the time. There may never be a time. You are Smoking Mirror too, a trickster and a tempter. Yet what you and I need now is not each other. We need a band of men, strong and faithful servants like the ones that we have lost. Men to carry my coffin."

A cool wind sighed through the deserted streets of Texcoco. It ruffled Toci's hair, and sent a shiver through her slim brown body. "There is no one here," she said. "We are alone."

"Perhaps. Yet there was something Martinez said that rang true. I have no way of knowing how long this city has been empty, but surely time enough has passed for someone to learn about it. There may be men in this city. Not its citizens, but those who come exploring. It seems most likely they would be enemies. But if we cannot find someone, we are in jeopardy here."

"The high priest," suggested Toci. "He will look for us."

"The blind man," said Sebastian. "I've thought of him. He will send a search party out for us eventually. But when? Until they come for us, there is no food for you, no blood for me."

"My blood is yours."

"Toci," Sebastian said. He touched her face. "You have given me enough. I need you as you are. I have no desire for more, and I will not see you transformed into a monster like myself."

"You are no monster," Toci said. "You are a god."

"A god with no subjects," said Sebastian. "Or only one. Come, Toci. We will be safer on the pyramid tonight: less visible, and more likely to see anyone approaching. My eyes are keen at night, but still it helps to have a vantage point."

He staggered to his feet and leaned heavily upon the priestess as she led him up the narrow steps. More than once he stumbled, but she never let him fall.

"Does it hurt?" she asked.

"No. It is dead."

At the summit, he let go of her and paced the edge of the terrace as he had the night before; but now his steps were slow and tortuous. He did not watch his feet, but kept his gaze on the silent city below him.

Toci stood in the center of the terrace and watched him grow straighter and stronger with each step he took. His eyes were never on her; he was struggling alone, still outwardly intent on his surveillance of the city.

He stopped abruptly, staring into the east. "Someone is coming," he whispered. "Get down, or they will see us against the sky."

Toci sank down on her bruised knees, then flat upon her belly. With her black robe and black hair, she seemed no more than a shadow slithering through the dim moonlight toward Sebastian. He had dropped down too, and lay prone upon the pavement, his face at the eastern edge of Smoking Mirror's pyramid. A night bird screamed somewhere in the distance.

"Do you see them?" asked Sebastian softly, as the priestess crept beside him.

"No. Where are they?"

"You will see them soon enough. They are coming this way. More than a score of men, and I would swear that they are heading directly toward us."

"There," said Toci in a breathless undertone.

The interlopers walked in darkness. They were small, swarthy men, naked but for loincloths, armed with spears and arrows.

"Weapons of wood," Sebastian said. "The only ones I fear."

The men walked single file through the narrow street until they passed into the courtyard at the base of Smoking Mirror's temple. They were almost directly beneath Sebastian and Toci.

"I know them," Toci whispered. "They are animals. A wild tribe with no king. I told you of them once before, and you laughed."

"Tell me again, quickly. They are going around to the other side of the pyramid, and I believe they mean to mount it."

"Animals. They kill for nothing. They have no god, only the bats."

"The bats?"

"I told you. Vampire bats. Animals that live on blood like you. You laughed when I told you."

"I am not laughing now. I hear them coming up the steps. We have only one chance. Can you understand their talk? Is their name for Smoking Mirror the same as yours?"

"Yes."

"Then lie there and wait for me. We shall see what kind of god I am." Sebastian rose slowly to his feet.

"Down!" gasped Toci. "They will kill you!"

"They will try," answered Sebastian, "but I shall change their minds."

Incoherent shouts came from below as Don Sebastian stood up against the waning moon. An arrow flew past him and rattled on the stones beside Toci. Sebastian raised his arms. A short spear seemed to strike one hand, but passed through it without apparent harm.

"Tezcatlipoca!" Sebastian shouted. He threw back his dark head and soared into the air. Two spears sped fruitlessly beneath him. His robe of red and white and black slipped limply to the ground; his pale flesh turned dark. Great webbed wings had sprouted from his shoulder blades. The hail of weapons ceased, and no one ventured to the summit of the pyramid. A vast silence embraced Texcoco. Half man, half bat, Sebastian floated hundreds of feet above the city claimed by Smoking Mirror.

He swept around the pyramid in a huge circle, then darted down, spreading more consternation among the terror-stricken men who sprawled along the steps. None of them screamed; none of them even moved. Sebastian skimmed the surface of the narrow stairway, and when he rose again one member of the tribe was caught in his strong hands.

The man kicked feebly, half dead from fright, and Sebastian climbed with him through the empty air. The huge wings flapped majestically, lifting man and monster until they were no more than specks against the stars. From above, the priestess heard a scream.

The cry was faint at first, like something heard in a forgotten dream, but it grew louder, and then louder still. Toci jumped up when she saw what was coming. The man Sebastian had chosen was plummeting through space, dropping like a stone from heights beyond imagination. His wail of horror rose till it was deafening; his flailing figure seemed to grow against the sky. Toci stepped back.

The man splattered on the stones atop the pyramid; his blood splashed over Toci. Nothing was left of him but split skin, shattered bones, and crimson jelly. Toci wiped his blood from her eyes and strode toward the stairway. Before she reached it, Sebastian swooped down beside her.

He became a man again. She touched his skin eagerly, ran her hands along his naked body, and kissed him fiercely. Willfully, she tore her lower lip against his fangs. She dropped down to her knees and kissed him once again, then rose to face the awestruck tribesmen, her face a mask of blood.

"This is your king!" she shouted. "This is your god! This is Smoking Mirror!"

Dozens of dark eyes looked anxiously up at her, but no one moved. Then, one by one, the men began to creep backward down the stairs.

"They are too much afraid," Sebastian said. "They will be no good to us or to themselves. I should not have killed that man."

"You did well, Tezcatlipoca."

Naked in the night, Sebastian felt his emaciated body stiffen at the sound of the name Toci had never called him before.

"You kept my life," the priestess said. "It is yours forever."

Sebastian wanted nothing more than to dismiss these men and take Toci at her word. But these might be the ones he had hoped for to replace his murdered escort, and he knew that he must win them to his side. "Tell them to stop," he told her, and Toci called out the command. Twenty-seven men froze like statuary.

"Where are these bats you say they worship?" he asked.

"At night, they are everywhere."

"Then I must find them. Keep these fellows here. They will obey you."

He ran his hands through her black hair, and he stared at her while his body changed again. Gray fur sprouted from his dead skin, wings wider than a man was tall sprang from his back. His face turned dark and blunt, and his still-human fingers traced a pattern upon Toci's breast.

"Keep them here," he said. Then he wheeled into the wind.

He was gone for long enough to worry his worshippers. Toci walked among them, up and down the steps, a blood-stained beauty they could scarcely comprehend. To some she spoke soothingly, to others she was sharp and threatening, but somehow she kept them together as the seemingly endless minutes dragged along.

At last Sebastian returned, and with him came a horde of little bats. They fluttered down in multitudes behind him, a swarm of miniature monsters, quick flapping bits of fur and leather. Their bright eyes gleamed where Don Sebastian's were dead, but their sharp teeth were very like his own.

Again Sebastian took human form, but still the black beasts clustered all around him. They covered his pale skin like a cloak of living leather. The men on the stairway looked at him with suddenly illuminated eyes.

"Tell them," said Sebastian, "these are my brothers."

The priestess spoke. Sebastian moved among the men, and Toci walked beside him. He bent to touch the men's heads, and more than one she kissed upon the cheek. And each man that either of the lovers touched rose up. Sebastian was alive with crawling creatures, each one nipping at his naked flesh. The tribesmen clustered round him eagerly, their faces flush with holy ecstasy. Red streams coursed down Sebastian's limbs, and Toci stood at his right hand.

"My brothers," Sebastian said again. Men and bats surrounded him. "These are my brothers."

15. The Feathered Serpent

HERNAN Cortez occupied the city of Texcoco on the last day of December 1520, in command of a great force, augmented by supplies and soldiers from the Spanish colonies of Cuba and Jamaica.

He issued orders that every native town owed him allegiance. All rebels were sold into slavery, except, of course, for those who died in the fight for their freedom; and the Spaniards never lost the allegiance of the Tlascalans, the tribe of Indians whose unswerving support had been theirs from the beginning. Perhaps they still adhered to the belief that Cortez was the Feathered Serpent, but as his power grew there was less and less need to bolster Spanish strength with claims upon the supernatural.

And yet the gods seemed to be with him. The hitherto unknown disease of smallpox had spread among the Mexicans, striking even the new emperor of Tenochtitlan, who was replaced by Cuauhtemoc, husband of one of Montezuma's daughters.

Cortez began to treat his men with some indifference. The gold that he had granted them on the night when they fled Tenochtitlan was gathered up, and most of it found its way into the coffers of the Spanish king and his commander. All Indian women captured were called in for branding, and none were returned to the common soldiers who had made wives or mistresses of them. His last order, before setting out for Texcoco on Christmas Day, was that his shipbuilder should begin construction of thirteen sloops that could patrol the waters of Lake Texcoco.

The Feathered Serpent from Spain appointed a puppet king, then set up his own headquarters in the palace. On the first day of 1521, he summoned Alfonso Martinez.

"The man is mad," the Spanish priest said. "He has been so for more than two months, since we first found him wandering around the lake. The tales he tells are past belief."

"No doubt," Cortez replied. "I have not seen him since he rejoined us. Yet I can hardly doubt his story that he saw Texcoco long before today; it is certain, just because he is alive, that he is the last man of our race to have set foot in Tenochtitlan. The interview should prove interesting, at least. Perhaps it will be of some use as well. I mean to glean the truth from his strange dreams. However weak his mind, he is our best informant."

Hernan Cortez sat upon the throne of Texcoco. The royal room was nearly empty, stripped of almost every trace of Aztec embellishment, though there were plans afoot to refurbish it. Six tried and trusted men stood beside the throne, their armor dulled, their sharp swords battered but still intact.

"Bring in Alfonso Martinez," Cortez commanded. Two men stepped forth to do his bidding.

The figure they escorted back into the king's chamber was grotesque. He had been fed, of course, yet his face had the sunken, bony look of a man near starvation. His eyes darted nervously from side to side, his hands shook from the aftereffects of a fever that not even native medicine could cool. His shoulders were stooped; his beard was sparse and sickly. His skin was an unpleasant shade of yellow. He wore some mismatched bits of scavenged armor, and each piece seemed too big for his small frame. Yet the priest had said that he refused to take them off, even when he slept.

Martinez was unaware of his commander's scrutiny. He was too busy looking at the man who was apparently on the brink of toppling an empire.

Cortez was suited to the part. Even though he was sitting, he was a man of considerable height, with broad shoulders and a thick chest. His hair and beard were dark, his face surprisingly pale. At his ease, in a sober black suit with white ruffles at the neck and wrists, Cortez looked more of a grandee than his birth would indicate; but this was the New World, where a man was judged more by his deeds than by his antecedents. And at thirty-five, Hernan Cortez was fortune's favorite. Yet there was something about him that disappointed Martinez. The conqueror's eyes were narrow and close-set; his mouth was small. His face suggested careful calculation more than bold heroics, however much his history might argue against it. Behind him stood one of the banners he had ordered years ago in Cuba. Embroidered in gold on the black field were a cross and the royal arms of Spain; beneath them was this legend: "Comrades, follow the sign of the Holy Cross with true faith, and through it we shall conquer."

The soldier and the alchemist examined each other, one completely relaxed, the other teetering on the brink of hysteria.

"I understand that you have been in Texcoco before," began Cortez.

"I have," croaked Martinez. "On the last night of the feast of Smoking Mirror. It was then that I killed eighteen of his jaguar knights."

Cortez decided there and then that the priest was right about this fellow's state of mind. He hardly seemed capable of killing a mosquito, much less of defeating a band of such intrepid warriors.

"I had to do it," Martinez continued. "I had to get away from Don Sebastian."

"Stop for a moment, please. Identify this Don Sebastian."

"Don Sebastian de Villanueva. He is Smoking Mirror, or so he claims."

"Stop again, please. Who or what is Smoking Mirror?"

"One of their gods, or one of their devils. Some of the Aztecs think that Don Sebastian is the incarnation of this fiend, much as Montezuma thought you were the one called Feathered Serpent."

"Parts of your tale have reached my ears before, physician, but only from the lips of other men. Yet one thing is sure. We checked the rolls, for all that it was hardly necessary, and found no man in all our company who bears the name you mention."

"Of course not!" answered Martinez. "He has been dead for more than thirty years."

"Ah," replied Cortez, suddenly grateful for the presence of half a dozen men-at-arms. This Martinez was clearly a lunatic, and very likely dangerous. Still, his wild stories might provide an evening's entertainment. Cortez stood up, and made an unobtrusive signal to his guards to keep close watch. Martinez noticed nothing but the conqueror's bowleggedness.

"Tell me more about this dead man," said Cortez.

"The Aztecs brought him to life again. This time, at least. The last time he did it himself."

"Then is he not one of our men who died in battle? A friend of yours, perhaps?"

"Oh, no," said Martinez. "He never fought for you. I brought him here, from Spain. I brought him in my pack."

Cortez exchanged a flickering smile with his guards. "It hardly seems big enough to hold a man," he said.

Martinez touched his pack, which he was said to keep beside him always. "It was only his head," he explained.

"And you carried the head of a corpse from Spain? It must have smelled pretty bad, after a time." One of the soldiers snorted, but Cortez silenced him with a swift glance.

"It was only his skull," explained Martinez. "I kept it with me for . . . for my medical studies. Besides, it was made of silver!"

"Then it was well worth having," Cortez said thoughtfully. "What other treasures have you in your pack?"

"Me?" gasped Martinez, as if he hoped the question might be meant for someone else. His eyes moved rapidly; his hand reached back to clutch all he possessed.

"Show us," Cortez commanded.

"There is nothing, really. Only a change of clothing and a bit of medicine. Nothing more." Martinez took only two steps toward the door, then the soldiers were upon him. He felt them pull the pack away from him, and remembered a similar event when the jaguar knights had robbed him of Sebastian's skull beneath the temple of Tezcatlipoca.

"Not again!" Martinez wailed.

He watched in horror as a burly guard emptied the pack upon the floor. Myriad golden rings and bracelets spilled out, together with a few small figurines. A gold bar clattered down behind them, followed by a jewel-encrusted human skull.

"I guessed as much," Cortez declared. "From the condition of the clothes you wear, it was evident you have no others. My nose told me as much." He pushed a path through the precious trinkets with his boot. "And no drugs, either. Reports have told me that you have not been much use as a physician since you rejoined us. I can see why."

"I have been ill myself," said Martinez.

"This is bad, physician. The order went out weeks ago that every man was to turn in his gold, so that the royal share could be collected. And the penalty for failure to comply was clearly stated: that each one who held back would lose everything. You have not paid your taxes, Martinez."

"You would not take it all!"

"You have disobeyed me. I have an obligation to the other men, the ones who did their duty." Cortez pushed at the jeweled skull with his toe. "And what is this? Your comrade Don Sebastian?"

"No, no! I told you. Don Sebastian is alive again in Tenochtitlan. Unless I killed him too. I meant to. This skull is an image of Smoking Mirror."

"But you said that this Sebastian was Smoking Mirror. What is the difference?"

"Listen to me!" screamed Martinez. "I know what you think of me. I know what everybody thinks. But I am telling you the truth! I have important information. This is not the skull I spoke about. The skull of Don Sebastian was brought back to life by that damned woman!" He reached out to touch Cortez, but six strong men kept him away.

"It will be more pleasant to converse from a reasonable distance," said Cortez. "I am sure you understand."

Martinez nodded.

"Very well. Release him. Tell me about this woman."

"She is his mistress, though she claims to be a maiden. A highborn Indian girl, who speaks for him to the Aztec chiefs. She has learned Spanish. She worships him."

"Send for the Lady Marina," Cortez told one of his guards in an undertone. "This fellow's fantasies must spring from something, and I begin to see the pattern."

This time Martinez was listening intently. Like every man in the army he had heard of Marina, the woman who claimed to be an Indian princess, who had been rescued from slavery by Cortez long before he reached Tenochtitlan, and who served now as his interpreter and his mistress. He had never thought before how similar her station was to that of Toci, but the realization only served to show him how important his own knowledge was. Quite clearly, the struggle for Mexico was a duel between Hernan Cortez and Don Sebastian de Villanueva, between the Feathered Serpent and Smoking Mirror. That each man had a native lover was only one more proof. But Martinez still had sense enough to suspect that Cortez would not be easy to convince.

"Believe me," pleaded Martinez, "for what I say is true. Smoking Mirror has a lady much like yours. I have not dreamed her. He is set against you, and he is the greatest threat to your success. I would not be surprised to learn that he has rallied all of Tenochtitlan against you after so much time. The gods fight in the skies, Feathered Serpent against Smoking Mirror, as you and Don Sebastian fight in Mexico."

"Tenochtitlan will fall," announced Cortez.

"There are at least a hundred thousand there to be subdued," protested Martinez.

"No doubt," Cortez agreed. "But we will take them. You have been with us since we moved against the province of Tepeaca.

The reports say that we killed at least fifty thousand there. Of course, they were not all banded together in the same city. But they fell. Tenochtitlan will do the same, I promise you."

"But you must beware of Don Sebastian!"

"Let him do his worst," Cortez said tolerantly. "God is with us, and His favor is worth more than any number of demonic serpents or bedeviled mirrors. All the news we hear tells us that the Aztecs have fallen victim to the pox. It is a new ailment to them, and it kills them faster than we could hope to do. I think I could sit here for a year, and then walk into Tenochtitlan unopposed."

"The pox will not kill Smoking Mirror."

"I suppose not, since you say he is already dead. And yet it does its work. The Indians have an ugly sort of vengeance, though, in this new lover's ailment, syphilis. It is a curse. No wonder that the Aztecs are so chaste."

"There is a cure for that," Martinez ventured. "The Aztecs know it. Let me help you."

"I was speaking in theory," Cortez announced, but he was blushing furiously. The five remaining men-at-arms did all they could to keep their faces grim.

"The Lady Marina," announced the sixth man as he came in through the door. Cortez attempted to compose himself by sinking down upon the throne of Texcoco.

The woman who came into the room was beautiful, garbed in the beaded gown of a Spanish noblewoman. But Martinez did his best to look past that, and past the elaborate high dressing of her thick, black hair. Attempting to keep his mind free from prejudice, he did his best to imagine her naked, the way that he had always tried to think of Toci.

They might have been sisters. Both had the same full lips, bright eyes, and golden skin. Yet Martinez decided, with mingled regret and pleasure, that Toci was far lovelier. In every feature the mistress of Cortez was just a trifle coarser, so that, finally, she seemed a caricature of the exquisite virgin Martinez had known. Perhaps it was no more than the incongruity of her European dress, but Martinez sensed subtler discrepancies. The Lady Ma-

162

rina looked to him like an opportunist, and for some reason he still hoped Toci was something more.

"Is this the woman you spoke of?" Cortez inquired.

"Of course not!" snapped Martinez. "If you think I'm a lunatic, why do you question me at all?"

"You have paid well for whatever time you take. Would you like to speak to her?"

"I have nothing to say to her," Martinez said boorishly.

Marina laughed, and Martinez saw at once that she had adopted the airs as well as the garments of a Spanish lady. He suspected that Cortez had spent much time instructing her.

"They are not the same," said Martinez. "The woman that I meant is much more beautiful."

The laughter stopped, and the Lady Marina looked at Martinez with a savage anger. She swept out of the room.

"I am not pleased with you, physician," said Cortez. His voice was quiet, but a vein in his forehead was throbbing.

"I am a simple man," said Martinez, "and not much good at giving compliments. Perhaps I am the idiot you take me for. But I swear to you that every word I say is true. My only wish is to prove myself to you. Why else would I run away from Don Sebastian? I was an honored man among the Aztecs, because I had brought back their god, and yet I gave it all away to seek you out. That much, at least, you must believe. How do you think that I survived for so long in Tenochtitlan?"

"If you were ever there. Much simpler to believe that you were lost in the retreat, and foraged for yourself until you rejoined us. Yet I do remember that we lost you once before, and you were returned alive in exchange for one of their heathen priests."

"Of course!" said Martinez. "I had almost forgotten. That was the night Toci brought Don Sebastian back to life! You should have seen it. I am the only white man to have witnessed it, and I know many such strange secrets. Just listen to me."

"All right, physician, I have a mystery for you. You know the tallest pyramid in Texcoco?"

"Indeed I do. That is Smoking Mirror's temple."

163

"Is it?" asked Cortez, genuinely surprised. "I scaled it yesterday, with some of my men, and we found something puzzling there. It was the body of a man. He had been dead for months."

"Was there a woman, too?"

"No. Now listen, Martinez, for this is very strange. There was almost nothing left of this man, yet there was more at work than mere decay. It looked as if he had been smashed to pulp against the summit of the pyramid, as if he had fallen from some tremendous height. Yet there is no higher spot in Texcoco. You say you know dark secrets. How do you explain it?"

The face of the alchemist was crumpled and shaking. "Sebastian!"

"What do you mean, physician?"

Martinez put a hand to his face as if to keep his quivering features still. "Don Sebastian dropped him," he said tonelessly.

"Dropped him?"

"From the sky. Didn't I tell you that Don Sebastian can fly?"

Cortez turned from him in disgust. "I see. We thought the man might have been crushed with rocks in some sort of sacrifice. None of us knew your friend Sebastian could fly."

"Of course he can fly! He is a vampire."

Cortez froze for a heartbeat, and cast a glance at the gold cross embroidered on his banner. His nurse had told him of such creatures when he was a mere child, and something of his boyhood fear came back to him, but he shook off the chill. "We will watch out for him," he said.

"Be warned," said Martinez. "He means to summon Smoking Mirror from the stars, and with the monster's power to destroy you."

"I shall be careful, Martinez. You saw one of their sacrifices, did you?"

"I witnessed dozens."

"That might be enough to turn the head of any man."

"Indeed," said Martinez. "Sometimes I wonder that I am not mad."

"All right, physician. You may go."

Martinez looked longingly at the floor. "Must I abandon all my treasure? Isn't my information worth something?"

"I suppose so," Cortez said sympathetically, and his guards looked at him in surprise. "Take the skull of your friend Sebastian."

"I told you that this isn't Don Sebastian," said Martinez, stooping to retrieve his prize and return it to his pack. "But you have listened to me with more courtesy than any man in all your army, and I thank you for that, at least. There is more honor for you in it, since I know you think me mad. God bless you for a gentleman!"

The alchemist had touched the right note; Cortez looked on him with new favor. Martinez backed toward the door, a soldier at each hand.

"There is one thing more," said Martinez.

"Come on," said one of the men-at-arms. "You've taken enough time."

"Wait," said Cortez from his throne. "I will hear him out."

"There is another threat to you," said Martinez. "I almost forgot, since it seems so trivial compared to Smoking Mirror."

"Go on."

"There is a conspiracy against you."

"Wait there," Cortez commanded. He beckoned the captain of his guards and whispered in the man's ear. "This Martinez is evidently off his head, yet I cannot ignore this sort of accusation. I would not worry your men unnecessarily. Take them out with you and leave us here alone. I shall be safe with him. I have my sword."

The captain of the guards reluctantly complied, and Cortez was left with no one but the little man in his ill-fitting armor.

"You fascinate me, Martinez. Tell me more. But keep your distance."

"I don't know all that I should. I think their plans are not yet laid. But they consider me an idiot, and they are not as careful with their speech as clever plotters should be. I believe they mean to assassinate you."

165

"So." Cortez shifted uneasily in the king's seat. "This tale is less fantastic than the others you have told me, but it is equally disturbing. It could not be my veterans. It must be some of the new men. I don't know why I listen to you, Martinez; but give me a name."

"It is too early to say. Nothing may come of it. You would not have me condemn a man for a bit of idle talk?"

"Take back your gold bar. But don't come any nearer than you must."

Martinez scuttled across the floor to snatch up his reward. "There is a man here," he whispered from halfway across the room, "who is the protégé of Cuba's governor. He does not speak well of you."

"I think I know the man you mean. How sure are you of this?"

"I need more time."

"So, Martinez, keep yours ears open, and act as crazy as you can. If you learn anything, report to me at once. The order will be given to admit you to my presence at any time of day or night. We shall give out the story that you are my court fool."

"Very clever," said Martinez, as he retreated.

"Physician!" barked Hernan Cortez. "Come back here! You have forgotten half your gold!"

It was not until several weeks later, when the chief of the conspirators was hanging from a palace window, that Cortez was sure he had made the correct decision in the matter of Alfonso Martinez. Yet one thing troubled him. The physician's story of a plot among the officers had proven all too accurate. Could it be, then, that there really was a walking corpse in Tenochtitlan, one whose sole ambition was to summon up the hordes of Hell to snatch away the Crown of Mexico?

16. The Plague

THE smallpox epidemic raged through Tenochtitlan like an army on horseback. No one knew the number of the dead. A king had died of the disease already, and thousands upon thousands of his subjects followed him. The city was filled with corpses, many of which remained unburied and unburned. Whole families fell and went unnoticed until the stench from their houses reached the street. Even then they were frequently ignored out of superstitious fear or sheer despair. The dead lay rotting where they dropped.

Sebastian sat brooding beneath the pyramid of Smoking Mirror. The tribesmen who worshipped the vampire bats had brought his coffin back from Texcoco, and now they formed his personal escort. A band of naked savages, they were as awed by Tenochtitlan as the city was by them, but they were unswerving in their loyalty to Don Sebastian. Toci informed him that their name for him was "He Who Flies." The god had found his followers at last.

But the god had not found his own god, and time was running short. Each messenger from the surrounding cities brought news that promised imminent disaster. Cortez triumphed everywhere; the best guess was that his army of subjugated Indians was almost equal to the population of this final Aztec stronghold, or more than a hundred thousand strong. Soon he would begin his siege upon the city in the lake. Until he did so, the plague did his work for him.

Sebastian kept Toci by his side as much as possible. His greatest fear was that she would fall victim to the disease, and he hoped she might be safer in the temple, isolated from contagion. He warned her against the cold baths with which the Aztecs suicidally tried to counteract the pox, and racked his brain in search of Spanish remedies. He even found himself wishing for Martinez, although he knew the man was no physician. Yet he might have helped somehow, and Sebastian's hatred of the little man grew deeper as he imagined Toci pockmarked and blistering with fever.

Yet life in the city went on. In May, while Cortez supervised completion of the mile-long canal that would put his thirteen sloops into the waters of Lake Texcoco, the spring feast of Smoking Mirror came due.

"It might be better if you did not attend," Sebastian said. "I am the only one in Tenochtitlan who can be certain he will not fall sick."

"No," said Toci. "I must go."

"I suppose you must, even as you must remain a virgin. Yet neither decision delights me. Of course you are a priestess, but sometimes I think you care more for the Smoking Mirror in the skies than you do for me."

"What do you want?" asked Toci earnestly. "I am for you. You want to see Tezcatlipoca, and you fear the sun. I go to see the sacrifice and you sleep. I go to tell you. What else? I love you."

Sebastian stood in the distorted room with its dull black walls and looked tenderly into her shining eyes. "I would not worry if I did not care for you," he said.

"Why do you speak backwards?"

Sebastian smiled. "Stand beside me, Toci, and I shall be more direct."

She stepped forward with no hesitation, and laughed to feel Sebastian's teeth nipping harmlessly at her throat. And yet there was no malice in her laughter, only a childlike pleasure. She knew no blood would flow, but she also knew that her complaisance satisfied her lord. The wounds that he had left upon her throat in Texcoco had long since healed.

"Be careful, Toci. But how can you beware of a disease?"

"It will not take me. I wait for something else."

"And what is that?"

"I wait for you. I will not die till you are ready."

"Then you will live forever."

"Maybe. It will be what Smoking Mirror wants."

He stroked her face in a familiar gesture. By now she was accustomed to his cold fingers, and thought that she would find the hot flesh of an ordinary man repugnant. She stroked his hands as they ran along her throat and brought his fingers to her lips.

"You are a fatalist," Sebastian said. "Where did you get such thoughts?"

"I have faith," Toci replied. She pulled his hands down until they rested on her heart and stared into his dead eyes. "I do not think. I know."

"I wish I were as sure," Sebastian said, "at least about the pox. I would keep you from the ceremony if I could. I shall be asleep in my coffin, and you will do as you choose. I hope there is some profit in the risk. This is Smoking Mirror's festival, and we certainly have need of him now. If we cannot evoke his power soon, Cortez will overrun us. We can hardly sit with folded hands, waiting until next autumn when the god returns; but I wonder what killing this boy will mean to us. This is the public ceremony, the Feast of Dry Things—no more, really, than a plea for rain to grow the corn. Tell me, Toci. Do you think Tezcatlipoca will sweep down from the sunny sky at the first sight of blood in his temple, destroy the Spanish forces, and set Tenochtitlan free?"

"Tomorrow will tell."

"How is the boy?"

"They say he is afraid."

Toci herself had no role in the sacrifice, but she stood at the foot of the black pyramid among the celebrants and watched. The crowd was hardly a crowd at all. Thousands of the Aztecs were dead of smallpox, and thousands more were ailing. Even among those who were well enough to attend, there was such a fear of plague that many had chosen to hide themselves at home on this great day of the great feast. And most of those who did attend stood well apart from one another, as if they sensed that no more than a touch might end their lives.

The day before, the idol of Tezcatlipoca had been brought forth from the vault and paraded through the streets, the blind high priest following behind it. The black statue was dressed in robes and jewels as if it were a man, and all who saw it wept for their sins. The weeping was more than ceremonial, especially this year, when the streets were lined with corpses, their faces covered with scabs that would never heal.

The Spaniards had built up an immunity to the disease, yet even among them it was a horror, for the epidemics that swept through Europe had killed many of them. Yet they had a good chance of surviving it with nothing more to show for the experience than pockmarks. Among the unexposed Aztecs, smallpox was almost always fatal. Each citizen of Tenochtitlan waited for the signs. At first there was no more than fever, a weak and giddy feeling that might be a dozen other illnesses, but then the marks would come just a few days later. Initially they were tiny lumps, like insect bites; sometimes they bled. Eventually the eruptions turned to blisters, and then to running sores. They covered the face, the arms, the back, and the chest; and they meant death.

The Aztecs feared the smallpox more than they feared Cortez. It was small wonder that so few of them turned out even to honor Smoking Mirror.

A second procession preceded the sacrifice. The idol was brought out again, carried by the priests of Tezcatlipoca, who had abandoned their black robes for this one day to don brilliant red and green and gold. Their faces were darkened with soot, and blood streamed over them from self-inflicted wounds. They had been fasting for five days.

Young men and women who were the acolytes of the temple came forth next, their faces brightly painted, their arms and legs adorned with scarlet plumes. Around their necks they wore many necklaces of toasted corn, and they passed among the noblemen to offer them the necklaces. Toci sighed to see so many courageous warriors shrink even slightly back from contact with another human being, but at length this ceremony was performed.

The citizens of Tenochtitlan moved reluctantly forward to reach the lower steps of the pyramid. While the statue of the god sat silently between braziers of burning incense, they made their offerings. Jewels and gold and cloth and featherwork were laid upon the stairs; the poor brought merely food, but it was welcome, for only this charity could end the fast of Smoking Mirror's priests.

The gifts were gathered up and carried into the temple, where a band of maidens, each with a black circle painted around her mouth, walked among the dignitaries of the cult, serving the sacred meal. Toci ate with all the others whose lives were dedicated to Tezcatlipoca, sitting cross-legged in the crooked chamber in the depths of the black pyramid. Sebastian slept among them as they feasted.

The afternoon was well along before the food was gone, and the time for the sacrifice was near. When Toci stepped again into the day, she was surprised to see how little light there was. The sun would not set for some time, but it was now overcast with clouds. Anxiously, she scanned the ominous sky, remembering Sebastian's question, and half expecting some uncanny being to drop down on Tenochtitlan.

The high priest and five of his underlings waited at the summit of the temple while the crowd made way for the young man who was to die. Unlike other sacrificial victims, he had been chosen an entire year before, the handsomest of all the prisoners of war on hand. Toci studied his appearance, not for the first time, and decided that he was a most suitable offering for what she knew to be the greatest of the gods.

His headdress was made of gold, covered with white plumes

that hung over his face; his bracelets, rings, and earrings were of gold as well, as were the small bells on his ankles that jingled when he walked. Garlands of flowers covered him; jewels flashed on his throat and wrists. A disk of white stone hung at his chest, reversing the image of the smoking mirror that Sebastian wore. The boy had a fringed white loincloth, and a richly woven blanket of black and red.

Toci had concluded that Tezcatlipoca would be pleased with such a splendid sacrifice, but when the young prisoner moved past her, she saw that he was trembling. This was unthinkable. It would never do to send a coward to meet Smoking Mirror. If this youth could not contain himself, he should have been drugged; but now it was too late for that.

No doubt it was hard for him to bid Tenochtitlan farewell, since for a year he had been granted all the honors of a king. His four brides walked behind him weeping, and at the foot of the temple they abandoned him. In his right hand he held a small bundle of flutes, the very ones that he had played throughout the city, symbols of his leisure. And now, as he mounted the black stairway alone, he cast the flutes down one by one and broke them on the steps beneath his feet. He faltered only when he reached the top; teetering dizzily at the edge of the platform as if his body had rebelled against his forward progress. Toci held her breath for an instant, then watched him right himself and step forward to meet the priests.

Drums played, and music sounded from around the pyramid. This was the greatest of the Aztec sacrifices, its victim the most honored. His body would not be cast coldly down the steps like all the others, but carried in reverence back to the ground by solemn priests. There would be no feasting on fragments of his flesh; only his heart would be removed, and after it had been held aloft by the high priest, it would be burned.

The old blind priest, still dressed in black, stood at a distance while his five aides surrounded the young man bedecked with gold. They led him toward the sacrificial stone, while Toci prayed that this offering might win Smoking Mirror's favor. Yet the gift to the god was shaking once again when he kneeled before the high priest, and when the others lifted off the brightly colored blanket that covered his back and chest. They stretched him out upon the stone, and then they stopped.

One of them shouted; another pointed. Then, one by one, they moved away from the young man. Toci peered up at them in bewilderment. The crowd stirred anxiously. The priests were staring at their hands in horror.

The young man was no coward. His trembling had not been caused by fear, but by a fever, for he was a victim of the plague. His feathered headdress and his robe of black and red had hidden the telltale spots on his face and shoulders. A priest ran screaming down the pyramid; another followed him. The people rushed back from them as they would from wild beasts. Panic filled the public square.

Smallpox put an end to the ceremony honoring Smoking Mirror. With cries and wails the worshippers departed, some of them fleeing headlong through the streets. They mourned not only the presence of the plague, but also the fact that they had offered up a tainted sacrifice. The city had offended Smoking Mirror. The nobles left more slowly, with flourishes of feathered cloaks, but most of them had cast aside their necklaces of corn as if they were contaminated.

Toci stood alone in the great plaza while the world grew dark. Tezcatlipoca's victim sat up on the great stone slab, demanding to be killed. He could hardly be blamed for preferring the black knife to the pox, yet his behavior had disgraced Tenochtitlan and he had frightened off the very men who might have stopped his suffering. He got up, looked around the terrace atop the temple, and saw no one there but the old high priest, huddled in upon himself like an ancient embryo.

The young man picked up the blanket that had covered him and then cast it aside. He stumbled down the steps and walked away to die alone.

Toci shivered in the dim shadow of the pyramid. The city seemed so deserted that it reminded her of Texcoco. Her thoughts were black, and nothing drew her from them until she heard the shouts that echoed through the empty plaza. They came from the peak of the temple. Toci turned her head to look, and saw the blind high priest crawling across the high terrace. Without hesitation she hurried up to him, and saw his old hands grope along the black stones in search of something he had lost. He screamed out his frustration, but ceased abruptly when his fingers touched the sacrificial dagger. Then he stood, a black figure against gray clouds, tears streaming down his wrinkled face. He held out his left hand and slashed the palm.

Toci stared as the black blade flashed again, this time hacking at the priest's forearm. She gasped to see how deep the wounds were; this was no ordinary penance. When he began to slice open his face, Toci could stand no more. She threw herself at the priest, grasping his right arm. The stones were slippery with his blood.

He fought frantically against her, even when she screamed her name. His bleeding hand clawed at her face and he kicked at her shins, but she was stronger. She pulled the knife out of his hand and pushed him away. He crumpled on the flagstones as Toci turned desperately to the sky. The sun was sinking and the clouds were darker than before. She panted heavily, her neck craning upward.

A raindrop struck her on the cheek.

Toci reached up to touch it, her eyes wide. The god had not forgotten them. The rain had come. She looked toward the old man at her feet, and what she saw showed her why he was the high priest. Gritting her teeth, she dug the black stone blade into her right arm. She could do no less than he had done. The rain was falling faster now, washing away the blood that ran from the gash in her arm, rattling on the pavement as she cut into the back of her left hand. Thunder boomed like Spanish cannons, and the storm broke with a vengeance. The priestess was drenched; the force of the downpour was so intense that it seemed to press her toward the earth, as if a giant's hand had stretched out from the sky to push against her.

"Smoking Mirror," she said.

The blind high priest was laughing. She could not hear him over the fury of the cloudburst, but she could see his mouth spread open in a toothless grin of triumph. His long gray hair was plastered over his eyes, his fingers stretched out to catch the raindrops.

Toci kneeled across from him, and she too reached out her hands to gather up Tezcatlipoca's storm. The old man and the young woman prayed together at the summit of the black pyramid while night fell imperceptibly on Tenochtitlan, hidden by the darkness of the clouds. They might have been the last remaining devotees of Smoking Mirror, except for one other buried hundreds of feet below. Wind whipped at them, and rain lashed at their faces.

They remained until a third figure appeared suddenly at the peak of the pyramid. Toci glanced up, and a flash of lightning showed her the face of Don Sebastian. He glared down at them for a moment, then reached out to grab the priestess by her shoulder, catching the high priest in his other hand.

"Get below!" he roared, his angry voice much louder than the driving rain. "Would you kill yourselves?"

He hurried them down the narrow steps and through the yawning skull that was the entrance to the pyramid. "To think I should be saddled with such a pair of allies!" Sebastian bellowed. "To sit out in the rain and court the pox! And this one an old man, already weak enough. Are you mad?"

"It rained," Toci protested, as he rushed her through claustrophobic corridors. "It rained!"

"That much is evident," Sebastian snapped. "Did it take you so long to notice it?"

"Listen to me," said Toci, her voice so full of feeling that it gave Sebastian pause.

"I will listen," he said more softly, "but only after you have dried yourself and changed your clothing. You will also see to the high priest. Then come to my chamber. I have news of my own, which also concerns the rain."

175

Toci did as she was told, leading the blind priest away. At each juncture of the twisted hallways she met anxious men who rushed by her without a word: priests, acolytes, jaguar knights, and even Sebastian's savage tribesmen. Oddly enough, each one of them carried a vessel: a jug, a bowl, or a vase.

Toci did her best to ignore this puzzling behavior until she had left the old man in the care of some temple maidens, and changed her dripping black robe. That done, she ran to meet Sebastian.

"Stand by that brazier," he told her, "and warm yourself."

Flattered by his concern, Toci moved closer to the flame. She pulled her long, damp hair over her shoulders and dried it by the fire. "The boy was sick," she said. "He had the marks. There was no sacrifice. The people ran away. The high priest gave his blood, and then the rain came."

"He was not the only one to give his blood," Sebastian said, reaching out to examine her hands and arms, "and I suspect that what you offered Smoking Mirror was most precious of all. No god could be indifferent to such a gift." He kissed her wounds, his tongue catching the last drops that lingered there.

Toci arched her back ecstatically, feeling again the now familiar mixture of pleasure and pain. "Smoking Mirror came," she said. "There was no sacrifice, but still he gave us rain."

Sebastian raised his head and spoke. "The god has an undoubted gift for irony. This is almost as amusing as the morning he announced his presence by leaving me a cripple. Damn Smoking Mirror, if he exists, and damn Hernan Cortez!"

"If he exists!" repeated Toci. "What else brought this rain?"

"Whatever always brings the rain," Sebastian said.

"What is wrong? We failed the god, but he gave us his blessing."

"He gave us no more than an ugly joke. This may be the last water Tenochtitlan will ever see."

"What is wrong?" Toci asked again.

"The water is stopped," Sebastian said. "You saw the men go out with jugs not long ago? I have given orders that every man and woman in the city should do the same. What we collect from

Smoking Mirror's rain may be the only water we shall have, unless the people try to drink the salty sludge of Lake Texcoco."

"But the aqueduct—"

"Exactly. The aqueduct—the city's only source of fresh, clean water. For weeks I had a tribesman stationed there, with no other order than to report to me. I had no doubt of what Cortez would do. Any general would do the same. I warned King Cuauhtemoc to guard it, but his army has been decimated by the plague. It would not have mattered much in any case, for the men who attacked the aqueduct today were insurmountable. Tens of thousands of them, mostly rebellious vassals of Tenochtitlan. They think the Spanish Crown will treat them better, fools that they are! While Smoking Mirror smiled and gave us rain, Cortez cut off the aqueduct."

Toci put her arms around Sebastian. "It begins," she said.

"It does indeed. While you and that blind fool sat up there bleeding into the rain, they took the western causeway and cut off the city's sole supply of water. And they did more. Another force has cut off the causeway to the south. Only the northern route out of the city is still open, and I can promise you that it will be shut soon. We are besieged, Toci. We are surrounded. And you tell me that Smoking Mirror came!"

The priestess raised her head, her eyes awash with tears.

"Forgive me, Toci. You did all you could do, and what you bought with your sweet blood may save the city yet. But what kind of god is this, to grant us little favors while he lets our enemies run wild? I'd like to meet him face to face, the way the legends say one can. If all it takes is bravery and will, he'd see his dripping heart in my cold hands and feel his bones disintegrate beneath my rotten foot. Where is this Smoking Mirror?"

"He is here," said Toci as she wept.

Sebastian tried to smile, then turned away toward the black stone wall.

17. City of Blood

ON June 1, 1521, thirteen newly constructed Spanish brigantines slid down the waters of the canal Cortez had built and floated off across the waters of Lake Texcoco. A roar of triumph went up from the assembled army, and on a nearby island the Aztec outpost set off a signal fire. The battle for Tenochtitlan had begun in earnest.

The ships swept toward the city in the lake, their long oars flashing, their white sails billowing. And from the city, close to a thousand Aztec war canoes set out to meet them, the warriors gazing in awe at the line of vessels which, however small by European standards, loomed over them like eagles over hummingbirds.

The canvases swelled, and the monstrous ships built by the Feathered Serpent bore down upon the Aztecs. There was no battle; there was only slaughter. The huge bows of the brigantines plowed through the light canoes, leaving little but splinters in their wake. Hundreds of men were thrown screaming into the salty water, crushed and drowning. Muskets and artillery sent smoky explosions from both sides of each ship, sinking more of the small boats and killing more of their crews. The surviving Aztecs turned tail at once, not even taking time to shoot a single arrow. Most of them ignored the cries of their sinking comrades, and those who did stop to take drowning men on board were sitting targets for the Spanish guns. Yet even flight did not bring safety. The big sailing ships were faster than canoes, and they cut continuous swaths through the ranks of their beleaguered enemies, while ceaseless volleys sank the stragglers. Under a sunny sky, the Spaniards took complete command of Lake Texcoco. Only a handful of canoes crept back to Tenochtitlan and slipped into the narrow canals where brigantines could not pursue them.

Sebastian took the news with little grace, but less fury than Toci had anticipated. "I warned them," he said bitterly, "but they would not listen. I suppose it was impossible for them to imagine just how badly things were bound to go, and I suspect they would have tried it anyway. Your people have courage, Toci, if nothing else, and they could not sit idly by and grant Cortez their lake. Their courage cost them much. Perhaps now King Cuauhtemoc will be ready to take my advice."

"What will you tell him?"

"About the ships, nothing. Even if we could get the timber, the skill to build our own fleet does not exist here, nor would there be trained men to sail. I am no sailor myself, nor am I a shipbuilder. I wish at least I were human again, so that I could go out by day and lead troops into battle. This Hernan Cortez would learn a few things about fighting then, I promise you."

"You will fight in the dark, as Smoking Mirror does."

"And as the Aztecs never do, unless I change their minds. At least I have my own platoon, a band of savages who love the night. We will give the Spaniards something to remember before the city falls."

"Then must it fall?"

"It appears inevitable. They have as many men as we do, and also ships, guns, food, and water. The only thing we have that they do not is plague."

"We have the gods," said Toci firmly.

"We shall need them. What maddens me is that each night I spend in warfare will mean another night lost to the search for Smoking Mirror. And yet we may at least gain time by fighting. I hope it will be time enough."

"Smoking Mirror is with us. It rains again tonight."

"Thanks for that. The rainy season will hamper Cortez, I think, and for a while the city may not die of thirst. Yet we must have food as well, and I see only one way to get it. The causeways are cut off, and apparently the lake is lost to us as well. But thirteen ships cannot guard so large a lake, especially at night. Canoes could slip through and reach the shore. There must be towns there where Tenochtitlan has friends. Surely the king will see the logic in at least that sort of night maneuver, and from it others may spring."

Toci nodded, then walked across the subterranean chamber to stand before the idol. "He will help us," she said.

"He seems to favor you as much as I do. We have that much in common. It was your blood that brought the rains, and I like it myself. But if we were really brothers, Smoking Mirror would send me some guns, or some ships. I am not fond of either, really. A cannon first took my life, and left this pretty scar across my eye. Yet they are useful things. And those damned ships! I would as soon fight soldiers armed with wooden stakes."

Toci reached out to stroke his arm, but Sebastian did not notice. He was lost in thought. "Stakes . . ." he said, and then fell silent for a moment. "It might work. Send for my men, Toci, and send for carpenters. There will not be time enough tonight, but we can be ready by tomorrow. It cannot solve all our problems, but if the first attempt succeeds, it will help a bit."

"What is it? Tell me."

"You will see soon enough."

On the next night she did see something, but still could not understand it. Sebastian set out for the lake, accompanied by his personal guard and a number of jaguar knights, all of them struggling under the weight of numerous gigantic wooden stakes, as thick as tree trunks and almost as long, one end of each cut to a sharp point. And still Sebastian would not explain their use.

"If the plan succeeds, you will hear of it," he said. "If not, I shall gain nothing by boasting of my ingenuity. Wait for us. There is no way for you to help, and there may be some danger. Look for us by dawn."

Cortez sailed around Tenochtitlan and made his camp near the southern causeway, the one that offered the shortest route into the city. Two of his most trusted lieutenants were stationed with thousands of men at the northern and the western causeways. Tenochtitlan was bottled up, and for the moment Cortez was content to wait, planning his strategy and watching the effect of his blockade.

The first attempt to break through it came almost at once, and close to Cortez. The southern waters of Lake Texcoco were thick with tall reeds, numerous enough to provide cover for canoes. Early one afternoon, a handful of the Aztec boats slipped from the reeds and headed for the distant shore. At once a trumpet signaled from the camp, where a lookout had been stationed in a captured Aztec tower near the foot of the causeway. Cortez himself climbed up to watch, accompanied by Alfonso Martinez.

"Good," said the commander as he peered across the lake. "Our two brigantines are coming already. We are too fast for them. These savages should have learned something from our last battle."

"They seem to have learned a little," said Martinez; "at least enough to cut and run. They're turning their canoes and heading back for the reeds."

"Much good may it do them. The reeds are no protection, and our ships will surely overtake them before they can reach real safety in the canals."

The brigantines tore through the stand of reeds in hot pursuit of the hidden enemy, then suddenly stopped dead, faster than any ship should, as if they had run into an invisible barrier. A tremendous noise of tearing wood echoed across the lake, joined with the bewildered shouts of Spanish sailors.

"Witchcraft!" said Martinez.

Cortez stared silently at the stranded brigantines. The shrill cacophony of the horns and whistles of Aztec warriors rose from the reeds, and hundreds of Indian arrows were launched into the air. Within moments, the decks of the stricken vessels were covered with fallen men.

"A trap," Cortez shouted. "Those ships are caught in something, and there's no way we can help. I can't see what's going on, but there must be a whole fleet of canoes hidden there. The ones that came out were only decoys. This is intolerable!"

He watched ashen-faced, while half-naked warriors swarmed over the sides of the ships. They did their work with astonishing speed; the long row of war canoes sped away for Tenochtitlan before there was any chance to summon other brigantines. The two ships trapped in the reeds were well aflame, certain to be destroyed before anything could be done. The two captains and most of their crews were dead, and Hernan Cortez was seething with frustration.

Hours passed before he determined the cause of the disaster. Some time ago, probably before his men had first approached the southern causeway, the Aztecs had floated a collection of huge logs out to the reeds and driven them down into the bed of Lake Texcoco, so that their tops were a foot or two below the surface. They provided no impediment to small canoes, but when the low-riding brigantines ran onto the stakes, they were as helpless as if they had run aground.

"Ingenious," said Cortez. "Who would have thought these savages could be so clever?"

"It was not the savages," said Martinez darkly.

"What? No matter, they will pay for their audacity. Tomorrow we march on Tenochtitlan."

"March carefully, then, and march by day. I see the hand of Don Sebastian in this."

The hand of Don Sebastian was clenched in triumph when he heard the news. Toci had assembled all the tribesmen to awaken him at sunset, and he rose to walk among them, embracing each one in turn as if he were a happy soldier and not an animated corpse.

"It means next to nothing, of course," he said at length, "yet it delights me nonetheless. A few Spaniards will have cause to remember us, and now perhaps the Aztecs will see the virtues of fighting at night. We should prepare tonight, and make a raid after the sun falls tomorrow."

Sebastian's plan did not come to fruition, however, for Cortez struck shortly after dawn, and his attack left the city reeling. The assault on Tenochtitlan came from all three causeways at once. The troops in the north and west had longer distances to go, and succeeded in no more than distracting large numbers of the defenders. Cortez, however, penetrated into the heart of the city.

The emperor Cuauhtemoc had ordered his men to break down each of the many bridges that interrupted the causeways, so that the Spaniards and their thousands of Indian allies marched only a short distance before they reached a gap. Across the water from the gap Cortez saw a strong stone barricade. Hundreds of Aztec warriors stood behind it, loosing clouds of arrows against their enemies. The fire of the besiegers could not destroy the rampart, but Cortez did not despair. He called up two of his brigantines, which sailed unimpeded around the wall of stone to use their guns on the defenders. The Aztecs retreated with great losses, and the attackers made their way across the gap. Cortez left orders that the breach should be filled with the stones that had defended it, then led his men toward the next broken bridge. Cavalry and cannon followed him over the rough reconstruction.

Each of the defense posts fell in the same manner until the Spaniards stood at the outskirts of Tenochtitlan. The people of the city were appalled to see how quickly all their barricades were broken; the besiegers seemed unstoppable. Yet within the city itself the Spaniards had no chance to use the ships. Now the fighting would be man to man, or so it seemed. But supplies from Spain had left Cortez well armed, and withering gunfire drove the Mexicans steadily backward while hundreds fell before the onslaught of the small harquebus and the huge cannon.

In their enthusiasm, the Spaniards overlooked the danger in their new position. Inside the city, they were surrounded. The Aztecs were not only in front of them, but on every side. The Spanish ranks were broken as hordes of screaming soldiers rushed down on them, and Cortez was forced to retreat. But that night, as the rain began to fall, he had cause for satisfaction. In one day he had destroyed the most important Aztec defenses, and proved that he could enter Tenochtitlan when he pleased.

The next morning, he set out again. Alfonso Martinez marched close beside him, encouraged by the stories of the preceding day's success and determined to take his share of loot. He expected to walk straight to Montezuma's treasure house, but he was disappointed. As in a dream, Cortez discovered that he must relieve the deeds of yesterday.

"The bridges are down again," he muttered to himself. "Don't these people sleep?"

"Sebastian," whispered Martinez, only to be rewarded with a glance so withering that he sought refuge in the rear.

Methodically, Cortez proceeded as he had before, and by noon he reached the public square, in the heart of the city. There he sent his men to the sprawling palace where they had been housed by Montezuma almost a year before. The building was made of stone, but its beams and roofs and towers were made of wood. The Spanish torches caught.

Flames streamed through the interior and the fire burst into view, a blinding sheet of red and gold, so hot that men retreated from it smelling their singed beards. The long beams turned to cinders, and the home of Montezuma's father collapsed upon itself with a roar like thunder.

Torches blazing, the Spaniards rushed on to the menagerie. Here, where Montezuma had collected all the creatures of his world, the buildings were unfortified. The house of birds, an airy structure delicately fashioned from thin shafts of wood, went up like kindling. The uncanny screams of the trapped creatures rose like voices from the pit of Hell. Birds struggled toward the sky, half-burned and trailing smoke. A few flapped weakly on wings that were afire, then plummeted to earth. Only a handful escaped, among them a pair of eagles that soared through the flames, exchanged harsh cries, and glided toward the distant mountains.

Sebastian crawled from his coffin with the smell of smoke in his nostrils, and listened grimly to Toci's report. Cortez had dropped back again at nightfall, so there was no one to challenge the dead wizard and the young priestess as they mounted Smoking Mirror's pyramid. They stood under the cloudy sky and watched the smoldering wreckage of Tenochtitlan's treasures. Embers glowed crimson in the shadows, while groups of men and women ran back and forth between the ruins and the canals, shouting to each other as they carried water to put out the flames.

"Too late for that," Sebastian said. "Will it be this easy for Cortez?"

"No," said Toci. "We build again."

"Of course, Toci. And really he has damaged nothing of significance. No doubt he thinks the loss will bring despair to the city, but from what you tell me, he has done nothing but steel the resolve of his enemies. Yet I don't like those fires. It is not pleasant to imagine that this pyramid might be consumed while I lie beneath it."

"Stone," said Toci, stamping her foot on the terrace. "No wood. Nothing that will burn."

"It is well. Then I have nothing to fear except cannon balls bringing the pile of black stone down upon me. Better not to think of it; better still to prevent it if I can. We must begin the counterattacks tonight."

Sebastian's first assault caught the Spaniards entirely off guard. He chose the southern causeway, more out of hatred for Cortez than from any strategic reason. Down it crept a small army of archers, led by the phantom many of them called Smoking Mirror. In support came dozens of canoes, sliding silently through the waters until they were within shooting distance of the Spanish camp.

Alfonso Martinez, never a good sleeper, was one of the few awake when the feathered shafts began to fall. He jumped up screaming from the muddy ground, thanking every power in Heaven and Hell that he was never without his armor. For more than a minute the effect of the attack was devastating. The arrows came so thickly that they might have been hail, and countless men were killed before they could awaken. Martinez, after his first shout, put both hands over his head and rolled himself into a ball, never looking up until he sensed that the attack was over. Sebastian's warriors had come and gone as quickly as a summer shower, but what they left behind was death.

Martinez ran to the tent where Cortez slept, and found the commander outside, buckling on his sword. "You see?" said Martinez. "I warned you they would fight at night. You cannot expect them to be like other Indians, not when Don Sebastian leads them. And now you see why I wear my armor all the time. You never can tell, can you?"

Cortez rubbed the sleep from his eyes and squinted at the corpses all around him. "You weary me, Martinez," he said. "You seem to be an idiot, yet time and again you turn out to be right. I will give orders for the men to sleep in their armor. Our native allies will have to do the best they can; sometimes I think we've too many of them anyway. Now, get away from me. Go ply your trade among the wounded!"

For days the war continued as before, with maneuvers by the Spaniards in the sunlight, and sorties from the defenders, inflicting vengeance when the sun was gone. For all his assaults, Cortez felt himself stalemated. He gave orders that his native troops should construct rude buildings to house his men, and for a time he ceased to make attacks. Each night, the Aztecs broke down the bridges once again. He thought of posting guards, but gave his reasons against it in a dispatch to the Spanish emperor. His Indian allies would not do battle after dark, and his few hundred Spaniards were too valuable to be deprived of sleep. He decided on a war of attrition, waiting to see what smallpox and starvation might do to the spirit of Tenochtitlan.

He stood by his decision until the last night of June, when the enemy launched a devastating attack on all three causeways. Many were slain; this was the anniversary of the *"noche triste,"* that sad night a year before, when the Spaniards had been driven from the city in disgrace.

Cortez saw the little physician the next morning. "Mention that name," he growled, "and I shall have you thrown into the lake. We have enough to worry about, without you trying to frighten the men with your old wives' tales."

Finally, Cortez decided to move. His goal was the marketplace in the northwestern corner of the city. Once established there, the Spanish forces at the northern and the western causeways could combine, forming an impregnable outpost within the city itself. The last orders Cortez gave before the march concerned the necessity for filling in the gaps where the bridges had been, which he said was much more crucial than a quick advance. With luck, all would go well, but it was always vital to leave a path in the event of a retreat.

Martinez wisely decided that he would keep well to the rear and supervise the work of filling the canals. Dead men have no use for gold, and he suspected that the day might be a hard one, especially because he sensed that the commander had made a decision against his own better judgment.

The advance went well at first—so well that it worried Cortez, who watched the Aztecs fall back with such alacrity that he began to fear a trap. The commander took a small group of men and abandoned his own post to reconnoiter. As he rushed to meet the rest of his scattered forces, he heard the blast of a horn from atop the great pyramid, the horn that could only be blown by the emperor of Mexico.

When he reached the path that most of his men had taken, Cortez found his worst fears confirmed. Before him stretched a broken bridge, the surface of the water interrupted by only a few boulders, not even enough to serve as a footpath. As he stood cursing, he heard the sound of running feet, followed by the distant sound of Aztec war cries. Before he had a chance to move, Cortez was overwhelmed.

His own forces rushed wildly down upon him. It was not a retreat, but a rout. Hundreds of men threw themselves into the canal, only to be trampled and drowned by comrades running frantically for safety. In a moment the Spanish forces were mixed with those of the Aztecs, and suddenly a dozen brown-skinned men had Cortez in their hands. A black stone sword chopped into his leg, and he fell writhing into the mud.

Two of his aides rushed to his defense, and paid for his life with their own. Someone's arm flopped down on the half-conscious Cortez, the blood from its stump spattering his face. The roar of battle made him dizzy, and the air was thick with spears and arrows.

More dead than alive, Cortez was escorted back to camp, surviving only because he had been on the right side of the gap his men had neglected to fill. He slipped into the ranks of his Indian troops and disappeared from the scene of battle.

The forces of Cortez had fled in disarray, and it was only the gunboats that prevented their foes from overtaking them. The expedition was a calamity. There was no record of the Indian allies slain, but the number must have been in the thousands. Seven precious horses and two of the cannon had been captured, and the Spanish soldiers had been decimated. The deaths would have been bad enough, but subsequent events showed that more than sixty had been taken alive.

Beyond the lake, Cortez sprawled on a blanket while Martinez cleaned his wound. "Sebastian," muttered the commander. "Don't say it! He had nothing to do with it. The sun was shining, physician. It was nothing more than savage strength, and our own incompetence. There is no Sebastian."

"You could see him now, if you could stand," replied Martinez, as he wrapped a bandage around the commander's wounded leg. An Aztec drum throbbed in the distance, and Cortez felt his leg respond in kind.

"What? Show him to me, physician. I challenge you!"

"You won't like what you see, no more than your soldiers do."

"Stand me up, Martinez! Call for men! Where is he?"

"Far off, but not far enough," said Martinez, offering Cortez his arm. Two pages joined him, and together they dragged Hernan Cortez into the night.

Cortez had insisted that he be carried to the camp on the western causeway; he was less than a mile from the great plaza. The night was clear, and torches illuminated the distant pyramid of the war god. With all the clarity of fever, Cortez saw black-robed priests dragging naked white men up the steps.

"See that one?" said Martinez. "The one at the top there, whose robes are red and white and black. The one with the knife. The one who's cutting out their hearts. That is Don Sebastian."

Cortez was almost convinced that he could hear the screams of his slaughtered comrades, and he knew without a doubt that some of those dying men had been his attendants.

"That little man?" he sneered. "I can hardly make him out. That doll? That puppet? He is some priest, and not a ghost."

"Whatever you say," replied Martinez. "But that is Don Sebastian."

The drumbeat rolled across the lake as Cortez sank down upon his blanket. That night he had a dream.

A glowing green mist filled his tent, and then a man stepped out from it. His face was dead white, his eyes sunken and dull. His black hair hung to his shoulders; his black mustache drooped below his chin. A hideous pale scar ran down the left side of his grim countenance. His robes were as Martinez had described them.

Cortez attempted to cry out. He heard a feeble croak, and knew it for his own voice. His skin crawled as if a family of snakes were creeping over it. He tried to raise a hand, and found that he could not.

"I could kill you now," Sebastian said, "but gentlemen do not fight wars that way. I need not explain, I trust. I shall pretend that you are a man of honor, whatever I hear to the contrary. I long to meet you in single combat, Hernan Cortez, but it will never be. We are both cripples, I fear. You may recover, but I shall not. Look."

The ghost raised up its robes and lifted up one leg. Cortez turned sick at the sight of it. The foot was gray and withered, as if it had been dead for a lifetime. Bones gleamed faintly through the rotten flesh.

"We share the same wound," Sebastian said, "but mine is permanent. It came not from a man, but from the sun. From a god, perhaps. From Smoking Mirror. I am your opposite, you know—I might almost say your mirror image, except that I cast no reflection. But the Aztecs take us both for gods, and the two they name us for are ones that struggle in the sky. Tell me, Hernan Cortez, do you feel like a god?"

Cortez managed to shake his head.

"Nor do I. But we do not choose the roles we play. And yet I think you crave divinity, or at least the power you think it brings. In that, at least, we are much alike. But you are too much of this world; your ambitions do not extend beyond this life. I have been a soldier, like you, and I learned that conquest comes to nothing. What matters is what the mind conceives for the future. Not the next battle, but the next life. And so I cling to belief in Smoking Mirror, however alien it may be, in the hope that I may achieve his incarnation and be free at last of this accursed planet."

Cortez could only stare in disbelief.

"I have known men like you before," Sebastian said. "My brother was one. He believed too much of what he was told, and death caught him unprepared. He was burning in the hell that he devised while you were still a boy. Wordly power is all vanity, you know. Of course you do. Even your priests say as much, but few men believe them until it is too late. Consider this, Hernan Cortez. I came here as a naked skull. I have been dead for decades, and still my trials are not done. I promise you this much, that you will return to this city as I first approached it. A man will bring your fleshless head to Tenochtitlan, and you will know it. I imagine you will win this war, but it will bring you nothing. You will never know peace, unless the gods are kinder than I think."

Cortez plucked weakly at his blanket, wondering when the dream would end, or whether it was a dream at all.

"I would not weary you," Sebastian said, his pale features dissolving into fog. "Sleep, conquistador. Tell Martinez that I was here, and that I shall see him again."

The green mist slipped away and Cortez collapsed. When the physician called the next day, his commander thought it wiser to say nothing. And after a while he forgot the dream.

18. A Wheel of Gold

THE Spanish troops were virtually idle while Cortez recovered from his wound. After their disastrous defeat, no one dared suggest that it was wrong to sit and wait, or even that it was wrong to endure the Aztec night attacks without reprisals. It was time for retrenchment, and a stricken commander was not the only problem. The supplies of powder and shot were running dangerously low, and the Indian allies were discouraged. Many of them had slipped away, their hatred for the Aztec overlords insufficient for the prospect of a long and fruitless siege. They began to believe the priests who shouted from the temples telling them that Tenochtitlan would never fall.

The expedition might have failed, if not for Spain. A ship arrived at Veracruz, and from that distant port came the ammunition that would turn the tide. Cortez was up to greet the first arrivals of these invaluable supplies, limping a bit, but clearly in command. He ordered a council of war.

"There is only one way to take the city," declared Cortez, "and that is to destroy it. We have been in and out of it more times than I can count, but nothing we can do has much effect. The causeways and canals impede us at every turn, and must be eliminated. The water must be converted into dry land."

His lieutenants stirred nervously and looked at him in some bewilderment.

"Some of you think, perhaps, that I am just as mad as my friend Martinez here. You wonder why I keep him by my side. It happens that his thoughts on this subject are much like my own."

Martinez smiled shyly and lowered his eyes.

"Our failures and successes in this campaign have depended almost entirely upon our use of the canals. When we have taken time to fill them, we have won. Surely none of you will dispute that." Here Cortez glanced pleasantly at several of his more careless officers. "So. We shall fill in everything, and then we shall have room to move. Work slowly; take one building at a time. And when you have it, tear it down! Cast the rubble into the water, and soon there will be land for the swift progress of the cannon and the cavalry. It seems a shame to lose this royal prize, but only when we level Tenochtitlan will it be ours."

"It won't be easy," someone said.

"But not as hard as you think," countered Cortez. "I have already spoken to our native allies, and the scheme delights their savage souls. They showed me a tool they have, something like a hoe, well suited to the work. They will be glad to pull apart the city that has ruled over them for centuries. Our guns will protect them, and there will be no stopping us. I only hope the Aztec king, Cuauhtemoc, will be humbled enough to surrender while there is still something left standing."

"Is this the festival of Xilonen?" Sebastian asked.

"Yes," Toci replied. "The goddess of the young corn."

"And a virgin is sacrificed?"

Toci nodded.

"I remember that Martinez did not enjoy it. It hardly seems possible that a year has passed since then. Will the sacrifice be made?"

Toci looked doubtful, but could not bring herself to answer.

"Cortez is near her temple, is he? Well, perhaps there will be time enough. It hardly matters. The way the war is going, there will be no one left to gather the harvest. And no one left to celebrate the gathering by greeting the return of Smoking Mirror in the fall. We cannot wait for that, or we shall certainly fail. Who follows the corn goddess?"

"The god of war," said Toci.

"The chief god of Tenochtitlan, the one whose pyramid rises above all the rest. No doubt the city needs his help, but it is slow in coming. What concerns me is that he is only another manifestation of Smoking Mirror."

"There is the red Tezcatlipoca, and the black. Huitzilopochtli, the war god, is their little brother. His name is Hummingbird Wizard."

"A wizard like his brother. And his holiday falls so as to coincide with Leo, perhaps the strongest sign in the Zodiac. And Smoking Mirror is the Great Bear."

"I do not understand."

"I am looking for the night, Toci, the best night when we may hope to conjure up your god to set us free. I doubt that even Smoking Mirror's magic can save the entire city now, but surely his power represents a chance for us to escape Cortez and the disaster he will bring, even if it means trading this world for the stars. So I study the stars, by the systems of your people and my own, searching for the most propitious time to summon Smoking Mirror. Consider it, and consult with your high priest. There must be another chance for us."

Toci nodded again, and Sebastian was so intent upon his own concerns that he failed to notice the expression on her face.

"Enough of this," he said, casting his charts upon the mica floor of the subterranean chamber. "I must look at the city."

"Again?" asked the priestess. "Cortez is there."

"The Spaniards sleep at night, Toci, and there is not much danger. I need to know how well the siege progresses. No, do not follow me. You see enough of this by day, and there is always the possibility that someone will be about. I will not have you raped and murdered by my countrymen."

Sebastian limped through the twisted corridors beneath the

temple, by now as familiar to him as the passages of his ancestral castle in the north of Spain. At length he reached the street. Nothing in his unnaturally prolonged life could compare with what he saw there.

The beautiful city of Tenochtitlan was in ruins. The outskirts had been razed, and from those ruins Cortez had proceeded inward, his troops attacking from the south, the north, and the west. Day by day the monuments had fallen, the buildings destroyed one at a time, and slowly the Aztecs were driven toward the marketplace in the center of the city. The great plaza where kings and gods dwelled together had been almost entirely destroyed; the palaces were gone, and only the gigantic pyramids of Huitzilopochtli and Tezcatlipoca still remained. Cortez had decided that they were too strong to be knocked down with ease, and almost impossible to burn. The two temples stood alone, huge piles of stone in a wasteland of devastation. The war had passed them by, if only for the moment.

Just a few priests remained with Sebastian and Toci in the black pyramid, together with what remained of the tribe they had found in Texcoco and a handful of the once-proud jaguar knights. Toci had pleaded with them, and the blind high priest had threatened, but only Sebastian's displays of wizardry had kept them out of the fray. They were the last defenders of a forgotten outpost.

More than once Cortez had offered terms, but the emperor Cuauhtemoc steadfastly refused them. He had learned too well the lesson of Montezuma, and his stubbornness was encouraged by the priests of every cult in Mexico. Better to die, said these seers, than to be slaves of the treacherous Spanish.

Almost two weeks ago, the plan to bring food into the city by canoe had failed. At first the men had come back empty-handed; then they had not come back. No friends of Tenochtitlan remained along the shores of Lake Texcoco, and now that the besiegers had moved in, there was no chance to use the lake in any case. There was now no food. The Aztecs fed on the roots and grass that grew within the city. The people captured vermin when they could, and sucked juice from the hard bodies of the insects that they caught. Women ate their babies. Yet still there was no thought of surrender.

Smallpox and starvation had done their work well. Corpses rotted in the streets and houses, and all efforts to dispose of them had been abandoned. The living lay beside the dead in humble dwellings, too weak to move when enemies approached to bring their roofs crashing down upon their heads. A pestilence sprang up from the corruption of the unburied dead, killing as many as the pox. The stench of mortality hung over Tenochtitlan.

Through these scenes of horror Sebastian stalked, his magic useless against the massed might of a continent. Cortez might provide the leadership, but the Mexicans were destroying themselves, the rivalry among their factions opening the way for a few thousand to take command of millions.

Sebastian saw an old man crawling down what once had been a street, and pitied him until he saw the bony hands reach out to catch a small green lizard. The old man smiled as he bit off the squirming head.

Sebastian stood beside him. "We must eat," he said in Spanish, but his companion did not understand. Nonetheless the old man nodded, the cold blood dripping down his chin.

The vampire was half starved himself, and he regarded the squatting figure with a speculative eye. But the creature that he saw was already in the embrace of death, hardly worth the taking. Sebastian needed not only sustenance for himself, but food for the dozens who waited in the pyramid. Smoking Mirror passed the old man by. Yet fires had turned the sky before Sebastian to the color of blood, and somewhere ahead of him a dim figure scurried through the shadows. No doubt it was another starving Aztec; what the vampire wanted was a well-fed Spaniard, his fat face flushed with triumph.

More than once it had occurred to Sebastian that he could infiltrate a Spanish camp, transforming himself into a wisp of fog. The idea of killing Cortez tempted him, but he rejected it. It was too late. Not even the death of their commander would stop the invaders now. They had won. Tenochtitlan was a dead city, though too staggered to give up the ghost.

There was one man Don Sebastian hoped to see, but he was not Cortez. He was a smaller man, with a thin beard and stooped shoulders, wearing a pack that was most likely filled with gold. Hernan Cortez might lay waste to a civilization, but Alfonso Martinez had done something still more unforgivable. He had betrayed Don Sebastian de Villanueva, and that, at least, must be avenged.

Sebastian picked his way through the rubble in the streets. Some of the bodies were fresh, Sebastian observed, but what of it? He would never stoop to drink the blood of a corpse.

He wondered if there might be looters abroad at night. The wealth of Tenochtitlan might tempt any man, but Cortez kept good discipline among his own troops, and to his allies gold and jewels were merely trinkets. And only a fool of either race would wander through these ruins by himself. Sebastian's chance of meeting anyone was small.

He walked beside a broad canal, its depths so choked with stones and timber and corpses that he could easily have walked across it. The brackish water lapped quietly against the banks, and a light rain began to fall.

He was sick of the sight of death. It had been his companion on countless battlefields throughout his life, and it had slept beside him in his coffin through the long days since his transformation. He had killed before, and even now he was searching for an opportunity to kill again, but he had never seen anything like Tenochtitlan. The city was a charnelhouse. A cloud of corruption seeped up from the slain, who soaked in the rain all night and baked in the sun all day. Swarms of flies were their only mourners and rats their only heirs. Suppressing the first shudder he had felt in decades, he moved toward the scene of that day's battle.

Something splashed in the canal. The sound was weak, but Sebastian whirled to investigate its source. A heap of bodies clogged the intersection of two waterways, and from them came a bubbling groan. The vampire stiffened, then moved toward the carrion pile.

He spied a pale hand crawling over muddy rocks, and then an armored back that moved. Sebastian hurried forward, ignoring what his feet were forced to touch. He lifted up the Spanish soldier, as tenderly as a father with a stricken son. A bloody gash trailed across the man's forehead and his helmet had been battered in. One of his eyes bulged unnaturally. Still, he was alive.

"Don't die now," Sebastian whispered. "We need you."

He took his captive by the arm, relieved to find that it did not drop away, and dragged him through the human rubble to the street. There he leaned over to examine his find more closely.

"You'll live long enough," he said. "And your death, when it comes, will not be meaningless."

The soldier groaned again, then coughed. His mouth was full of blood and water.

"Just a few minutes more," Sebastian assured him. "We have not far to go."

Dragging his prize behind him, he shuffled through the ruins toward the black pyramid.

As July drew to a close, Cortez joined forces with his lieutenant Pedro de Alvarado, the man whose slaughter of the dancers more than a year before had begun the war between the Aztecs and the Spaniards. Cortez crossed the last canal between them, his progress impeded only briefly by a bedraggled crew of emaciated Aztec warriors. The Spaniards did not move too near the water until it had been filled in by the labor of their Indian allies, and if a number of those workers died completing their task, there were many thousands more.

As Cortez rode over the broken stones and broken bodies, he saw flames in the west. They seemed to be rising from a nearby temple, and for a moment he imagined that some cult was conducting an unholy rite there, perhaps a ceremony to curse the invaders. But when he drew closer to the fire, he realized to his delight that the conflagration was Alvarado's work. The armies of the south and west had joined, leaving behind them acres of utter devastation. More than three-quarters of the city had been completely leveled, and now the two paths of terror had merged into one. As soon as the remaining troops moved in from the north, the vise would close, leaving the surviving Aztecs with nowhere to hide.

The two contingents of the Spanish force rushed to embrace each other over the brown bodies of their friends and foes. They met in the marketplace of Tlatelolco, where in happier days the people of the city had exchanged their wares. Cortez and Alvarado took their horses into the huge enclosure whose countless porticoes and pavilions marked the sites where merchants traded their weavings and carvings for vegetables and grain. The square was empty, but despairing Aztecs lined the roofs.

Martinez watched from a safe distance. There seemed to be no fight left in the people of Tenochtitlan, but their spirit was not what worried Martinez. Reports of a most disturbing nature touched on a topic close to the alchemist's heart. Alvarado's men claimed that they had heard shouts from the vanquished priests, repeated so often that a translation had been possible. The Aztecs were taunting their conquerors with the information that they had buried all the city's treasure where no man would ever find it.

The thought drove Martinez close to madness, and his only consolation was that he did not entirely believe the story. Certainly the Aztecs were capable of such barbarism, but it seemed hardly possible that they had found the time to hide the wealth of an entire empire. They might do so in the days remaining to them, but surely some booty still remained. Where could they have put it all? He thought of the lake and its far shores and almost despaired, but then reminded himself that Cortez had controlled the waters of Texcoco for some time.

Martinez did not move, but his brain was working furiously. His mind was wracked by the horrors he had seen in Mexico, but still he knew what he wanted. The gold might be anywhere; the chance to seek it out might never come, but Martinez was determined to try for his share.

He kept well to the rear for the next few days, anticipating at least one more big battle. And at each sunset he cursed himself because he had not yet hit upon a plan for finding Montezuma's gold.

The battle he expected finally came. The marketplace was constantly filled with old men, women, and children—who offered no resistance, but seemed to form a shield for the soldiers who must be lurking somewhere. Three times Cortez called on them to surrender, promising to treat them well. It was imperative to clear the way, he said, and if they did not move he had no choice but to unloose his Indian allies.

The people stood quietly in the marketplace, as if they did not have the strength to move. They were like sheep awaiting slaughter, and at last their butchers came.

Martinez felt himself drawn irresistibly toward the scene, despite his fear, despite his disapproval. He had seen men kill each other before, but he had never seen anything like this.

A few rocks fell from the rooftops; otherwise the Aztec defense was negligible. Gunfire kept the Aztecs so well confined within the square that Martinez was able to observe the action with next to no danger to himself. He saw an infant smashed against a wall and its mother cut in two. An old man lay in the dust while half a dozen warriors flattened his head with their war clubs. A woman slumped in front of him, her back feathered with arrows. A small boy caught a cannonball as if it were a toy; it carried him into a canal.

These were the stragglers. Where the fighting was hottest, there was nothing to be seen except a flailing throng of flesh. The screams were deafening, the smoke blinding. Spears and arrows hissed like snakes; swords and clubs rose and fell like clockwork. Martinez turned away and noticed, to his surprise, that the water behind him had turned red. He had heard of such a thing, but always assumed that it was simply poetic exaggeration. This was real. The canals were bright with human blood.

The attack was so successful that the victors could hardly climb over the bodies of their victims to reach more. Even Cortez was shocked. He wrote in his reports that more than twelve thousand had been killed in this one afternoon, and then he called a truce.

King Cuauhtemoc offered to meet with Cortez, but day after day he failed to appear. It was clear to Martinez, as it would be soon to everyone, that the Aztecs were playing for time; they were evidently determined to fight to the bitter end, and then beyond.

The truce tempted Alfonso Martinez. Ostensibly there was no fighting anywhere; perhaps a man might be safe alone in the city. And certainly this was the perfect chance for the priests to make good their promise by burying the treasure of Tenochtitlan. For two nights Martinez held himself in check; on the third he slipped out of his quarters. A little piece of gold sufficed to bribe the guard. He would have let the lunatic physician out for nothing. The campfires burned behind Martinez. He was alone.

The city was black, its broken buildings like the ancient ruins of some forgotten civilization. A few minutes beyond the Spanish headquarters, Martinez ran into his first heap of corpses. The darkness obscured them, but he could not block out their reek. He tried to hold his breath until he passed them, but it was no use. The dead and their unholy stench were everywhere.

A light rain trickled down from the gray sky, drops pattering against his armor. The sound dismayed him; he began to fear that he was making too much noise. He knew he should go back, but something drove him forward. He had traveled thousands of miles for this. He had braved vampires and demons, endured war and famine, countenanced cannibalism and human sacrifice. The time had surely come for his reward.

He imagined how the guard would laugh at him if he crept back so soon, and he kept on. He scarcely realized where he was going. The gold might be anywhere, but he was moving slowly south.

The thought occurred to him that some of the bodies piled around him might be worth investigating. He spotted one covered with limp white feathers; perhaps it was a chief. Martinez sloshed through a puddle that he hoped was only water and reached out a trembling hand. He groped for an instant, then pulled away with an involuntary gasp. His fingers were coated with something thick and sticky. He ran for the canal and dipped his hand into the water, choking back his nausea as best he could. When he stood up, Sebastian was beside him.

Martinez drew his sword, stared at it for a moment, then handed it to Don Sebastian. The vampire tossed it carelessly away.

"You were coming to the pyramid," Sebastian said.

"Was I?" Martinez blinked against the water that dripped from the visor of his helmet.

"Nothing else but blight lies in this direction, and it would be a good place to look for gold."

"No doubt. Funny that I didn't think of you."

"Part of you remembered, Martinez. Part of you wanted me."

"There was not much else for me to do, was there?"

Sebastian did not reply. He beckoned, and Martinez fell into step beside him. Smoking Mirror's temple lay that way.

"I shall show you my treasure," Sebastian said. They walked together through the rain.

"The priestess," said Martinez. "Is she still alive?"

"She is."

"Shall I see her again?"

"I think not, Martinez. You disappointed her, you know."

"I am not like you. I told you more than once. I was not ready to reach out and grasp at stars. There was no place for me in your schemes, and Cortez was no better. I shall have neither gold nor glory."

"You shall have gold enough, I promise you."

They stopped before the black pyramid. The area around it had been cleaned of corpses.

"Has Smoking Mirror come to set you free?"

"Not yet, Martinez."

"He'd better hurry. I wish I could go with you. Perhaps in my next life."

"Perhaps."

"I should go," said Martinez; but he stood quite still.

"Come, Martinez. There is nowhere for you to go. You would not get far, and you would miss the splendid death that I have planned for you."

"Your treasure?"

"Wait for me here."

Martinez watched Sebastian mount the steps, a tall pale figure whose Aztec robes of red and white and black no longer seemed incongruous. He might have been a native priest.

Sebastian sat on the top step and then reached back toward the terrace. He pulled an object toward the ledge.

"Look at this, Martinez," he called down. "The Aztec calendar. One I never showed you. It was too precious. But I have learned all I can from it, and now it shall be yours."

The vampire stood on the brink of the terrace, the gigantic calendar clutched in his pale fingers. He lifted it above his head, a wheel of solid gold. No mortal could have carried it. Thicker than a man's arm, it was half as tall as Sebastian. Martinez expected him to throw it down from the pyramid at once, but Sebastian was not yet ready.

"See how it gleams, Martinez," Sebastian shouted. "It is the moon! It is the sun!"

"Let me look for a moment," Martinez said, his head raised toward the sky. "It is beautiful. You were right. That is the gold I wanted all along."

Time stopped for an instant, and in that span Martinez saw each marking on the disc in bold relief. And more than that, he read their meaning. Each hieroglyphic was a message from a god, and in their twisted symmetry he understood the secrets of his fate. He knew now what Sebastian had tried to tell him, and he would remember it. His quest was ended.

"Thank you," said Martinez, and even as he spoke Sebastian cast the glimmering disc from the heights of Smoking Mirror's temple.

The false physician bowed his head, and the heavy wheel of gold came spinning down on him like some gigantic coin.

19. Heart of the Earth

THE eleventh night of August," Sebastian said.

"What is that?" asked Toci.

"It is the best night left to us for what we have to do, the night after the war god's festival is over. It seems to be a day of no importance, only the beginning of the feast you call the Fall of Fruit. Yet my calculations have convinced me that something will happen then. There is a discrepancy between your calendar and my charts of the Zodiac, and I have done what I could to correlate them. I believe I am right, Toci, but come and look."

She kneeled beside him on the mica floor, much of which was covered by two huge parchment sheets. On each of them was inscribed a circle, divided into segments marked with hieroglyphics. Sebastian leaned over the two charts, using the stick of charcoal with which he had drawn them as a pointer.

"This is the Aztec calendar," he said, gesturing to his left. "Beside it is a map of the stars as they will be on that night, constructed according to the rules of Spanish astrologers. You have eighteen months but we have twelve, each of them named for the constellation that is strongest in the heavens at the time. This is the month we call Leo; his name means a wild beast, something like your jaguar. The eleventh day of August is the twentieth degree of Leo, much more auspicious for our purposes than the nineteenth, even if it means bypassing the climax of Huitzilopochtli's holiday. The influence of the war god should still be lingering then, and in any case it is not war we seek."

Toci looked down at the charts, then up at Sebastian. She seemed puzzled.

"Perhaps this will help you to see it," Sebastian said. He gathered up the twin sheets of parchment and placed one over the other. Then he stood and held the two charts close to a brazier's flame. The light shone through, and suddenly both diagrams became visible, one against the other. Sebastian adjusted them meticulously.

"Now look," he said. "Your map of the year and my map of the stars. Can you see how the two of them are aligned? This line represents the change between the two feasts, and just after it is the night represented by this horoscope. Look at this mark, here. We call it Venus, but you told me that the same star represents the Feathered Serpent. When I learned that, I thought there might be a way to read the Aztec diagram against the European one. Actually, of course, it is Arabic. You remember when I told you of them? Well, never mind that now. The important thing is that it does all come together."

"Show me," Toci said.

"We call this Mars," Sebastian went on, "this glyph made of a circle and a dart. He is our god of war, and should correspond to yours. See how he stands in relation to the Feathered Serpent. I think it means Cortez will win the war, although we hardly need a horoscope to tell us that. But look at these other stars. This one, I believe, is Toci."

"Toci?"

"Your goddess, the one you call 'Grandmother,' or 'Heart of the Earth.' She is old and wise, and moves with great deliberation. She is the planet with the ring of light around her body, the one that we call Saturn."

"And where is Smoking Mirror?"

"I wish I knew. No planet that we can see corresponds to him, but certainly one exists. Our sorcerers insist that there are planets we cannot see, whose presence affects us nonetheless. I wish

I had my cards, or that I had taken the time to make some. Then I could show you his face. We cannot see his home, but we have a picture of him, and it is much like one of yours. He is a skeleton. I cannot chart his course, but the god we have who stands for Smoking Mirror is called Pluto."

"A dead god? And in hiding?"

"Precisely. But there are signs of his presence. I know from you that Smoking Mirror is the Great Bear; at least that is our name for the group of stars you showed me. That is a constellation that plays only a minor part in our astrology. It is marked here. By reckoning the attributes, Smoking Mirror should be Scorpio, and yet his festivals fall in Libra and in Taurus. But look again at the Great Bear. Then note this planet, Jupiter, the one we call the god of fortune. See how they have combined? And look at the moon. I have never seen a chart like this. I promise you this is the night when Smoking Mirror's power will be at its height."

"You see more than I see," Toci said, "but you do not see Sebastian. Your face tells me more than these pictures. I know you speak the truth. You have found the hour?"

"Only three more days," Sebastian replied. "I wonder if Cortez will grant them to us."

"Our king will fight."

"I want these final days, but I wonder what their price will be. There has been too much killing. How many more must die to grant me the opportunity for this last experiment?"

"No," said Toci firmly. "They have forgotten us. Tenochtitlan does not fight for Smoking Mirror. It fights to be free."

"Death before slavery," muttered Sebastian. "I wonder. It was not my choice, or I would never have become one of the undead. There is something to be learned here on this plane, and often a single lifetime is not enough. Nothing is enough. I stand here with my calculations and I believe in them. But what will happen when that night falls? How shall we summon Smoking Mirror?"

Toci took him by the arm with a surprising strength and turned him round to face her. "Smoking Mirror will be there. As you say, 'I promise you.'"

Sebastian stared into her shining eyes. "So be it," he said. "We shall trust each other, Toci, though neither of us understands just what the other means."

The priestess kissed his cold lips, as if to seal the bargain. Then she stepped away.

"Three days," Sebastian said. "King Cuauhtemoc has kept Cortez at bay with his talk of peace, but he will certainly be forced to fight soon, unless he chooses to surrender. And meanwhile the Spanish are constructing that damned catapult. It is a strange device, Toci; it might be strong enough to knock down Tezcatlipoca's temple."

Day by day the emissaries went back and forth between the Spaniards and the Aztecs. The uneasy truce was close to collapse. Cuauhtemoc promised to meet with Cortez, but did not. Some of his chiefs appeared, however, to explain that their emperor was ill. At the next appointment the same chiefs arrived, saying that Cuauhtemoc feared an ambush. Cortez agreed to give him one more chance, and warned him of the consequences if he did not comply.

There was a soldier in the camp, one Sotelo, who talked loudly about his experiences in the Italian wars. He had observed the working of the great siege engines there, and was confident that he could build one. It would be powerful enough to break through any building in Tenochtitlan, or so the self-styled engineer insisted. Cortez endured the fellow's boasting for as long as he could, then ordered him to build a catapult.

Lime and stone were hauled into the empty square, along with ropes and timbers. The carpenters set to work, and the sound of their hammers rang through the empty streets. A hideous structure of beams and pulleys rose above the roofs. Two gigantic slings were sewn together from carefully selected hides; they were big enough to hold a boulder. As an afterthought, Cortez ordered that the weapon be equipped with wheels. If it worked, there would be no point in confining it to this one locality. A hundred Indian allies struggled to lift the ponderous engine so that axles could be slipped beneath it. When the sun set, Sotelo was still making delicate adjustments of the ropes and cords, and promising that it would be ready by morning.

That night it rained again. Guards were stationed all around the catapult, grumbling at the drizzle, and the mist, and the sickening miasma that rose from the unburied bodies of their foes. The men felt extraneous; the Aztecs were completely cowed, and it was reasonable to assume that they had no idea what this machine could do.

None of the guards noticed the wisp of fog floating above their heads, its color more green than gray. None of them observed it hovering over the catapult, and none of them saw the long pale hands that materialized out of the cloud. Thin fingers reached forth from the mist to touch a pulley and draw back a cord. In a few seconds the hands were gone, and the green cloud drifted south.

The next morning, Cortez marched into the marketplace. He waited impatiently for the arrival of Cuauhtemoc, convinced that he would never come. When the Aztec messengers arrived with new excuses, Cortez was ready for them.

The command was given, and a platoon of Indian workers rolled a huge rock up the ramp. Sotelo supervised while it was set in place. The engine of destruction was aimed toward one of the temples that bordered the marketplace. The leather sling was filled. Windlasses turned, and ropes grew taut.

Sotelo released the stone, while his audience gave one collective gasp. The boulder flew into the sky.

Then it dropped straight down again, crushing the catapult to splinters.

There was a moment of stunned silence, and then the starving citizens of Tenochtitlan burst into laughter. The flight of the stone had been so ludicrous that not even the Spaniards could contain themselves. They laughed too; thousands of delighted voices rose in a sound that would never be heard in the city again.

Sotelo stood beside his ruined catapult, his protestations of innocence drowned out by the general hilarity. He blushed furiously and turned away.

Cortez was red-faced too, but more from fury than from shame. He ordered an immediate retreat, then made his plans for the final assault on the city. Cortez, who had been driving the Aztecs steadily to the north, now gave the order for the troops in the north to advance, supported by the entire fleet of ships. Cuauhtemoc's retreat would be cut off, and further defense of the city would be impossible. A few days' work would make the Spaniards masters of Tenochtitlan.

The massacres began again.

Sebastian brooded beneath the black pyramid. He stared at his charts for hours, alternately consoled by their exactitude and depressed by their apparent uselessness. His frustration took form in endless pacing back and forth, and his restlessness communicated itself to his men, who wanted nothing more than to go out and fight. Sebastian himself remained inside the temple; he had seen enough. Toci did her best to soothe him, yet Sebastian noticed a change in her. It was more than despair at the plight of her people. She was withdrawn and meditative.

Finally the night they had been waiting for arrived. At sunset Toci touched the panel in the dull black wall, and the stone turned back, exposing Sebastian's earth-filled coffin. The priestess lifted up the lid, and the master of the pyramid crawled out into the shadows.

"How goes the siege?" he asked at once, and listened to Toci's catalogue of horrors with no show of emotion.

"At least this pyramid still stands," Sebastian said. "The wreck of the catapult has left us enough time. Now there is nothing for us to do but to await Smoking Mirror."

"We must call him," Toci said.

"Indeed," replied Sebastian. "And have you found a way to summon him?"

Toci nodded, and Sebastian looked at her in amazement. Her eyes were unnaturally bright, her dark features a mask of fierce determination.

"How?" Sebastian asked her.

"You know," said Toci.

Sebastian did not reply. Instead he stared at her as if he hoped to read whatever mysteries were hidden behind her enigmatic expression.

"We shall speak of it later," he said at length. "For now, you may tell the men that they are free to go and fight if they still wish it. They can do nothing more for us after this night, and I would not deprive them of their pleasure."

Toci slipped out of the room without a word, and Sebastian gathered up his charts. He glanced at them for a few seconds, then rolled them up and carried them to the corner where a brazier burned. The parchments burst into flame almost at once; their fitful light sent Sebastian's shadow leaping over the sloping ceiling of the subterranean room.

"They left as soon as I told them they could go," Toci said as she returned to him. "The high priest is here, and four jaguar knights. That is all."

"The high priest," Sebastian said. "Does he know what you intend to do?"

"I told him today."

"And he approves?"

"He said it would be best, whether the god comes or not."

"And what will he do?"

"He will not come here. He said this is sacred, for us alone. He will go up on the pyramid and call on Smoking Mirror."

Sebastian took both her hands in his. "There is no need for you to do this thing," he said. "The Spaniards will not kill you; you are too beautiful. You could wait here until Cuauhtemoc surrenders, and perhaps your future life would be a pleasant one. Some chief might take you for a bride and make you a great lady."

Toci spat on the mica floor. "I am not the woman who sleeps beside Cortez," she said indignantly. "I have only one husband, and tonight he comes to me."

The vampire kissed her, and then stepped away. "I wonder what the chances are . . ." he said. "Surely Smoking Mirror has never had such a noble sacrifice, but it must not be offered for nothing."

"Not for nothing," Toci said. "For love."

"Listen, Toci. I have given this much thought. How do these gods approach the earth? And what are they? Are they beings like ourselves? Or are they bodiless intelligence? Perhaps they are pure energy, a force like fire or light. But whatever they are, they reach us through the power of our own wills. They do not travel through the stars in ships, as a sailor might, but through the minds of those who wait for them. Our strength feeds them, as the blood of living men and women feeds me."

"This is why you are Smoking Mirror."

"But even gods die, Toci. Consider the gods of Rome. No, you know nothing of them. The stars bear their names, the ones I told you of, like Venus and Jupiter and Saturn. And the city that worshipped them had conquered all the world. But men forgot those gods, who once walked among them, and now they come no more. I fear the same is true of Smoking Mirror. How many are there left to call on him? Only the two of us, and five men up above. Can that be enough to draw him down to us?"

"You say the gods are dead," Toci replied, "but they have become stars. And the stars still shine."

"Then this is truly what you want?"

"This is what I want, and it is what you want. You always wanted it. You know the story of Tezcatlipoca; you told it to Martinez. Smoking Mirror waits in darkness for someone to come, then offers up his heart. If you have the courage to take it, you will be blessed. He gives what you wish, if you are strong enough to wish it."

"His heart," Sebastian said. "The heart of the earth."

"Take what you want," said Toci, "and we shall see the Smoking Mirror."

She slipped out of her black robe and walked naked to the sacrificial slab. The virgin priestess sat cross-legged on the stone, waiting for the appointed hour.

20. The Smoking Mirror

A BAND of eager warriors rushed from Smoking Mirror's temple. Some of them were jaguar knights who had been assigned to guard the pyramid; the others were Don Sebastian's own troops, members of the savage tribe that worshipped vampire bats. They were fresh soldiers, who had been kept out of the battle of Tenochtitlan for many days, and not long ago Sebastian had fed them well.

Atop the pyramid, the blind high priest listened to them hurrying across the plaza. He guessed that they would not return alive, but nonetheless he sensed the same longing in the four men who had been ordered to stay behind and help him in his invocations. He felt the heat from their torches, and a cool breeze that promised rain before the night was gone. Aromatic incense helped to mask the odor from the streets beow, and the flavor of the sacred potion he had shared with Toci was still bitter in his mouth. Pictures formed behind his sightless eyes.

He envisioned the devastation of the city, and for a moment he was grateful that he could no longer see. He summoned up the image of the young men who were running off to die, then thought with more satisfaction of the two lovers hidden hundreds of feet beneath him. He turned his dead eyes toward the sky, away from them, and dreamed of Smoking Mirror.

His trembling fingers reached out into the air around him, as though it had a substance he could feel, and the four acolytes stepped back to give him room. One of them handed him the bejeweled skull that had been retrieved from the pack strapped to the crushed corpse of Alfonso Martinez. The high priest kissed the skull and fell into a trance.

Something called him from his contemplations, though, and he shook himself awake, uncertain of how much time had passed. There was a disturbance in the public square at the foot of the pyramid. He heard the sound of running feet, and angry voices shouting. At once his thoughts returned to earth. He did not need to ask his acolytes to understand what had happened. The attack of Smoking Mirror's men had turned into a rout. Jaguar knights would surely stand and die, but the tribesmen had no such training, and they had fled the onslaught of the enemy, leading their pursuers back to the only home they knew and to the god who would protect them. They had hurried back to Don Sebastian, and thus betrayed him in the final hour.

The old high priest cast the sacred skull down toward the noise of fighting men and listened to it splinter on the distant flagstones. For an instant the clash of arms was stilled, and he imagined all the soldiers staring up at the peak of the pyramid to discover the source of the strange missile. He called for his staff of office, a stout stick taller than any man, capped at one end with a heavy ornament of gold. Clutching this formidable weapon in both hands, he gave swift orders to the soldiers who stood beside him. If the Spaniards could be lured up to the platform, it would take them that much longer to find the secret chamber in the heart of the temple.

The torches were doused against black rocks, their pungent smoke filling the blind priest's nostrils. He heard men moving up the narrow stairway: first his allies, then his enemies. Swords clashed and soldiers screamed. He retreated from the steps as his four guards advanced, listening with satisfaction as a brazier scraped along the stones, and smiling at the howl of agony when its smoldering incense caught someone in the face.

The mixture of peyote, mushrooms, and morning glory seeds had made his senses unnaturally acute. The clash of armor, the gasps for breath, the bite of steel or stone in flesh, even the whistling of weapons through the air, all served to form a picture in his mind. No sighted observer could have been more aware of every detail of the struggle on the stairs. He judged that the Spaniards were more than halfway up the steps, but still he would not allow his quartet of jaguar knights to venture down. Each second that could be gained might make a difference.

He tried to count the number of those below him, studying the voices and their placement. He estimated half a dozen tribesmen, and at least twice as many Spaniards. But by the time the first man reached the summit, the numbers had grown smaller. Finally, he commanded his four knights to move forward. He had no doubt of who would win the fight; over his vision of battling warriors floated the hollow face of Smoking Mirror.

The wail of someone tumbling down the stairs was so distorted that there was no telling who had fallen, but his loyal soldiers shouted out the progress of the conflict to him when they could. It was not until the last of their voices died away that he stepped forth from the darkness beyond the stairs, the final defender of Tezcatlipoca's temple.

Their heavy breathing told him of several men, closing in upon him in a semicircle. He came to meet them, an old man leaning on his stick. And as he hoped, they tried to capture him alive.

When they were close enough, he lifted his long staff and sent it wheeling through the air. He heard the satisfying thuds and felt the impact in his arms as the golden figure at the far end of his stick caught two separate men. He spun in a circle, his weapon longer than any sword, and felt another enemy go down.

And then the steel shaft from a Spanish crossbow caught him in the throat.

Toci lay curled up on the stone slab, her body cushioned by her own black garments, and by Sebastian's robes of black and white and red. She looked up into his face as he leaned over her, his bright fangs bared.

"Not all at once," the priestess said. "Take my love before you take my life."

Sebastian kneeled beside the sacrificial altar so that his face was close to hers. She turned toward him, leaning on one elbow, her long black hair covering her like a cloak. Sebastian stroked it with pale fingers, then gently pushed it back, uncovering her golden flesh.

"Now is the time," said Toci.

She took one deep breath, then sank down upon her back, drawing the vampire to her with both hands. They kissed as gently as if they were strangers, their lips barely touching. She felt Sebastian slip up to lie beside her on the stone.

Sebastian kissed her once again, this time with more intensity. He clutched her shoulders, rolling on his side to pull the full length of her body close to his, her warmth against his chill. The still embrace continued for a moment, interrupted only by Sebastian's continual caresses. He felt Toci's warm breath against his cheek, and heard her shuddering sighs. He nipped her soft throat tenderly, then drew away, letting her sink down again, her bright black tresses like a blanket under her.

Sebastian kneeled between her open legs and gazed down at her familiar features, seeing them as if for the first time. Her brown eyes gleamed with anxious expectation, her nostrils flared, her full lips quivered. She arched her back, lifting her small, exquisite breasts to meet his eager hands. Her soft flesh seemed to writhe beneath his touch, and when her nipples hardened he bent low to give them delicate bites.

Toci reached out to touch his face, and as he raised his head, his black hair fell around it like a dark halo. The faint light from the braziers turned his pale cheeks red and gold as he ran his fingers along the inside of her thighs. His strong hands grasped her slim hips, and Toci felt him slipping into her. She gasped at the short, sharp pain, but then it passed away and they were one.

The priestess who had been a virgin saw the slanted ceiling

spinning overhead. Her intoxicated eyes went wide, and every fiber of her being pulsated with independent life. She rocked beneath her lover, her legs wrapped around his waist. Bursts of passion coursed through the drugged visions that she saw; Sebastian's eyes were stars. Smoking Mirror had taken her for his bride when she was still a child, and finally their wedding night had come. This was the sacrifice that would call the god down from the skies, the god whose only law was to take what he desired, the god who had already found a partial incarnation in the dead flesh of Don Sebastian de Villanueva. And now that Sebastian was pure appetite, there could be no barriers between his spirit and the dazzling force that was the Smoking Mirror. But Toci could no longer consider her decision; she could only watch the whirling images of the god, who was at once a dark statue, a pale man, and a silver skull. Her moans rose into an ecstatic scream, and she fell back upon the sacrificial stone.

Six Spanish soldiers stood outside the doorway to the pyramid, examining the black stone skull whose open mouth invited them to enter.

"Nothing in there," one of them said.

"No? Where do you think those five up top came from? This part of the city's supposed to be cleaned out, but those barbarians were guarding something. This might be where they hid the gold."

"And it might be where they hide their soldiers. Do you want to go in and see?"

"There can't be anybody left. They'd all have come out to fight us."

"Anyway, we should get back. We'll catch hell if any officer finds out we chased those men back here. It's against orders."

"They'll forget that if we bring Cortez a fortune, won't they? And a promotion wouldn't hurt, now the war's almost over and the fun's about to start."

"I don't like this place. I heard something about it. All their gods are devils, but this one frightens even the Aztecs."

"What was that? Somebody screamed!"

"I'm going back. We need a cannon for this accursed pile."

"And I'm going in. Women and gold sound good enough to me, especially when there's no officer around to tell us how to behave. Who's with me? Come on!"

"Your love is like your bite," murmured Toci. "It hurts at first, but not for long." She lay in Don Sebastian's arms, her skin covered with a shiny dew of perspiration.

"Is this not enough for you, Toci? Do you insist on death?"

"This is the night you chose. You took part of me; now take all. And Tezcatlipoca will welcome us."

"If he does not come, you will be dead."

"I die tonight, or I die tomorrow, when Cortez comes. Believe, Sebastian. This is the way, I promise you."

Sebastian's faith might waver, but his desire was unswerving. The lovely creature he embraced was begging him to take her blood, and even as he pitied her, he felt the hunger rise within him. He took her roughly by the throat, as if he hoped that she might stop him with a cry for mercy. But Toci only threw back her head and wrapped her arms around him.

Sebastian ran his fingers along her body, cherishing every touch. His lips were at her jugular. He thought of her dead, then imagined her rising the next night as a vampire like himself. But would there be another night? And what chance would two of the living dead have to survive in a city conquered by Cortez? They were not proof against the wooden spears and arrows carried by tens of thousands of the Indian allies. The only hope lay with Smoking Mirror, whose faithful followers had been reduced to a pathetic handful.

Sebastian cast his doubts aside and sank his sharp teeth into Toci's throat.

Even then, a protest from her might have stopped him. Her life was precious, and there was nothing he could offer her in exchange for it except the dream that something might sweep down from the stars to rescue them. But Toci held him closer than before, her body stiffening, her breath coming in spasms.

Her hot blood pulsed over his tongue with each throb of her wildly beating heart, its salty sweetness laced with the mysterious drugs of Mexico. A fever overcame Sebastian, and as he sucked the life out of his lover he saw the world turn red. Her fingers raked his face spasmodically; to him they felt as if they were already bones.

Then Toci's slim brown hands dropped down, and her blood came more slowly. Her heart was failing.

"The god is here," she whispered. "You are Tezcatlipoca, my Sebastian. . . . You are the only Smoking Mirror."

Her words reverberated through the black chamber, sending a shock of horror through Sebastian. He lifted up his head so suddenly that he tore a piece out of her throat. Her blood splashed over the altar.

"Toci!" he shouted. "What do you mean?"

A small smile twisted her lips; her eyes were glistening. There was no reproach in her steady gaze, only tenderness.

"Toci!"

The light went out of her eyes, and she slumped back against the stone.

Sebastian stepped away from her. Toci's golden skin had turned hideously pale; her slim body was unexpectedly gaunt. Clotting blood dripped slowly from the ugly rip his teeth had left when he pulled away from her. His intoxicated gaze distorted every detail so that he could hardly bear to look at her.

Sick at heart, he stood beside the stone slab while the moments passed, waiting for something he no longer expected. The black room was still. No god appeared.

The subterranean room was suddenly very small. The dull and twisted walls seemed to press in upon Sebastian. For the first time, he noticed every dusty cobweb and every puddle of dried blood. The chamber was a tomb, weighed down by countless tons of dark and heavy stone. The drugs from Toci's veins showed Sebastian no visions, only a pitilessly detailed picture of his own surroundings. A naked corpse limped back and forth inside this black and bloody trap, alone except for the woman it had murdered.

Sebastian's head throbbed and voices rang in his ears. They spoke in Spanish, and they were coming closer.

He realized abruptly that the sounds he heard were not delusions. Spanish soldiers had invaded the temple, and they were working their way through the twisting passageways toward the little room where their dead countryman stood alone.

Sebastian prepared himself to meet them. Shutting his eyes against the sight of the slaughtered priestess, he gathered up his robes and put them on. As he did so, he noticed to his dim confusion that the sacred disc hanging from his neck had changed from black to gold.

Sebastian shook off his surprise, determined to control his reeling brain. His first decision was to rid the room of light. It made no sense to guide his enemies directly to his lair. He knocked the two burning braziers to the floor and stamped on the burning coals with his naked feet, noting with grim satisfaction the way his gray, withered right foot began to smoke and smolder.

The voices were louder now, yet somehow they were more distant, echoing along endless corridors that seemed to stretch a century away. And the room had not gone dark. The fires were all out, but the chamber was illuminated by some faint phosphorescence. Sebastian turned toward the entrance; it was thick with shadows. He looked down at the glassy mica floor, and through its half-transparent surface he saw the full moon beaming up at him.

"Sebastian," whispered someone behind him.

He whirled at the sound, convinced that it was Toci speaking, and when he faced her corpse he saw that its bloodless flesh had been transformed into a figure of rich, black obsidian.

The shining statue spoke again; he saw its dark lips move. "Tezcatlipoca," it said, "Smoking Mirror." The sound of cymbals rippled through the pyramid, and spicy incense filled the stagnant air.

He staggered toward the altar, to gaze in wonder at the perfect replica of his beloved. She was as beautiful as she had ever been, each swelling slope and curve of her face and figure embodied in the gleaming stone. The muttering of Spaniards became as faint as the buzzing of insects, and he waited for the voice of the priestess to come again. Instead, the glistening statue rose.

He reached out to touch her cheek, but at his touch the living statue disappeared, leaving him with nothing to embrace but throbbing darkness.

Somewhere a bell rang. Sebastian raised his hands above his head and saw the ceiling of his dismal prison turn to glass. A universe of stars shone down upon him.

Sebastian spun around, and, as he did so, he saw each of the slanting walls of his dark chamber turn transparent. He was in the center of a jewel, bright and multifaceted. From each slanted wall there rose a flight of stairs, stretching off into infinity. He watched a silver skull bounce down each set of steps, rolling up gigantically against the glassy surfaces until he was surrounded by images of his own mortality.

Sebastian screamed, covered with filth and blood and death.

A cleansing wave of blue and green rolled down each stairway, washing away the multitude of skulls, and he realized that the waves were made of fire.

It occurred to him that he had experienced all of this before. He remembered it, and he was calm, even when his gemlike cell broke away from Tenochtitlan to drop dizzyingly into the sky.

He soared through the starry universe in a twelve-sided crystal cage, the distant points of brightness rushing by so quickly that they turned to flickering streaks of white. He spun head over heels in a giddy flight that put his wings to shame.

Toci appeared before him, her face so huge that it blotted out the stars. "We have won," she said. "Tezcatlipoca."

The shining polyhedron flew toward her and sank into the darkness of her eyes. Passing through the darkness, Sebastian felt himself turned round about, and what he saw behind him was his own gigantic face, fading into distance as he dropped away.

The stars were specks of gold and silver against a background of black silk when Sebastian came to rest. Suspended in infinity, he reached out to touch the translucent sides of his bright prison. One of the walls swung open, and the blind high priest stepped through. The hollow sockets of his eyes were filled with diamonds.

"We are the last," said the old man. "Gods never die, but men do, and they announce the death of gods who have forgotten them. Smoking Mirror has forgotten Mexico, but he has not forgotten us. His priestess waits for you, the bride of the stars."

The high priest touched his own forehead and dwindled away to nothing.

Sebastian heard Toci calling to him, and felt himself dissolving into light. His glowing body rose into a shower of dazzling brightness as he reached out to embrace the universe, and in each of its endless worlds he sensed the presence of his beloved. He had become the Smoking Mirror, and she was his reflection.

The walls around him shattered, and finally he was free.

21. The Conqueror

CORTEZ and several of his officers stood inside the tilted chamber at the bottom of Tezcatlipoca's temple. The night was far advanced, and outside the rain was falling heavily.

"Reprimand the men who left their posts," said Cortez. "There is no gold here, nor any Aztec warrior. Nothing but that heathen idol."

"Look at that dried blood, though," said an eager young officer. "It's caked to the floor. And the incense! The place smells worse than the street we passed through. How many lost souls have spent their last moments here, I wonder?"

"There shall be no more," Cortez replied. "Call up the cannon. This abomination must be destroyed. And if they have anything hidden here, we shall find it among the broken stones."

The men filed out, but the young officer lingered for a moment. "Look at the walls," he said. "They're made of that black glass. You can see yourself in them."

On that night, August 11, 1521, the heavy thunderstorm produced a rare phenomenon. A ball of lightning streaked across the sky, sparks trailing behind it, and disappeared into the darkness of the lake. It might have been a visitation from one of the gods, but in their present plight the Aztecs could only regard this sign in the heavens as an ill omen.

Two days later, King Cuauhtemoc surrendered the city of Tenochtitlan. Hernan Cortez and his allies took possession of the ruins eighteen days before the festival of the goddess called "Heart of the Earth." Her feast was not celebrated, nor were any of the others that had always followed. The gods were gone.

Cortez died in 1547, after years of neglect by the fickle court of Spain. He had his time of triumph, but political enemies kept him from the honors he sought, and he squandered most of his fortune. He was buried in Spain, but twenty-two years later his body was exhumed and transported to Mexico City, the capital he had built with slave labor on the ruins of Tenochtitlan. In 1823, after the war for independence, public indignation against the man who had conquered Mexico for Spain grew so great that plans were made to burn what was left of Cortez. Officers of the church were forced to hide the body, and did it so successfully that it was lost for more than a century. Archaeologists finally uncovered it in 1946, hidden behind the walls of an old chapel. The little casket was covered with a cross of gold; the broken bones inside it were wrapped in white silk trimmed with black lace. There was little left of the conquistador except a yellowed skull.